Canticle
of the
Spear

S.C. TERLECKY

Cover by Mihail Uvarov

This is a work of fiction. Names, characters, organizations, places, events, and incidents are either products of the author's imagination or are used fictitiously.

Special thanks to Mom, Dad, Jared, Linda Jackson,
Jake Meinerding, Christine Pingleton, and Kay Verch for
beta reading, editing, and encouragement. Also a huge
thank you to my wife Ashley for putting up with my time
consuming hobby of fiction writing.

Also by S.C. Terlecky

American Relic

Author website: https://scterlecky.wordpress.com/

For Ravenna and Evanna

Canticle
of the
Spear

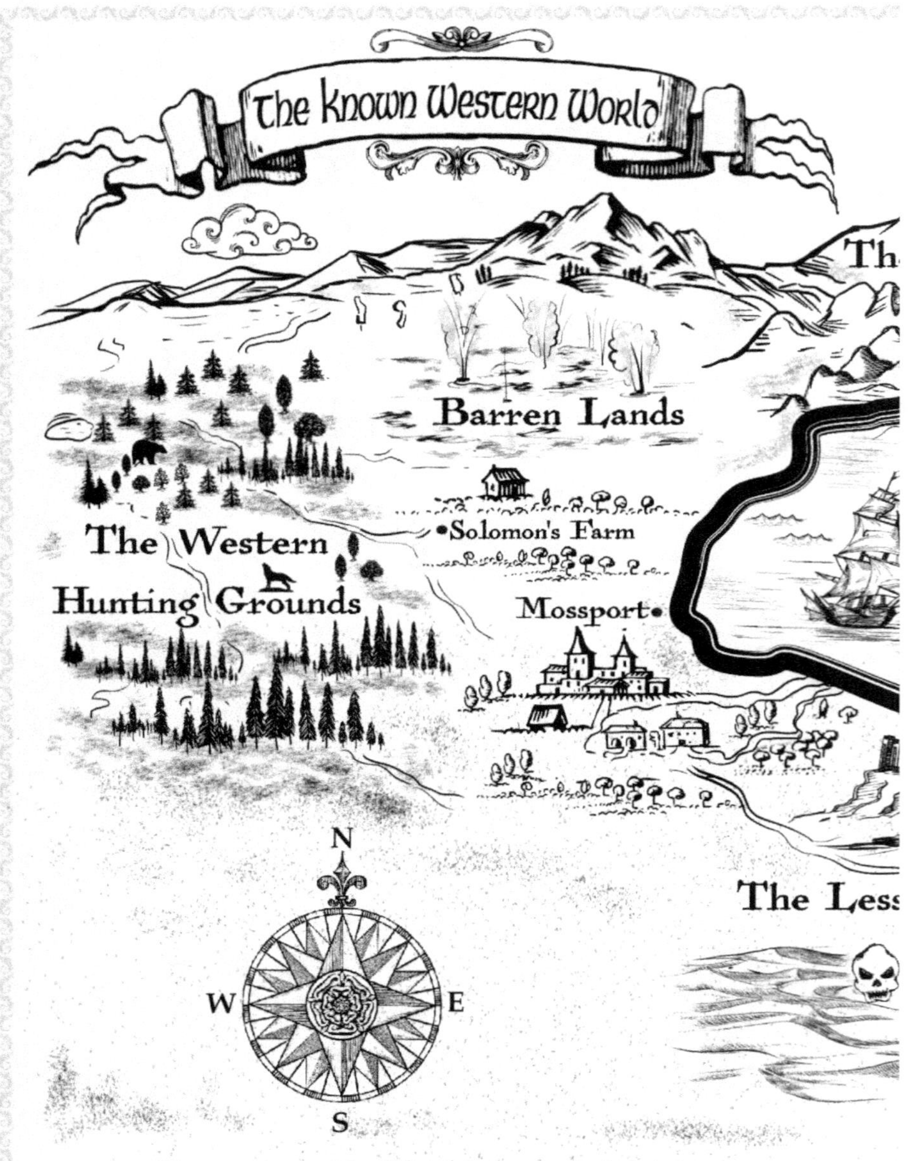

The Known Western World
Th
Barren Lands
Solomon's Farm
The Western
Hunting Grounds
Mossport
The Less
N
W
E
S

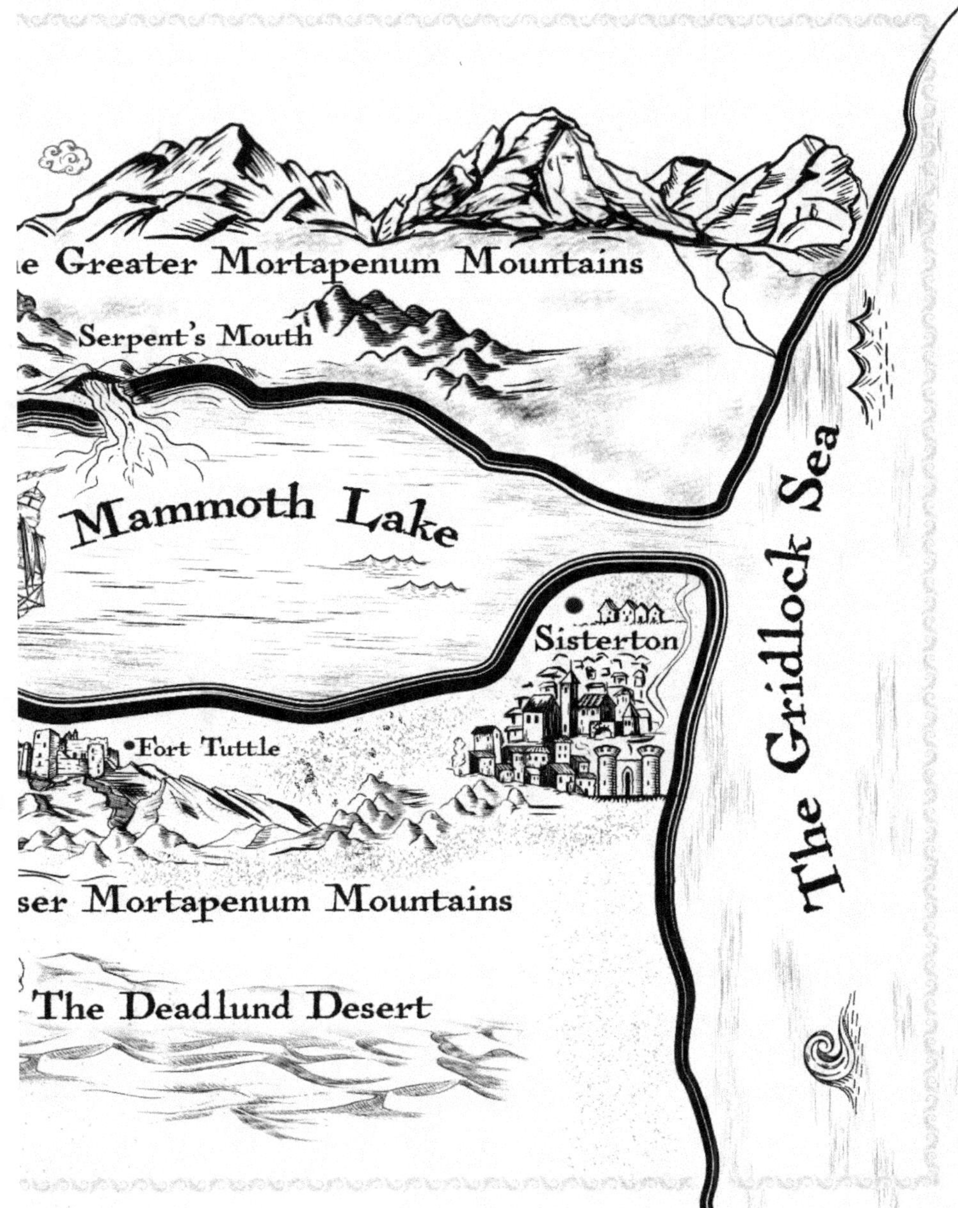
The Greater Mortapenum Mountains
Serpent's Mouth
Mammoth Lake
Sisterton
Fort Tuttle
The Gridlock Sea
ser Mortapenum Mountains
The Deadlund Desert

Chapter I

THE CAPTAIN OF *The Rose Tattoo* marched back and forth on the weathered deck, scratching his peppered beard, deep in thought. His vessel was clean and orderly, though she had been in service longer than most on the sea. Her bow boasted a unique wood carving of a single giant rose with thorns. The unforgiving sun and elements had faded the once bright red flower to a hue of brown since its last touch-up. The ancient flower was a symbol worn by many a gray-haired sailor who had at some point swabbed her decks. The ship was the type that many a sailor started with, but not one that sailors tended to stay on for long. It was old enough that people could only guess as to what the original meaning of the symbol had been. After all, a rose could be placed on a casket as easily as in a wedding bouquet. And red meant blood as often as it meant love. She'd seen both extremes of her numerous owners' fortunes, but no matter the swing of luck, good or bad, it had usually led to another man's hands on her helm. It was an unlikely twist of fate that led to this, the second stint of Captain Gordon.

Few captains at it long enough hadn't seen their share of misfortune. It was the experience of failure that taught the captain and the crew the true worth of the man in charge. Often enough, for the sailing trade, the trick was surviving long enough to see things twice. The perils of life aboard a ship were multifaceted. Many fear Mother Nature the most when alone on the water, but the wiser seaman knew that often, the greater threat came from the mixture of souls aboard.

Captain Gordon had dealt with thievery before and was quick to root it out. The provisions were dwindling too quickly for the one-week passage from the massive Port Sisterton to the loneliest port on the western shore of the Great Mammoth Lake. His planning for trips was meticulous, and his crew, while somewhat green, was dutiful and knew better than to sneak extra food and drink from their hardened captain. He had perceived on a few occasions the smell of liquor in the breeze, only to check his men's breath to find nothing. They all now likely thought him mad. Perhaps they believed he'd been in the sun too long. Let any mate suggest it openly; he'd rope them around the main mast and whip them until they passed out. The sea was no place for so much as a hint of insubordination.

The old captain had a nose unrivaled by any other. A simple belch in his presence resulted in a correct assessment of the mate's diet the previous day. Gordon could smell and identify a seaport before he could see it. He could read subtle notes in the air like a pianist reads sheet music. He knew if he searched long enough, he'd uproot the bottle he was searching for. It had to be out here, on the open deck. Perhaps the evidence was stashed in the cargo crates on the front of the ship.

As he approached the front of the ship, his crew did their best to look busy, as if they hadn't noticed their captain wandering to and fro all morning. The wind whipped at the faded cloth cover, roped down to protect the excess cargo the captain had taken on board. The captain hesitated and then lifted the cloth for a sniff.

The smells of sweat, mud, and alcohol registered in his brain simultaneously as fingers tightly enclosed the captain's gullet, rendering him unable to cry out. He was pulled fully underneath the covering and fell to his knees, trying to gasp for breath.

"Now we have a problem," whispered the man cutting off his oxygen supply. The captain shuddered at the sight of him. His hair, as well as his beard, was long, ragged and caked with mud. He had a black tattoo of a raven on his neck, still scabbing over from its recent addition to his pale skin. There was dried blood on his clothes but no obvious injury to the man, which made the captain guess as to its origin. But it was the stowaway's eyes that frightened Gordon the most. They were vertical black slits, just like a cat's. There was only one man the captain had heard of with a trait so rare.

"Perhaps you can help me solve a riddle," said the man with a husky, gravelly voice. His glazed, demented pupils were inflamed with red from drink. "Imagine a scenario where I get off your ship with none of your crew the wiser that I was here, including you."

The captain tried to whisper his plea to the madman. Instead of listening, the mud-plastered drunkard pulled the captain closer until their faces were nearly touching.

"Whisper softly, Captain. Your life depends on how you choose your words." His grip lessened enough for the captain to speak.

"I can pay you, friend," Gordon whispered under duress. "Tell me the price and you shall have it!"

The cat-eyed man smiled. "I have no friends. Your coin will buy me nothing, but your silence buys me time. With regard to the latter, I have my own idea to assure it. This is your chance to change my mind." The smile was not warm; his tongue danced between his teeth like a hissing viper, calculating its next strike.

The captain kept his eyes closed, swallowed, and tried to think quickly. The lack of oxygen made it harder than usual. "What about a ransom for my silence?"

"I assured you it would do no good." The grip tightened around the captain's neck again.

"I know, good sir. But if you would return said ransom whenever you chose to leave wherever it is you're going, it would give me incentive to keep silent."

"Stop addressing me with flattery," the man snarled. "You couldn't guess how many souls I've killed to end up on your ship." With his threat came a pause, and with it, likely some consideration to the captain's proposal.

Gordon allowed his eyes to open for just the slightest sliver of light. Perhaps the man truly didn't want to kill him. This was his chance to lay everything on the table. Folding meant fatality. "I carry something on board that is worth more than money to me," he whispered.

The stowaway leaned in closer, his spirited breath making the captain's face contort. "What do you carry?"

"A map, hand drawn by the infamous Horton Conner."

The drunken man sneered. "You offer me the map of a madman? Perhaps I should examine your head after I cleave it open."

"If he was crazy, why hasn't anyone…ever proved him wrong? Th… this is the only verified map he ever drew. I…I carry it on me, wherever I go." The captain reached a shaky hand slowly into his vest and produced a leather cylinder. "If I place it in your care, you guarantee my silence. I would like to get it back."

The stowaway loosened his grip to accept the container. He removed the cork to slide out a faded, yellowed, rolled-up piece of parchment. He released the captain's neck and unrolled the paper to find an aged map. "Your offer is unexpected." He rubbed his face with the hand that had formerly strangled Gordon. "I believe you've bought an extension of life, Captain. But remember, if you cross me, I'll find out, and when I do, you'll never break your word again."

The captain sat there a moment, catching his breath.

The wild-eyed man continued. "And if your word is true, I will find you again regardless, to return your map and reward you handsomely."

"Reward?" asked the captain, perking up his ears.

"I have need of your ship. My riches all lie overseas."

"Riches? Why are you here?" asked the captain.

"The same reason you gave me your map. Survival. Don't pretend you don't know who I am."

Gordon hesitated to say the name. He knew the mud was to hide the red hair and red beard. He had seen posters with the name of an ominous outlaw soldier on the run from the law.

"You're Hellion Swash."

"There it is. Good. Let that sink in a moment. If you don't think you can keep it to yourself, you'd be better off to lop off your tongue now." A sharp blade appeared in Hellion's hand, outstretched to the captain.

The captain's hand went instinctively to his mouth as if protecting it.

"Captain Gordon? You alright?" The voice came from the deck of the ship.

"You have my word," he whispered. "I'll sneak you to shore at night. No one will ever know." Then he cleared his voice. "Yes, I'm fine, Linden. Get back to work, damn it!" He slipped out of the cloth, back into the world of fresh air and bright light.

HELLION PONDERED IN his solitude. No matter what happened going forward, he would always be hunted. If the captain's tongue became loose when he sailed east to Sisterton, the mercenary army would just come sooner for him. They'd been watching all the ports on Mammoth Lake as well as the Gridlock Sea. All merchandise and passengers were logged and scrutinized at the ports. His unique characteristics had almost betrayed him thrice on this journey alone. Luckily for him, dead men tell no tales. That one truth had given him great comfort in the past, which made him pause to consider what had been different this time. Was Hellion Swash losing his edge?

He took another snort from his flask. He had lost nothing. He exhaled slowly, confident in his decision. The boredom from the solitude of daytime was what bothered him the most. He never went out until night, which left one option for daytime when he couldn't sleep. Whiskey.

He was a despicable, miserable, ruined man, and he was only three and twenty years. Despite the misery, he was resilient and hadn't made plans for any dirt naps yet. In fact, it was a direct consequence of his resiliency that he had survived childhood. He'd always had just one skill in this life. He could fight. He found his way into the fighting rings at age twelve as a skinny, nameless orphan. But after notching twenty straight wins on the streets, the alias Hellion Swash began to gain fame.

Everything started to turn around in his life while he was winning. The problems came when his fights drew such a crowd that he had enough coin in his pocket to live on. As soon as he was comfortable in a rented room with a roof over his head, a man had shown up telling him he had to lose his next fight. He was small but very quick, so he laughed the angry man away, saying, "No one can beat me." But when the man returned, he didn't convince the youngster with his fists. No, he used a metal bar and nearly killed the boy. After that, the boy threw his first fight.

For the next two years the boy only won when he was supposed to win. He often made more money when he lost than when he won. While his income steadily rose, his self-respect plummeted. He hated the man for making him do it, but he hated himself even more. He had become a willing slave. Letting people's fists collide with your skull would prove to be a short career.

Hellion shook his head to clear the unpleasant memories. He knew he'd made not only the correct choice but the only choice with a future. If he'd killed the captain, he would have to kill the crew. Then he'd have to sail alone on the largest freshwater lake known to civilization and hope to avoid imprisonment should he find an actual port. He would stick to his original plan. His new life would begin in the settlement of Mossport.

Chapter 2

THE LONE FUR trader emerged on the hillside, soundlessly slipping through the spines of the sinister comb of trees and into the vivid sunlight. He lifted a hand to shield his eyes. Behind him appeared a tall, shaggy black horse. Its saddle and packs were filled with skins, herbs, and anything else the man could use to barter for supplies. At first glance the man's age would be a tricky guess. The faded clothes and fatigued gait hinted at a lifetime of experience, but his eyes would suggest otherwise. Of course, one would need to get close enough to see through the brown hair that shielded them. He'd been on his own the last five years. Apprenticed by the only man who rivaled his own skill in the wilderness, this was one of the few times he'd stepped out of his element…the elements. He could count the times he'd visited civilization on one hand, and he'd never stayed long.

The only town he'd ever seen lay down the hillside on the shore of what he would describe as the ocean. But unlike the sea, the water was not salty. The body of water happened to be one of the largest lakes yet discovered. The supply of the lake came from the impenetrable mountains to the north, and what lay beyond that, no one claimed to know. The small town was a faint echo of the distant orchestra of human society. It quickly faded into an immediate surrounding area farmed with wheat, corn, and potatoes mostly. The livestock included sheep, poultry, and goats.

The weather of the town had a tendency to be severe, particularly in winter. Worse, there were no roads to the town. If the Great Mammoth Lake, as it was called, froze over, no supplies could be delivered until it melted. The people were hardy. Most were friendly but also wary of traveling too far away from the only civilization reachable by land. The bolder inhabitants had a tendency of not returning after venturing too far.

A very select few made their living in the dense wilderness that lay to the west of the gray-skied, rocky, moss-covered settlement for which the town was named. These people tended to be very good at staying alive. In these people's small circles, no one was more respected than the man gazing upon the port now, Pike Granger. He wasn't scared of the unknown. He thrived in it.

As he approached Mossport from afar on the clear afternoon, he gazed north to glimpse the Mortapenum Mountains. They rose skyward more like a wall than an actual mountain range. They marked the end of the map, for no one had ever found a way to pass the impenetrable barrier. Some speculated the world ended and there was nothing beyond the rock walls. Others believed the mountains guarded the afterlife, a place they might all see someday. One man claimed to have been on the other side. His story was beguiled and scrutinized and had since become more of a story for children rather than recorded history. While never accepted as anything other than the ravings of a madman, the only book ever published by Horton Conner had made its way into nearly every library worldwide in the mere century since its publication. Even Granger owned a copy in his cabin to go with the handful of books left behind by his mentor.

The woods to the west impeded the advancement of civilization almost as well as the mountains to the north. The other reason for the lack of roads to the settlement was a vast desert to the south. The south shore of Mammoth Lake was bordered by a smaller mountain range known as the Lesser Mortapenums. The gigantic rocks that formed the smaller range tumbled downward and sprawled into the sands of the Deadlund Desert.

When Pike Granger appeared on the dirt road leading into the little town, people took notice of the strange man. He was a little taller than most in Mossport, and his dress was purely functional for his occupation. He wore a crude vest of animal hide with what could only be described as a cape covering his shoulders and ending near his knees. His pants appeared to be fashioned from wool but had nearly as many leather patches as original green wool left. His hair was long, and his beard hadn't been trimmed since his last visit to town, a full year ago the previous spring. He looked wild, and to those unfamiliar with him, dangerous.

The huntsman tied his horse to the front of Grom's Trade Shop and lugged off a shoulderful of hides from his impressive steed's back as the front door of the shop opened. In the doorway stood a bald-headed shopkeeper, one of the few inhabitants in town with recognition in their eyes.

"Granger! It's been too long!" The jovial owner for which the shop was named had a habit of befriending every customer he had. Most people liked him for his friendly personality, but many were also careful not to be too free lipped in the man's presence. In his store, the only general store in town, personal secrets and indiscretions flew out the door like free samples in a pastry kitchen. "I can see the dry spell hasn't hindered your season at all. The produce farmers have been doing rain dances every night. We've never had a spring without rain."

Pike shrugged. "I suppose that's what comes from the mild winter. If this year's total is half of last year's, I can't really complain."

Grom patted the great horse on the shoulder and it reared up with a low whinny, causing him to flee to safety.

"Sorry, Grom," said Pike, running his hand down the steed's neck to calm it. "Clyde isn't what you'd call a people-friendly horse."

Grom laughed, slapping his leg a safe distance away. "Hargh! I wouldn't call him a broke horse neither. How many times that wild beast throw you off?"

"Just once."

Grom shook his head in amazement. He motioned for Pike to follow. "I'd sooner put a saddle on a wild moose myself."

"How are the prices on hides back east?" asked the hunter, carrying the first load of fur into the store behind the shopkeeper.

"I hate to tell you the city folk are more concerned with fashion than warmth these days. The raccoon and opossum hides won't get you as much as last year." He paused, clearing some space on his counter previously occupied by order and inventory sheets. "We'll just go through one batch at a time like always." He sorted the hides into separate piles based on species. When he unrolled the final, heaviest specimen, he smiled with eyes wide in amazement. "A monster bear is always in fashion. They'll pay well for this one. It must have been gigantic!"

"It might be my biggest yet," said Pike, smiling. "This one was hunting me and Clyde more than the other way around, but the story probably won't affect the price."

"Nay, but it should. How long are you in town fer?"

"Probably as long as it takes to unload the skins and get a few supplies. Is my credit restored from last year's run?"

"For the amount you spend, you might as well be the richest man this side of Sisterton." Grom paused, getting serious for a second. "The reason I ask is there's a way for you to make the next ten years' wages now if you don't mind hanging around town."

Pike smiled, "Now Grom, don't get me involved in anything illegal; I know I'm not street smart, but even I know coin like that doesn't come the regular way."

Grom held his hands up in defense. "I'd never suggest something like that, friend. But you see we have a real problem here besides the drought. Something has been terrorizing the livestock since spring began. There's a beast about that's taken dozens of animals."

The huntsman stood quietly for a minute after listening. "No one's gotten it yet?" he asked, surprised. "That's a lot of money for one animal, Grom."

The shopkeeper nodded his head knowingly. "I'm putting up a large part of that bounty. This town can't survive a harsh winter if we lose too much livestock. After a mild one, everyone knows how the next one will be. What's more than that is everyone's afraid to go. We already upped the reward three times. The last group of men that went out twelve days ago, well…they never came back yet. We have reason to believe they're dead."

"How do you know they aren't just lost? Twelve days isn't so long."

Grom looked at the ground. "One of their horses made it back a few days past. Poor animal had a bite the size of a watermelon missing from its hind quarters. It shouldn't have been able to make it back in such bad shape, but the horse was so traumatized it couldn't stop. We had to put the poor beast down. I've never seen such terror in an animal's eyes."

"We dealing with a bear or wolf?"

"Neither."

Pike looked at him, confused. "You don't know what it is?"

"No sir," said Grom gingerly. "But we think it's bigger than anything ever recorded out here. I like you, Granger. I don't think you ought to go by yourself."

Pike laughed. "You don't have much faith in me."

"Oh, I do. I know you'll find it. But you need someone to watch your back. Six good men, all in their prime, are gone. I was talking with a newcomer to town a few days back. He might be interested in joining you."

"I'm not much of a babysitter, Grom."

"This guy acts like he's used to being on his own too. Just let me ask around and see if I can find where he's staying. I'll even pay for your room tonight."

"You seem dead set on it," said Pike with a sigh. He preferred doing things his own way more often than not. "Fine. Send him to the Mammoth Inn if you find him. But I'll warn you now, if he looks like a liability, I'm leaving him here."

Chapter 3

CLYDE WARILY CARRIED Pike Granger down the main strip of town. The large specimen of a horse was not accustomed to the number of people that loitered in the street. The horse's eyes glanced suspiciously as he passed by the flower-scented candlemaker, the noisy smithy's shop, and the sweet aroma from the bakery before arriving to a place his rider had seen but never visited. Situated on the shore side of the Mossport lane of businesses stood the largest building Pike had ever laid eyes on. The three-storied Mammoth Inn. He dismounted and led Clyde around the back of the building, instantly feeling the coarse wind that ripped off the gigantic lake. Clyde's gray nostrils flared at the seaside smells that were unfamiliar to him. Pike gently rubbed the horse's neck to settle his nerves before leading him into the stable. Then Granger tossed the stable boy two coins and requested double grain for his companion. Next, he took the horse's saddle off because even if the boy could reach it, Clyde probably wouldn't tolerate it. Pike threw his saddle bag and gear over his shoulder and took a quick glance around. Clyde wasted no time in digging into the hay provided in his rack. Satisfied with his horse's lodging, Pike walked around front to settle his own.

It was closer to evening than midday by the time he entered the front door. The great room was warmed by a large fireplace, and a few men sat drinking at a table. Pike looked around for a moment before a young woman came out of the kitchen with a tray of drinks. She motioned that she would be right with him.

After serving the men at the table, she directed him to the far end of the bar.

"What grade of room you looking for?" she asked, eyeing him up and down.

"The regular kind, I suppose," he replied, feeling uncertain about his response. "How'd you know I needed a room?"

"I know you're not from town, and you don't strike me as the type to socialize," she replied, glancing at his hunting knife and the bow hanging on his back.

"I'll take your least expensive room, as long as it has a large enough bed. Tonight is actually being paid for by Grom, but anything beyond that is my responsibility."

"I think I have a room that might work for you," she said, staring off like she was in deep thought. "It's one of my better ones, but at least you'll fit in the bed. I'll give you or Grom or whoever's paying a fair deal on it, but I have to request you go straight to the bathhouse before I let you inside." Her face looked firm.

Pike felt embarrassed. It was an unfamiliar situation. Was the woman trying to be rude? "I'm sorry, if you'd rather I took a different room or the stable I…"

"Don't be ridiculous," she interrupted. "I'll have a bath drawn up for you now. I'll send for a barber at once. If you're going to enjoy my best room, I want you to feel good and look good at the same time. Might be I'm just curious what you look like under that hair and grime." She said it without a smile.

Pike was untrained in the ways of behaving around women, but he knew better than to be rude. "Best room? Why I think I just might enjoy a bath, Miss…"

"Jada."

"That's a really pretty name, Miss Jada," he replied, feeling foolish. "I'm Pike Granger."

The bartender's eyes rose. "I think I've heard of you before," she said with just a hint of softness in her expression.

"Well, I hope it wasn't something embarrassing," replied Pike.

"I wouldn't tell you if it was. But don't worry, it wasn't." She winked at him, confounding him so much he didn't know how to respond. "Well, don't just stand there, follow me up to the washroom. I'll get you set up."

As Pike followed the young lady up the stairs that rose from the far end of the bar, he felt as if there was something familiar about her. Almost like a tune he'd heard before but couldn't put his finger on when or where he'd heard it. He wasn't sure if she was being humorous or strange, but being in her presence seemed to cloud his thoughts.

"Now, Mr. Granger," she said, snapping his thoughts back into the hallway where they now stood. In front of him was the entrance to the washroom. "You'll want to be back down in the main room early because we have good entertainment tonight, and you'll have a hard time getting a seat if you don't. I'll throw in a meal with your room, but drinks will be extra. You can set your bags down in the corner there," she motioned to a bench against the wall, "and just leave your dirty clothes next to the tub. I'll have them laundered and returned to you tomorrow. The stable boy will haul up your water in a few minutes, and I'll make sure your room is ready for you. Anything else? Oh yes, I forgot to fetch the barber. I'll send him shortly. Any other requests?"

Pike felt breathless for the woman as she rattled off her instructions so quickly. "Uh, no, Miss Jada."

"Good then," she said patting his back. "I'll see you tonight." With that, she raced off down the hall.

A MUCH CLEANER version of Pike Granger descended the stairs for dinner that night. His face had been scrubbed and shaven while his hair was trimmed and tamed with a comb, although it was still lengthy enough with the slightest curl reaching his shoulders. He wore a newer and cleaner pair of charcoal wool pants with a long-sleeved navy cotton shirt. When he had looked in the mirror, he'd been surprised at how young he appeared without a beard. He felt both confident and foolish at the same time. At least he wouldn't have to stay in town for too long.

As Jada had said, the long tables were filling up quickly with towns-people. The wooden tabletops were already damp from the spillage of ale from overserved customers. Pike found an open chair at the bar and sat down to take in his surroundings.

The far corner of the large room had a wooden platform that rose up about a foot higher than the rest of the dining area. An old man with a long gray beard was unpacking his fiddle from its case. All the tables directly surrounding the platform had been filled to capacity. The fire in the middle of the room was now a roaring flame, with plenty of wood piled up to keep it going into the night. The chimney rose high and was decorated with stag, elk, and moose antlers until it reached the immensely high ceiling. The door to the road opened frequently with thirsty newcomers. There were now three serving girls hustling around with trays on their shoulders. Many of the men in the room were speaking loudly to one another, almost shouting in their conversation. It was more people in a room than Pike had ever seen.

"You can't be the same man I sent upstairs earlier this afternoon." Jada had reappeared behind the bar. "What do you think of your room?"

Pike wasn't sure how she'd found time to change her clothes and fashion her hair, but she looked different than earlier in the day. She had been attractive before, but now she looked like a real lady. "It's the nicest I've ever stayed in, Miss Jada. I hope you don't mind my saying, you sure look pretty tonight."

Her mouth opened up in wonder at the compliment. "You hear that, boys?" she asked the other men sitting at the bar. "That is how you address your barmaid properly. Now, Mr. Pike, what does a gentleman like yourself prefer to drink?"

"I'll have what he's having," replied Pike, pointing to the man next to him who sat staring blankly at his cup.

"House ale it is," she replied and jetted into the kitchen.

Jada returned within minutes with fresh bread and butter and a mug of ale. The bread was better than anything Pike had eaten in recent memory. "Your stew will be out in a few minutes. Anything else I can get you?"

"Maybe the recipe for this bread. This is delicious."

She laughed and then raised her eyebrows. "You just wait until you try my stew. I'll have you coming into town every week after just one bite."

Pike smiled thinking about the week's journey that had seen him from his cabin into town. The man sitting next to Pike continued to stare at his drink with intermittent peeks at the bread Pike was tearing open. He was a middle-aged man with very rough-looking hands, most likely from years of farming. The man looked downtrodden, almost downright sad.

"Have some bread, friend," said the hunter, handing his neighbor a piece of bread. "You look troubled."

The man eagerly accepted the bread and took a large bite, tearing the flakey crust in two. He chewed quickly, then swallowed his mouthful down with a large gulp of ale.

"Mighty kind of you, stranger," he replied. "Tell me, young man, where are you from?"

"West," replied Pike.

The man perked up upon hearing his response. "You haven't had any run-ins with any unusual creatures, have you?"

"Nothing out of the usual that I've come across. Just the typical elk, bear, cougar, and the like. I've heard you folk might have some type of man-eater on the loose.

"Tales don't do justice to seeing it, young man."

Pike turned sideways to the man. "Is this why you look so troubled? Tell me, what did you see?"

The man gripped his mug tightly with both hands. "It was unnatural. Too dark to see anything but the outline. Ran on two hind legs, taller than two men stacked on top of each other."

Pike's reaction conveyed his disbelief of the story. "Is there anything helpful you can tell me if I am to hunt this beast down?"

The man patted Pike's hand. "You seem like a good man, but don't be a fool. The animal now has a taste for human flesh. We'll have to wait for the army to arrive before we put an end to whatever's been attacking us. There's no sense in losing any more men out there."

Jada came bursting through the kitchen doors with a large bowl of steaming stew.

Pike replied confidently, "I will track this monster you speak of, and when I find it, I'll put an end to your fears."

Jada looked at him, her face horrified. "You will kill the beast?" The conversations stopped, and now everyone around the bar seemed to be listening.

"Yes," replied Pike firmly.

Laughter and howls were the only replies he received.

Then the stories were yelled out for all to hear.

"The beast ripped a full-grown ram in half!" one man yelled.

"I saw it carry off two goats!" yelled another. "One under each arm!"

Pike Granger crossed his arms, annoyed at the mockery surrounding him. The yells eventually died down to a murmur as he sat quietly with no reply. He tried to pretend he couldn't hear the continued insults, now being whispered. He turned his attention to the stew and sat in silence. The ale continued to flow, and his neighbors eventually lost interest in the strange man and went back to their private conversations. After some time, the outburst became a distant memory and the fiddler started working his bow. All the attention quickly turned toward the stage. The wiry man with the long beard stomped one foot and danced his bow across the instrument's strings. Pike had never heard such a pleasing sound and was instantaneously mesmerized by the music. The first song he called out was "Waves on the Mammoth," which referred to a ship lost in a storm on the big lake that never was found. It was an intricate arrangement with a refrain that grew louder with each verse. The sound awoke something inside the hunter. It felt as if he had an extra sense that the sound was feeding. *What sorcery is this?* He marveled at the goose bumps forming on his arms before he promptly rubbed them away.

The old fiddler was both an excellent musician and storyteller. It seemed as if everyone had forgotten about Pike's existence by the end of the first song. While Granger thoroughly liked the music, it also made him feel unsettled. It was at times like these he wished the Baron was still with him. The old man had taught him so much before he disappeared. Pike shook his head to clear his thoughts. He had plans to make, and no one here would seem to be of any help. He turned his back on the music, pushed his empty mug away from him, and started to stand up when he felt a hand on his shoulder.

Chapter 4

G RANGER SPUN AROUND to see an average-size man in a short-brimmed hat wearing dark glasses. He was a pale man, with a freshly shaven face, sporting black wool pants, a white collared shirt, and a long black coat. His tinted lenses were large and obscured much of his face.

"Are you the one called Pike?" the man asked, almost in a harsh whisper.

"I am," replied the hunter. "Who are you?"

The man seemingly ignored the question. "Grom said you needed help tracking down the man-eater," the stranger said.

Pike looked the man up and down, unable to hide the skepticism on his brow. The man's wardrobe was more suited to town life than any type of outdoorsman work.

"Perhaps Grom made it sound that way," he replied dismissively. "Have you ever had any experience hunting or tracking?"

The man in the hat smiled darkly. "Not animals."

"Well, you probably don't belong out there then. Especially the way the people around here are talking. Let me save us both some significant time and hassle. I already told Grom when he mentioned you earlier; it's not a good idea for anyone to come with me."

If his response fazed the man behind the shades, he didn't show it. "I'm going after it either way," he replied matter-of-factly. "If you're worried about splitting the pot, imagine getting nothing when I haul back the trophy."

Pike huffed. "I can see you're a confident man. May I ask why you're wearing a hat and glasses in this dark, warm bar room?"

"It's not for fashion," came the hoarse reply.

"I don't care much about that. I would be worried about what you'll show up in to go tracking with me." Pike couldn't suppress a smile. "At least tell me a little about yourself before I decide."

The man's lips tightened. Was he angry or just deep in thought?

"I can tell you this. I don't need your help. Your friend Grom hunted me down because you're staying here tonight. The reason I came was for the free drinks. Speaking of which…" he flagged down Jada and yelled in his harsh whisper, "A bottle of your strongest spirits on Grom's tab, please!"

Pike studied the man. What could be seen of his cleanly shaven face was a firm jaw, an air of malice, and the expression of a man who took himself too seriously. It was also possible the man's confidence was a bluff to split Pike's bounty. He did not look to be the type of man the Baron would have associated with.

"I'm sorry to offend you," began Pike. "Grom is a good man, and while he thinks he's looking out for me, he is not truly my friend. I don't have any friends. I work best alone. As I said, he told me he'd be sending you against my wishes."

"Whatever your thoughts are regarding me, they're likely wrong," replied the stranger. "But you're wiser than most to admit you have no friends. I wish I'd have known that in a former life."

Jada returned just then with a bottle and a glass.

"You can keep the glass, ma'am." The words grated like gravel crushed underfoot. He grabbed the bottle and put it to his lips. With his head tilted back, he relished the long swig of potent liquor.

"Your former life must not have been long ago, judging by your age," replied Pike. "I've always been told a man must believe in something to be complete. If not friends, then family. If not family, then community. If not community, perhaps nature itself." He could hear the Baron's voice in his head while he repeated it.

The stranger started laughing and nearly spit out his second gulp of alcohol. "Do you buy into that selfless bullshit? The world's an ugly, cruel place. To deny that is foolishness."

"Well, I believe in something bigger than me."

"Ha!" laughed the stranger. "There's the difference between us. I only believe in myself."

"Where has that gotten you so far?"

The man set his bottle next to Pike and looked serious for a moment. "It's kept me on the sunny side of the dirt for this long—a place not many I come in contact with tend to stay too long, regardless of their belief. Maybe I'm just lucky, or maybe I'm a part of a bigger plan, as you say. Maybe my crooked, ugly, moth-eaten ass has been kept around to meet you!" He laughed deeply and slapped Pike on the shoulder before gripping the bottle again.

Now it was Pike's turn to be offended. He rose to full height and spoke his mind down to the stranger. "You're a twisted, cocky, selfish drunkard. I know I just met you, but I can't think of one good reason to take you with me. I'm sure you can't track. You have no supplies, no experience, no plan. You haven't even told me your name."

"You sound like my last woman," the man replied, nearly laughing. "But you left out my best trait."

"What's that? The ability to still stand after drinking a jug of alcohol that would kill most people?"

"I'd call that my second-best trait." The stranger leaned in closer to whisper to Granger. His voice almost had a metallic tone as he choked out his next words. "I'm the deadliest weapon ever unleashed on this old world. You can doubt me if you like. Many fools have. I can fight from morning to night, and I never get tired of killing. I was made for battle, and it sounds like you might need that."

Pike shook his head. "So you're a soldier now too? You realize I'm hunting an animal, not going to war."

The man grabbed Pike's arm and latched it so tightly he couldn't move. He lowered his glasses for Pike to see his furious, vertically split eyes. They were the eyes of a predator. "Keep your voice down," he growled between clenched teeth. "I am not your friend, but we can either help each other or hurt each other."

"What kind of demon are you?" asked Granger in astonishment, still unable to pull his arm away.

"I'm the kind that's been honest with you up front, even if you weren't listening. I'm the kind that keeps his word for bad or good. I'm the kind of guy you hate but despite that you want on your side. For lack of better words, I am the monster needed by you, because I see you, and you are no killer."

Granger was speechless for a moment as the merriment of the boisterous night continued around their lonely island of testosterone. The stare-down that ensued suggested they were at an impasse. It was decision time. Against all his better judgment and internal thoughts and even his common sense, Pike Granger finally relented.

"Since you're so hard set on this, I'll give you one chance," started Pike. "You have to give me your good word, as you put it, that you won't hinder my tracking. If you can't follow me, you'll do nothing but assure either the beast gets away or we die. Just remember, killing might be the goal of the hunt, but putting yourself in good position is the key to the ultimate goal."

The stranger clapped his hands, grinning. "Sounds poetic, my good tracker. I wouldn't know, of course. Shall we shake on our deal?" He extended a white hand toward Pike.

Pike reluctantly accepted the man's hand. *What am I getting myself into?* "And how shall I address you since you haven't given me your name?"

The white and gold flash of the man's smile appeared instantaneously.

"People call me a lot of things, mostly unrepeatable. How about you use one of my favorite nicknames. Call me Lion."

Normally, the gaudy name would have made the huntsman bubble over with laughter, but if the man was not totally full of lies, and Granger was starting to believe it possible he wasn't, the name was fitting of his personality. "Shall we turn in now for an early morning, Lion?" asked Pike.

"On the contrary, my tracker. Now we must celebrate our joining of talents! Barmaid! Another bottle, please, and this time my companion needs a glass!"

The look Jada gave Pike resembled a treed cougar. Sans roar, she produced the bottle and glass, but the hunter noted no more warmth from her eyes the remainder of the evening.

"Thanks, Dame," replied Lion. Then he continued as if she couldn't hear him. "That one's colder than the Mammoth come winter! We should bring her with us. One glare from Medusa and the beast might turn to stone!" He laughed heartily at his own joke, the result of the alcohol starting to mellow his tone toward Pike.

Pike looked apologetically at Jada as she stood stone-eyed with arms crossed, watching Lion.

"Don't mind that one, partner. A heart like that could never keep you warm at night." Lion poured Pike a drink and then raised his bottle in the air. "Listen here, and raise that glass. I think you'll like this. Let us drink."

Let us drink to past, present, and 'morrow,
To sweet love, may we give more than borrow,
To life, that it be fulfilled not hollow,
To all who can't drink away their sorrow,
Last to the dead, who we'll all soon follow!

Pike drank his glass and set it on the bar. "I thought you knew nothing of poetry? Very profound for a man who describes himself as you have."

Lion laughed with the butt of the bottle still high in the air. "I didn't make that up myself, you know."

"I think I like you more when you're drunk, Lion."

"You'll like me more when I kill that beast tomorrow."

Pike slapped his odd partner on the back. "Now I know you're telling stories."

The two men and the rest of the patrons continued drinking well into the morning. To the outside world, the problems of drought and monsters looked to be distant from the minds of the Mammoth Inn's guests tonight. The fiddler picked up his pace, and many took to dancing on the tabletops while clapping their hands with the pounding of the old fiddler's foot.

Lion was a strange man, but perhaps he would be able to work with Pike, as long as he listened. A second set of eyes could be helpful. The man didn't seem like the type to run off at the first sign of danger, at least. And if he was nothing else, Lion seemed to be brutally honest. Perhaps Grom had done well to pair him with Pike. Or perhaps it was just the alcohol that made it all sound like a good idea to the hunter.

Eventually the townspeople began filing out to head to their homes. Sunrise would come far too soon for many, Pike included. He made plans to meet Lion at Grom's shop in the afternoon.

Pike climbed the stairs to his room and washed his face in the basin set out for him. He half walked, half crawled into his large feather-stuffed bed and finally stared contentedly at the ceiling. He inhaled deeply from his clean surroundings, putting his arms behind his head. It only took a moment for him to drift into peacefulness.

A knock at the door would forever change how he'd remember this night.

Chapter 5

PIKE JOLTED UPRIGHT in bed, more alert than he'd thought possible given the current circumstances. His head hurt, throbbing with each pulse. He took his time putting his feet on the floor to steady himself. Had he imagined it?

There was another light knock on his door.

He rose to his feet and made his way toward the door, keeping his arms outstretched in case he lost his balance. He moved slowly, quietly. Halfway to the door, he thought it wise to keep a hand on the handle of his knife, which he realized he had never removed from his belt. When he reached the door, he quietly unbolted it and turned the brass knob slowly before pulling it toward him.

The flicker of a single candle danced its light on her face.

"Jada? What are you doing?" he asked, taking his hand off the knife.

Her eyes were wide in surprise as she realized he had been about to draw a blade on her.

"I came up here to try to talk some sense into you!" she replied angrily. "Do you really plan to hunt the monster?"

"Yes," he replied. "It's the only reason I'm not on my way back to my cabin."

"It will kill you," she said slowly. "Don't you understand that?" Her words picked up their pace. "If it doesn't, that man you're with? He's a scoundrel. I've seen his type before. He'll probably knife you and rob you the first chance he gets. Don't you see how stupid you're acting? This animal killed a group of six men!"

Pike took a breath, trying to rationalize his choice with the woman. "I've done this type of tracking since I could walk. I try to avoid boasting, but in truth I was made to do this. There's no one better for the job. I can really be of help to your town, so why would you be upset about that? Why are you even worried about me at all?"

Jada looked at Pike through narrowed eyes. "I fear you may be too simple-minded to understand."

Pike was confused. Why was she insulting him? "I may live simple, but that doesn't mean I'm a fool."

"Please tell me," she replied with begging eyes. "What can I do to convince you not to throw your life away? Could I convince you to stay here? Listen to how ridiculous I sound right now."

"You want *me* to stay with you?" asked the hunter.

"That's not what I said," Jada replied quickly. "I…suppose I could pay you to work for me."

"Work for you?" asked Pike, surprised. "You own this place?"

Jada folded her arms and stood sturdily holding the candle in her fist. "Of course, I own this place. You see how hard I work to keep it running."

There was silence for a moment.

"You're a remarkable woman," said Pike.

"Thank you," said Jada, her eyes still piercing and businesslike. "Is that all you have to say?"

Pike shrugged. "This is a real nice place, but I don't belong here."

"Don't you have any aspirations, Mr. Granger? What about building a business, or making a life in Mossport? What about a family?"

Pike cleared his throat almost apologetically. "I guess I just aspire to kill this beast."

"Fine," replied Jada curtly. "But just remember when you die alone out there, whether on this trip or on another, you could have had someone who actually cared about you. For some strange reason when I met you, I thought you might be different from the rest. My mistake. You're a bigger fool than the whole lot of them!"

"Whole lot of who?" asked Pike, confused.

"Men!" replied Jada, slamming the door in his face.

Was it something he had said? Should he apologize? He decided she was much too angry to talk to tonight. Maybe she had been drinking too? The Baron had warned him once that the ways of women could never be fully understood by a man. Perhaps that was an understatement. Even if he wasn't sure what had just happened, he decided he could try to smooth things over in the morning.

The next day Pike awoke later than usual. He ached and did not feel well rested but could no longer sleep. He washed his face and followed the smell of breakfast to the dining area. Very few people were in the great room now, and yet there was Jada, scrubbing the tables and motioning for him to take the same seat as the night before.

The heat of the great fire and close proximity of patrons had been replaced with a damp chill in the air and the start of a newer, but much smaller, fire. The quietness about the place was eerie after the boisterousness of the previous evening. The music and howling and cheers still echoed in Pike's ears, making the present scene seem sad and lonely.

Jada brought him a tray of soft-boiled eggs, biscuits, and sausage gravy. She hardly uttered a word to him at breakfast but would smile whenever he looked her way. The food was excellent, which shouldn't have surprised Pike after the stew from the night before.

Finally, he tried to break the silence. "If anything could change my mind, it would be your cooking," he said softly. "I do still need to settle my bill with you before I leave."

"It's already settled," she replied.

"I never paid you," he protested.

"If you want to repay me, come back alive," Jada replied matter-of-factly. "I know now you must go on your quest, so I hope you are successful."

"But last night…"

"Forget about last night," she replied.

How could he forget about last night? She'd come to his room late, surprised him in his drunken state, and then slammed the door in his face. The Baron had also told him that one of the secrets to good relationships with women was to always apologize. *For what?* he'd asked. *I'll let you know if I ever find out* was the reply.

"I'm sorry, Jada," he started, unsure of himself.

"For what?" she asked, surprised.

"I still don't know," he said, gathering up his gear. "But I will come back to visit you when we're done."

Jada didn't quite smile, but Pike thought he detected contentment from the woman before he walked out the door.

Chapter 6

THERE WAS NOTHING *quite equal to the feeling before battle. A true warrior's senses reached the next level of awareness in the hours before the fight. The man, deep in his own form of meditation, did not need his eyes open to know there was a soldier standing behind him. He could feel the heat given off by the unnaturally large man from several feet away. The man to his right held a long spear, as evidenced by the wind cutting a light hum against the sharp blade pointed toward the sky. To his left, he could smell alcohol on the breath of a man who had drunk too much. The man was quietly wiping his sweating palms on his tunic. He could feel the man shaking with either chill or fear.*

War was the ultimate test of a man. Hellion Swash breathed in deeply while raising his red-bearded face upward toward the sun with his eyes still closed. Barely visible under his signature red beard were his mercenary army numerals, tattooed upon his neck like every other soldier. It had taken him sixteen years in the world to find what he was made for. He almost smiled in pity thinking about the other men around him. Many were older than his twenty and three years, but none had more experience in hand-to-hand combat. He was the finest soldier the mercenary army had ever had. For the past seven years, he had volunteered to go wherever the death toll was expected to be highest. He was considered a weapons expert with a sword, spear, bow, and ax. His superiors described him on numerous occasions as the purest form of a true killer, and they paid him handsomely for his services.

So acute were his senses that he knew something was terribly wrong before he led his squad across the plain that morning. There was nothing he could do about it. Even if he had wanted to stop the advance, the order had already been given. His refusal would result in the gallows, and the task would be carried out by another in his place. But he could sense doubt in some of his men. And these men had known no fear the last time they had fought for Hellion. That was just one of the perks of being a seasoned fighter. It gave those around him confidence that they hadn't earned. Only he had survived the last thirty-two assignments.

He opened his eyes and gave his men no sign of his misgivings for what was to come. A messenger on a horse came riding full speed to his position. The rider waved a red cloth from the end of a long stick. It was the signal from the commander.

"Advance!" he shouted, stepping forward and feeling the coordinated movements of the men behind him. The enemy had previously retreated across the plain and settled into a low-lying field of trees and boulders. They had sought refuge from the arrows that had rained upon them and were now regrouped for a final defensive of their homeland. It would be futile, of course, but fighting until the last combatant was killed was expected by the mercenary army.

"Faster gait!" Hellion turned his march into a slow jog.

The men picked up their pace behind him as he quickly approached the halfway point to the battle. He could see the enemy peeking from behind rocks and trees, bows raised and ready to unleash their arrows into his men.

"Raise shields!" he barked at his men. There was no cover on the open plain, but there weren't enough archers to have a sufficient impact on his fifty men.

"War cry!" he howled at his men. They responded with whoops and blood-curdling screams that scared the enemy into shooting their first grouping of arrows too far out. Hellion smiled as the majority of arrows missed their mark. A few bounced off of shields, and one man caught one in

his foot. He roared with anger and jumped around in pain before running back into position and limping forward.

His men had now jogged past the halfway point. Not too much further now.

"Ready arms!" He pulled his longsword from its sheath on his back and heard metal bearing witness to the sky all around him. The second volley of arrows would let loose soon. It was time.

"Attack!" He screamed and ran full speed down the hill. He could feel the ground tremble beneath his men's feet. Their breaths labored from the speed. The flight of arrows again reached into the sky, undoubtedly about to end the lives of some of Hellion's men. But they followed him, as they always had, and it almost made Hellion begin to wonder if his suspicions were unfounded.

The arrows rained down amongst them, and within minutes, the lucky ones of his men joined him in the boulder field.

He batted down an enemy spear in front of him before kicking the first man to the ground and opening him up with his long sword. The sound of hand-to-hand combat echoed off the rocks as he and his men chopped their way through the poorly trained and ill-equipped victims in front of them. It was every man for himself from here to the end, just as Hellion had always preferred. The enemy had no coordination of manpower and were going to be picked off in the rock and tree field one by one.

Hellion looked left and right, deciding where to engage next, when he smelled a trace of alcohol in the wind. Someone was too close to his flank. He jumped left and swung his blade in defense but still caught a spear in his shoulder. He glimpsed its head coming out the front of his shoulder and knew the weapon well as he roared in pain and swung around to see a familiar face, stricken with terror.

"Traitor!" he yelled and took the man's legs with his sword.

HELLION SWASH WOKE and instantly grabbed his shoulder. The wound had since healed but not his memories. He squinted in the sunlight, realizing it had to be near midday already. He shook the memories from his head, picked up his wool duffle, and carefully brushed the hay off his clothes. It was far from the first time he'd slept in a stable, though if he'd had the coin, he would have gotten a room at the Mammoth. The air was chilly, which drew sharp contrast to his blood. It boiled with anticipation. Today would be a good day to kill.

He had enjoyed himself the previous night. He hadn't had an open tab at a bar for a good long while. Actually, it had been since he left the army. He could tell the hunter still didn't trust him. Smart man. At least the woodsman had made good conversation. Being on the run had its share of downfalls. One of them was not being able to converse with anyone. Any man with good wit needed to exercise it in dialogue from time to time. Perhaps he was now far enough away from the bounty hunters to enjoy life a little more. He'd already located and removed every posted reward sign in town since he'd arrived. Truth be told, they were already remarkably faded and didn't match his current look. Gone was his long red beard that instilled fear wherever he went. Captain Gordon had been even better than his word. He'd given Hellion a duffle of weapons along with supplies to change his appearance before smuggling him to land at night. The man would need to be paid accordingly. His hair was now cropped short and covered with a hat, and the darkened glasses would likely prove the most valuable of all his disguises. But even with his new look, he couldn't take chances.

Hellion's stomach rumbled with hunger, but it was already past time to head to Grom's shop. He had a feeling if he was late Pike would not hesitate to leave without him. Presently, he couldn't afford to miss out on the reward. He was tired of scavenging for food and sleeping outside. His only true skill was not of much use in the civilized world, and nearly a year on the run had drained him of all his resources. However, that would eventually change once the reward was forgotten, and he could board a ship passing through the heart of the mercenary army waters....

In the meantime he was also doing Pike a favor. The hunter might have more skill in tracking the animal, but he was not the same type of survivor that Hellion Swash was. When the time came, he would prove his worth.

He scratched at the raven tattoo on his neck. It was healing nicely now. He lived the life of his ink, flying from one destination to the next, always a scavenger. It was ironic considering he had not picked out the image himself. He'd been in a hurry, as with most days when you're being hunted, and the artist did not speak his language. The work was quick and covered his army numerals with above-average skill. However, the most important thing was that the man wouldn't talk.

Hellion made his way by foot back into town. On the outskirts, he saw the sign of perhaps the first place he'd visit once he had money. It was not open yet; rather, it was a place most often frequented when the sun went down. He had seen the telltale glow of the red lantern in the darkness the past few evenings. The faded boards and blanketed windows gave few other clues about what went on inside the walls, but Hellion was no stranger to the type of business conducted there.

He continued down the center of the street, not oblivious to the stares of the townspeople who probably wondered what business he had in their town. He had little doubt that as soon as he left, Grom would tell everyone in town why he had sought their settlement. It was to hunt the beast, of course; he smiled at his own brilliance, at the same time befuddling the onlookers he passed.

When he reached Grom's shop, he saw an extraordinarily large black horse tied in the front. He stopped in the middle of the street. It was too big for a civilian. It looked like a cavalry horse for battle. Was the army here? How could they know…unless the captain had talked? Still, just one horse meant only one man. If need be, he could dispatch the spy and slip away…again. He swung his duffel around to the front of his shoulder. He reached in and felt the leather-wrapped handle of his long sword. It was the only weapon that actually belonged to him. Well, technically, it belonged to the army, but such nuances weren't terribly important at the moment. Concealment of such an obvious weapon was important, especially in the little town of Mossport. If he needed it, it was ready.

He kicked open the front door of the business with a loud bang.

Chapter 7

PIKE JUMPED AT the sudden appearance of Lion in the doorway. "You know, we usually knock first around here," said a slightly alarmed Grom.

"You haven't left yet?" asked Hellion, staring at Pike.

Pike shook his head. "I gave you my word. Might be regretting it now, though. You look awful."

"Well, so do you, hunter." He managed a grimace behind his darkened lenses. "I'll be fine. Wipe that worried look off your face already. I'm just not a morning person...or afternoon for that matter."

Pike glared at Grom, who quickly broke eye contact with the tracker.

"I'm outfitting you two with supplies," Grom finally announced. "The payment will have to come out of your reward money."

"I'll pay for my half up front," announced Pike. "I don't like to be in debt."

Grom shrugged. "Well, however you want to do it is fine with me. I suppose you don't have a horse?" He glanced at Lion.

"No, I don't."

"I have a loaner you can borrow until you get back. If you're successful, I'll keep the fee minimal."

"I suppose I don't have much of a choice," replied Lion, looking at Pike.

"You aren't doubling up with me," replied Pike.

Grom helped the pair choose their supplies wisely. Pike already had some of what he needed, but the two combined would be very ill prepared for any length of time without Grom's aid. Items selected included a tent, sleeping rolls, wool blankets, canteens, a pan, jerky, flour, salt, potatoes, and coffee.

After bagging and securing their supplies on their horses, Grom briefed them on the last sighting of the beast.

"The last attack happened two weeks ago at Solomon's sheep farm to the north of town. Take the north road for a spell and turn west at the first dirt crossroad. You'll see his pastures from there. He can give you more information when you get there. You two better be careful."

"Thank you for everything, Grom," replied Pike. "Don't worry if we're gone awhile. We'll go slow and not take any chances."

Lion tipped his brimmed hat to Grom and climbed into the saddle of the bony tan horse named Harley. Pike took the lead, and the two sped north.

THE SKIES WERE blue, but the wind had picked up considerably when the pair rode up to the ranch house built of large dark logs from the western forest. The turbulent sound of the gusting air squashed any ability to hear the expected ranch melodies of livestock bleats or clanging hand tools. The property was surrounded by dry, brown grasslands, thanks to the lack of rain. The northern backdrop of the gigantic Mortapenum Mountains made the size of the farm buildings, the open plains, and even the entire town of Mossport itself pale with insignificance. It looked as if the ground had jumped toward the sky from the flat plain that the farm stood on. The only signs of life on the ranch were the frightened sheep that hung close together while they watched the two strangers approach. The whole compound had an eerie air, like it had witnessed something unspeakable.

Ferrell Solomon came out of the main barn to greet Pike and Lion.

"What's your business here, boys?" His voice cut through the wind with a serious tone.

"My name's Pike, and this is Lion." The hunter motioned to his right. "We're looking to track the animal that attacked your farm two weeks ago. Is there anything you can tell us about that night that might be useful?"

Ferrell, squinting in the afternoon sunlight, looked up at the pair of riders. "All I can show you is what I found." He took a few steps before looking back and motioning to the two men. "Come around behind the barn." The pair dismounted and followed the farmer behind his large hay barn.

"I heard the sheep bleating in the middle of the night. Whatever was out there had them terrified. I let out my trusty shepherd dog Ginny, grabbed my ax, and ran out the door. There wasn't much for moonlight that night, so I couldn't really see anything, but I followed Ginny's bark. The dog chased whatever it was far into the field. Then it must have stopped and turned around. I heard Ginny screech, and I swear I heard every one of her bones snap. I ran out to her, but it was gone. Probably a lucky thing for me. I found Ginny still breathing but with her back broke. Had to put her down. Shame, she was a good dog too. The next morning I was missing two sheep. It wasn't too hard to see which way it went because there were two streaks of blood on either side of its footprints."

"You're saying it hauled off two full-grown sheep?" asked Pike.

Ferrell shrugged his shoulders. "I imagine it carried one in each arm."

"Impossible," said Pike. "Why did you bring us back here?"

"To show you what you're up against." The rancher knelt in the pen where they were now standing. He picked up a wooden crate that protected a large square of dirt. "Take a good look at this imprint. This is what you're tracking."

Beside Ferrell Solomon, there was a perfect imprint in the clay. It was unlike anything Pike had ever seen. The size was more than twice the length of a man's footprint. The weight needed to press into the dry ground must have been equal to that of five men.

"Did your dog have bite marks, or was it raked by claws?" asked Lion.

"I couldn't find any marks. It was almost as if it grabbed on to my Ginny and snapped her in half. It has to be massive."

Lion pursed his lips and swore under his breath.

Pike was still crouched by the print. "It looks to have some large claws. Definitely larger than any bear I've ever come across." He followed the track to the barbwire fence that enclosed the pen behind the barn. He studied the wire, still intact with no remnants of fur or flesh in the barbs. "Looks like it jumped your fence. You can see where it landed and skidded over there on the other side. That's at least ten paces. No animal this size would be able to clear that distance."

"Believe me, friends, I'm just as baffled as you are right now. I know there are some big animals in those western forests, but I've never dreamed of anything like this," said Ferrell shakily.

Pike could see the farmer's fear. He looked beside him to see Lion staring up at the sky as if lost. "There isn't anything this big out there. I've spent my whole life out there, believe me. After we bring this thing back, I imagine people might start believing in monsters. But if it's still out there, we'll find it."

Lion snapped back to earth and gave a menacing smile.

"I just hope you don't end up like those other men that last went after it. I certainly wouldn't join you for all the gold in Mossport. Good luck to you both though."

Pike thanked him and mounted big Clyde. Lion did likewise with Harley and they headed north, the direction of the last known trail of the beast.

The sun was midway between noon and nightfall, and the wind now blew more gently from the west. The weather looked as though it should hold steady for the next few days. Pike's plan was to keep an eye open for a sign of the beast and hopefully find its main trail toward the town.

"Tell me, Lion, are you still sure you want to be on this hunt?"

"Ask me that after we collect the money," he said, adjusting his glasses. "I fear this tracking business is going to be a bore. I've always been told monsters don't exist. Add to that all this area to cover, I figure we'll be lucky if we ever find it."

Pike smiled. "That's why you were wise to come with me. All I need to do is to find some fresh sign. Once I do, we'll find where it lives. No matter what type of creature it is, it's just an animal when it's all said and done. It will have a home territory. It will probably leave markings to signify its territory. We'll pay close attention to the comings and goings of its tracks and any of its kills we find. As big as it is, it will need to eat a large amount. I'll be curious as to whether it travels high or low ground, dry or swampy. We are definitely going to find some trails, and big ones at that. We'll take our time and learn everything we can before we go for the kill." He made eye contact with Lion to make sure he understood. "They say it killed the last group that went charging blindly after it. We'll not make the same mistake."

Lion broke eye contact and went back to his uninterested gaze at the sky. "Don't take offense to this, but you sound intelligent for a simple hunter."

"I was educated, if that's what you're referring to."

"That would be unusual for many in these parts, I'm guessing," replied Lion.

"There's a lot you don't know about me." He paused. "Of course, you might say the same goes for me regarding your history."

Lion smiled. "Being educated doesn't make you smart. Not that I would know the first thing about being educated. But I am smart enough to realize the value of your tracking. And I think you'll soon appreciate my skills if you find the monster."

Chapter 8

JADA WAS FRUSTRATED. It was no small task operating her business on the edge of nowhere. She mostly saw the same people day in and day out, and whenever someone new did come into town, they rarely stayed long. She had worked hard and built up a good reputation of having the best food and entertainment in town. The only ingredient she lacked for growing with exponential success was a larger population of people. If that ever happened, it might also make it possible to finally meet a good man. The whole lot of them out here was especially thin for her liking.

It wasn't as if she hadn't had plenty of offers by unsuitable men to settle down. No, offers out here were easy to come by. Often, all one needed was a pulse. Jada tried to do as little as possible to encourage the local menfolk, but they seemed either blind to her prickliness or just didn't mind it. Some even hinted that they liked her crossness, which made it all the easier to tell them she wouldn't be interested if they were the last males on earth. Oftentimes, they needed it spelled out. Why should she settle for just any man?

Sometimes, whilst in her lonely bed at night, Jada would imagine that a dashing man would ride into town and completely fall in love with her. She knew it was vain and likely hopeless, but still it was nice to fantasize about. He would have to be a strong man, a flashy, charismatic man who would never be boring. And he would never get cross with her strong opinions. Alas, a good husband like that would need years of training, but she could envision herself accomplishing such a task. He would fill her life with the excitement and adventure that she'd dreamed about before traveling to this musty, stale old town.

And to think I almost thought the hunter could be a capable man. More likely than not, he was too much of a dunce to be trained how to love a woman properly. The fool will probably never make it back alive anyways.

These were the thoughts that tormented her mind as she served ale to her crowd tonight. Their compliments and whistles when she walked by would only be met with glares as usual. Jada was in no mood for pleasantries. She knew it was foolish and incredibly naïve, but a part of her wondered what could happen if he did manage to survive and return with the beast.

As unlikely as it might be, she really should be prepared in case he returned in triumph. Perhaps if she tried her spicy breaded fish, she could find the way to his heart through his belly. The stew had been good—he'd said as much—but no doubt it was a common meal. Perhaps he was looking for something a bit more exotic than regular old beef stew. *I can be exotic. Yes, perhaps the fish would be best.*

After listening to the same singer entertain all week, Jada had become weary of the repetitive songs. She was able to get some acts from Sisterton as long as she gave them a free room, free food, and decent pay. Such was the cost of business when you needed something in short supply. If only the town were bigger and she had more options. Why had she even come to Mossport in the first place? Oh, that's right, she was tired of the city. She had used her inheritance from her uncle to entrap herself in this old inn that the previous owner had been a little too quick to sell. That old man must have dropped to his knees and kissed the dirty ground of Sisterton when he rejoined civilization. After a week by water, if the weather had been good, he was probably telling the world how he'd pulled a fast one over a rich, dumb city girl. She ground her teeth together thinking about it. Perhaps his boat sank before he got across the Mammoth. It would serve the old deceiver right. People who were smart merely visited Mossport. Those that were fools chose to live there. And only the completely insane started a business there.

She now knew that this little town was likely as big as it would ever get. If only she'd known that three years ago. But youth and bad decisions went hand in hand. At least they had for her life so far. She'd always settled on the worst suitors when she'd lived in Sisterton. There was the judge's son who had seemed promising until she realized he preferred company with his own sex. Then there was the gangster who promised her the world, only to deliver himself stabbed to death at her door. Then there was the only boy who was ever truly good to her, whom she'd sent away after a one-week stint with a prize fighter. Dumb move there. The fighter turned out to be dumber than a box of rocks and had the nerve to dump her the next week. The last she'd heard about that nice boy, he'd become the captain of the police force. Before she'd come into her inheritance, she'd spent a brief time in the companionship industry. She shook her head in disgust, thinking about her string of bad choices.

Jada knew her looks would not stay with her forever, and with them her chance at having children would dry up soon after as well. She needed to make something happen soon.

Before the night's end, as the candles and fire were burning lower, she caught herself looking at the singer she'd ignored all night. He was singing a softer song now, and his features weren't hideous in the low light. His song was about a girl lost in the wilderness. He could have called it "Jada's Song."

And she walked all alone, unafraid of scary beasts;
And she walked all alone, with her back to the east;
No, she never looked behind, only forward would she go;
No, she never looked behind, at the troubles that she'd sowed.

Chapter 9

THE SUN WOULD soon be setting over the vast western forest, putting to bed the canticle of daylight. Pike kept an eye open for a safe place to set up camp. It would be a cool evening but far from freezing. The ground had become rockier since they'd started north, with both small and large pieces of rock jutting into the air out of the brownish, grassy plain. Pike found a rock that provided protection from the northwest, and they began setting up camp.

There was a nearby spring that flowed into a clear shallow pond that afforded the horses some fresh cold water. They tethered Harley and Clyde close to camp with enough rope to graze on the greener grass surrounding the spring. There wasn't much good firewood to be gathered, but they managed a decent fire with some dried shrubs. The day had been warm enough, but the night breeze made shelter a necessity.

Pike instructed Lion to clean and cut up some of the potatoes to be boiled above the fire. They each ate a few pieces of jerky with their salted potato chunks. It was no feast like the Mammoth Inn, but it had the calories they needed.

After dinner, they sat staring into the flames. Pike was mentally going over their list of supplies, making sure they would be prepared for whatever might lie ahead.

"What do you know about the mountains?" asked Lion, breaking the silence.

"Nothing different from the tales they tell children."

Lion crossed his arms. "I've heard tales in my travels, but you've lived your whole life in the shadow of these rocks. Believe me when I tell you I have seen some indescribable things in this world, but these mountains take the cake. You seriously have never tried to get through?"

"The stories are all nonsense," Pike replied. "They're just the result of an overly creative mind that had a fondness for drink and possibly mushrooms. Everyone fears the unknown. Even the western hunting grounds I travel and have lived in since I was a boy are said to be haunted and cursed. It's all farce. I've never seen anything that can't be explained. It's true they're dangerous to many who aren't seasoned woodsmen, but beyond that the biggest risks are exposure, starvation, and animal attacks. Although, with that said about tales of nonsense, getting through that rock mountain is truly impossible."

"So you've tried?"

"I admit that I've explored the mountain. It's impenetrable. Like an iron gate with no keyhole."

"What if something's changed?"

"Explain yourself, Lion."

Hellion smiled. "What if an earthquake opened up a crack in the mountain?"

"I've heard of such things, but no doubt someone would have felt that kind of shake of the ground. Your theory isn't new, by the way. People who actually believe Horton Conner's story think that's how he found a passageway through. The only problem is, no one has ever been able to find such a pass. If it did exist—and clearly I don't believe it did, but if it did—how would it have closed back up in the hundred years that have elapsed since he wrote about his journey?"

Hellion sat quietly thinking for a moment. "I've talked with people that very much believe what was written in that book."

"Well then, you've talked with fools."

"Maybe," replied Hellion. "I have a copy of *Adventure in the North Woods*, but I've never been able to read it for myself."

"A man who can't read carries around books? Someday you'll have to tell me your whole story, Lion. Then again, I've read the story myself numerous times, all the while proclaiming it as utter nonsense."

"Since you're such a learned man, why don't you tell me the short story of it then?"

"How much would you like it dumbed down?"

"I bet it makes you feel high and mighty being able to read and withhold information pertinent to our situation. You're lucky you had a family to teach you."

Pike could sense a twinge of sorrow buried within the man's insult. Rather than rile him up more, he allowed himself to play the role of story spinner.

"You know, I never knew my family," he started. "But that's not the story you want to hear right now. I guess I'll start with what are believed to be the facts before we get into the real silliness. The history of Mossport does confirm that Horton Conner went missing for a period of time somewhere around fifteen years. No one can account for where he was living, although I'd wager somewhere in the western woods, as it isn't hard to disappear out there. The story he told the people from town and the story he later wrote down were one and the same. He did not appear to be making the story up as he went or changing any parts. The final part of the factual piece of the story is that he did return wearing a necklace with what appeared to be a single tooth. It was the size of a man's hand and was reportedly bigger than could be obtained from any animal on this side of the globe."

"What's your theory on how he got that?"

"I never saw it, so I can't say. Maybe he carved it out of another bone to look like a tooth. In his book it sounds like he truly believes he was in another world. The writing is coherent and fairly easy to follow. He talks of gigantic beasts and native tribes and a different ecology…"

"What's that mean?"

"Ecology just means environment. In his use of the term, the scenery was different. There were different trees, plants, animals, bugs, and even people, or natives as he called them."

"Did he ever speak of treasure?" asked Lion in a stern tone.

Pike laughed. "You sound genuinely interested. To answer your question, yes and no. There's no description of a treasure cache in the book. Although it does mention that the mountains contain rare gems and such. It also hints that there are many other secrets the land holds. What better way to spark interest in your book though, right? How many fools waste their lives looking for mythical treasure?" Pike laughed, slapping his knee. "There's no such thing as hidden treasure. If it was there, that crazy loon would have hauled it out with him instead of writing a silly, albeit creative, story to make a few bucks."

Lion sat unamused with his arms folded. "Every land has its secrets. I've traveled enough to know that."

"Oh yeah?" asked Pike. "Why don't you tell me about your travels? Where have you been? What brought you here? What are you after?"

"I still have one more question for you," replied Lion.

"Shoot."

"Why couldn't Horton go back after he got out?"

Pike smiled. "That's the perfect part of his story. He wandered for years trying to find the entrance he used to get in and never found it. When he decided he'd been gone too long, he rafted through the underground river that cuts through the mountain and fell straight into Mammoth Lake. The name he used for the waterfall was the Serpent's Mouth. We still call it that today. It's a one-way deal; people have tried."

"It makes sense."

"Oh, it's perfect to defend his story. And that's why the fools you speak with still believe the nonsense."

Lion formed an evil grin. "I have a habit of hanging around fools."

"Clever. Now tell me about your travels."

"Maybe another time," he replied uncomfortably. "Why don't you get some rest and I'll keep first watch."

"Fine. Don't fall asleep or we'll probably end up in the beast's belly before we're awake."

With that, Pike lay his head down and let his mind wander. What would he do once they returned home with the animal? He would have more coin in his pocket than he could ever hope to spend in the wilderness. He began to think about Jada. She liked him, he'd decided. And, she could surely cook well enough. Yet, if it were up to her, he wouldn't be doing what he was born to do right now. Perhaps she would understand some day. He found himself exploring the endless possibilities of the future before he cursed himself for his wild imagination. He needed to focus on what was in front of him if he intended to survive and return to town successful. Women, he had been taught, had been the downfall of too many men in history. He didn't relish being added to that never-ending list.

Chapter 10

AT FIRST LIGHT, the pair was up and moving to break down and pack up their little camp. Each had only gotten a half night's sleep, but neither one complained about it. There would be worse hardships to come.

The cold night gave way to a warming day with clear skies and a blinding sun to the east. Lion's gaze remained on the mountains in the distance as they traveled, while Pike kept an eye on the ground. Ahead of them lay the barren lands. Steam arose from various pockets of ground, shooting boiling hot water hundreds of feet into the air. The travelers kept to the places where grass and shrubs grew, believing them to be a safe distance from the geysers that might surprise them at any moment. Around them lay the only puddles of water to be seen in months.

The horses were not fond of the scenery. Clyde twitched his ears forward and side to side, straining to listen for danger, while he warily advanced his master's chosen path. Harley followed behind, as the two decided it was safer to travel single file through the unforgiving landscape. Ahead, they spied a large cluster of tall trees in the hot, marshy surroundings. Pike led them in a circle around the trees before stopping and dismounting from his horse.

"Tell me, Lion. What do you think of these tracks?"

"They look like our own," was his reply.

"Exactly what I was thinking. Perhaps we've found the trail of the men who never came back. This grouping of trees seems to be the only landmark around for about a day's ride. I'll wager the group headed for it just as we have. The path leading in has been used frequently before them, but I see no prints resembling what we saw at Ferrell's farm."

"Shall we have a look?" asked Lion as he dismounted and drew his longsword.

Pike nodded and let Lion lead the way. He eagerly advanced into the thick brush, using his sword to help pick his way through as he led his horse behind him. Lion felt his loaner horse press its head against his back to protect itself from the backlash of branches in his wake.

The grove of trees stood on higher ground than the land that surrounded them. The thick branches gave way to an open forest inside, protected by the high canopy above. Pike was able to walk beside Lion once within.

"They definitely camped here." Pike pointed to a ring of rocks around a charred log. "It was probably after their first day of travel." The spot was wisely chosen, considering the current surroundings. The ground was dry, the wind was blocked, and it would be difficult to see the fire at night through the trees. They searched to see if there were any more clues left behind, but other than the fire and marks on the ground where at least six men had rested their heads, nothing seemed out of the ordinary.

There was still half the day's light left, and both agreed to try to cover as much ground as possible before dark. Pike led the way again, but now he was following a trail. It had now been fifteen days since the beast last attacked Ferrell's farm.

A disturbing sight awaited them an hour ahead. The previous party did not look like it had traveled single file after leaving camp. There was less threat of water geysers this far north, but the ground was still not to be trusted. To the right of the path were what remained of the heads of two perished horses. The vultures had been after them, probably before the poor beasts had even expired.

Pike and Lion dismounted. The ground looked to have given way beneath the horses. There was evidence of a struggle on the animals' part and a rope remained that had been used to try to pull them out. All efforts had, of course, proved unsuccessful. The birds scattered but refused to go far from their precious meal. Now both Clyde and Harley were snorting heavily, eyes white with fear.

"We stay single file, leading the horses behind us. If the ground feels soft beneath your feet, the horses' hooves will punch so deep we'll never get them out. Without the horses this far north, we would have to turn back." Lion nodded in agreement.

They continued on, methodically following successful tracks from the previous party. From here forward, they would have been left with four horses for six men.

In this barren landscape they were exposed to the afternoon light and a steady west wind. After a few hours of slow moving, they were within sight of thick pines that would no doubt mean solid ground again. They pushed onward with purpose.

The path they followed led into the pines at dusk. Here they found the remnants of another campsite. This one was not as well picked up as the last. With fewer horses, the party had had to leave some supplies behind. Pike and Lion found a heavy pot, some canned rations, a heavy double-bladed ax, two pairs of saddle bags, and a small shovel. They also found a few empty bottles of bourbon.

"It's late enough that we best settle here for the night," said Pike.

"Aye, it seems our fate is falling into step with the last souls out here."

"True, but there is no evidence of a struggle." Pike looked at the sky. "It doesn't look like rain is coming anytime soon. Though we could use some, no rain means the trail will still be intact tomorrow. Let's get our gear unpacked." He swung his leg off his horse and dismounted. "This should go without saying," he continued quietly, "but I'll say it anyways. We have to be extra careful from here on out. The foundation of the mountain is not too far away. That mountain base is as far north as anything can reach, which makes it a natural highway for anything traveling out here. No loud noises and no roaring fires would be prudent. I'll take first watch tonight."

Thankfully, it was another uneventful night. The trackers again packed up early the next morning. They took the rations left behind by the previous party. Pike decided to scratch a short message into the large pot that had been left behind. He reasoned it would be good to mark their trail in case reinforcements came looking for them. He roughly scratched with his knife into the upside-down kettle *Pike and Lion, forty days until change of season, no sighting of creature or previous trackers.* At least there would be some clues left behind should they not return.

Now that the ground allowed for riding rather than leading the horses, they covered the landscape more quickly. The path weaved around gigantic boulders that could almost be described as having been thrown from the mountain to block their approach. The pines continued here, though only where they could get a root down in the rocky ground. Tracking was now becoming much more difficult, but the flow of the land left few natural choices for the trail to veer off without warning.

Eventually, they reached the steep base of the Mortapenum Mountains. As described, there was no plausible way to climb the incline that seemingly rose straight from the ground to the sky. Looking up, there might have been one ledge available for a foothold, but it was many times higher than the highest stone throw could reach. The path turned west here. To head east would continue to the north shore of the Mammoth.

"I don't like this," stated Lion. "Every move we make is predictable. Whatever we are hunting will know we are coming. Either it runs far before we arrive or lies in wait to ambush us. We need an element of surprise. There's no way to flank an opponent when you're boxed in."

Pike gave Lion a sideways glance. He dismounted and stretched his legs, all the while keeping his eyes on Lion. "If I had to guess, I'd say you have a military background."

"Took you long enough to figure that out, hunter."

"If you're as good as you claim at killing, why would you leave the army?" asked Pike.

"The less you know the better."

Pike was getting annoyed with all the secrecy. "Obviously something happened," he prodded. "Obviously your real name isn't Lion. You put on a tough appearance, but I'm guessing there are many other things you're not telling me. I'm guessing you're on the run from the army. No?"

"Trying to make me angry isn't going to get you anywhere," said Lion through clenched teeth.

"Maybe not, but neither is you lying to me."

"I've told you no lies."

Pike walked up to Lion, who still sat in his saddle. He smiled up at him. "Your name's not Lion."

"I told you that's a nickname."

"Well, give me one damn truth out of your mouth before we continue. I have no idea who you are and what type of training you have. The only reason I care is because at some point on this trip my life might end up in your hands or vice versa. Knowing the facts affects the choices we make. The choices we make may be life or death."

Lion started chuckling.

"Is there anything funny about what I just said?" asked Pike angrily.

"You have no clue who I am." He slipped off his horse and approached the bigger man with his chest flared and removed his glasses to reveal those menacing eyes looking deep into the man. "My name is Hellion Swash, Pike." He stuck out a hand, which Pike did not take. "Lion is actually a part of my name and thus not a lie. I've been 100 percent honest with you and this is where you turn on me? We're about to split an enormous, life-changing bounty, and now you're having second thoughts about me, about my capabilities? This extended hand you're sneering at has ended more lives than the total population of your piss pot of a town. I told you the truth about me the first time we met. Did I sugarcoat anything? I'm a lot of bad things, but I am not a liar."

Pike took a step back. "I saw a sign for you last season when I came into town."

"And you'll find none now as I've taken them all down."

Pike was puzzled. "They said you're a monster. A thief, a murderer, a pirate when it suits you."

"I am what they made me," he said soberly. "There'll be no tears when I'm gone. Got no one I can trust. If anyone finds out, they'll be after that reward. That's why I omitted so much of my past."

Pike was silent for a moment in thought before responding, "I will keep your secret."

Hellion chuckled. "I've heard that once before." Then he glared menacingly back. "I pulled the bastard's very knife out of my back and stuck it through his eye before I escaped. So much for trusting people."

"You'll have so much money when we're done you can pay off whatever grievance the army has against you for deserting."

"Some debts are due in blood."

"Yours or the army's?"

"Both."

"Why are they really after you…Hellion?"

"Because I got too good at my job," he said with that dangerous smile.

Chapter 11

GROM, THE SHOPKEEPER, had lived in North Grove all his life. Sure, he had visited Sisterton on many occasions, but he was Mossport, through and through. He worked in the store as a boy for his father, as his father had done before him. His family was among the first to settle in Mossport nearly two hundred years prior. He had seen his fair share of hard winters and pestilences that made life difficult for the townspeople. There was the massive flooding just a few years back and the outbreak of the pox before that. Frontier life could be brutal. Now, there was the beast to contend with. If the town's livestock continued to be decimated, families would not survive the upcoming winter. The grain harvest would also no doubt be lighter than usual due to the prolonged drought conditions. A town that didn't survive winter wouldn't need to buy supplies from him. A loss of business could cause him to close his doors. If his doors closed, the town would surely fail as well.

It was for these reasons that he needed to be sure the hunter would succeed. That was why he had pushed so hard for a capable partner to help Pike. The man in the darkened glasses who had showed up asking about the bounty days before certainly looked serious enough for the payoff. Hopefully, he would turn out to be a good partner for Pike.

Grom had added very generously to the reward being offered for the beast. Was it too much of a stretch for the two men to pull off what a greater number had failed at already? True, Pike survived and even flourished where most men wouldn't last a fortnight alone. But this monster they hunted could not be a beast native to the region. Grom secretly feared it had somehow come from beyond the Mortapentums. If the tales from his family were true, he shuddered at the odds the two men were up against.

Grom's grandfather had actually known the infamous Horton Conner, author of *Adventure in the North Woods*. What was more telling was that privately, he had believed Horton's tale in full. Horton had disappeared for fifteen years before showing up again. Where could the man have been? Grom owned an original version of Conner's book and had read it many times, accepting it as fact. That truth was not something he talked about publicly for two reasons. The first was because the townsfolk would think him a fool, and the latter because people would not feel safe if they were aware of the forces that reigned on the other side of the mountain.

Conner had written about other-worldly vegetation, animals as big as houses, and warring natives. *On the northern side of the mountain, man is lower on the food chain,* he wrote. *There are forces at work besides nature that must be accounted for if one wishes to survive.* The tale would go on to describe how he was adopted into a tribe of natives and became a teacher of sorts. In turn, he had learned of the foretelling that spoke of his arrival to the natives in the North. At his own admission, Conner had used this story to gain influence on the people. At the same time, he advanced their tribal communities for the better, he claimed.

While he wrote kindly of the people and experiences he enjoyed beyond the Mortapenums, Horton Conner also had a clear warning regarding the North. He had prophesied, *If ever a piece of their world were to cross into our own, it would result in the destruction of Mossport and all beyond. Nothing must ever be permitted to move from North to South.* And now, perhaps this warning was coming to fruition.

Grom had already helped send six people to their death, and now he had most likely sent their greatest weapon with an unknown wanderer to the same fate. It was true the first six were nothing more than plain ranchers, unskilled with a bow or sword, but they had numbers on their side and they still had not returned. What else could Grom do, short of going himself? That certainly wouldn't do any good for anyone, especially himself. And so he worked on in his shop, pretending everything was normal, all the while sweating heavily at the gravity of the situation.

The townspeople were not without worry themselves, but they had no idea of the danger they might be in. They were scared of the beast like a child is of the dark. They still had yet to grasp the direness of the situation at hand. If they had, they would be on the next boat out of Mossport. However, if things went as Grom hoped, they would never know the peril they were truly in.

With these thoughts in his head, Grom sat down to pen another letter requesting aid for a strange unidentified beast attacking livestock. He was careful not to give out too much information, which could portray his letter as more of a foolish prank than an urgent request. His previous attempts had not even registered a response from Sisterton. He decided to cut out the middleman, the city, and instead addressed his urgent request to the lone garrison stationed on Mammoth Lake. Fort Tuttle.

Chapter 12

THE TWO MEN were hours into their march west along the rock wall. The mountain was just as Pike remembered it, continuous rock as far as the eye could see. How could such seamless perfection exist in a world full of randomness? As of yet, they had failed to see so much as a crack in the steep precipice. Pike motioned to Hellion to stop as he peered ahead, but Swash had already seen what had caught his attention. The canvas flap of a tent fluttered in the wind. There was no other sound to be heard, save the fresh zephyr and the horses huffing and snorting. Only the breath of nature had the audacity to disturb the scene.

Cautiously, they approached. Before them lay the ruins of the final campsite. Packs were scattered, empty and strewn with dried blood. The ropes that had tied the remaining horses hung limp from the nearby pines, having been frayed or slashed. The bodies, both man and beast, were nowhere to be found.

"They were asleep when this happened," said Pike. "Something was watching them. It may even be watching us now."

Hellion drew his sword and turned in a circle to assure himself they were not under attack.

"We know it has attacked the village at night." Pike examined the scene closer. "The horses got away, at least initially. Grom said one made it back. They had to have been terrified to break these ropes." He glanced at his own black stallion sniffing the ground beside him. "Do you see any prints from the beast…Hellion?"

Swash swore aloud. "None."

"There should be tracks here, like the horses'. Either this creature can fly, or it cleaned up its own tracks and hid the bodies. I'm not sure which option is more frightening." He continued looking around the tents and surrounding area with a look of confusion.

"Should we consider reinforcements?"

"It's already too late for that, my soldier friend. Something knew we were coming. We best prepare for nightfall if we mean to survive."

Hellion swore again. "What's your plan, hunter?"

Pike shrugged his shoulders. "I guess we'll just have to play stupid."

Hellion spat on the ground, then he smiled with that crazy gleam in his eye. "Feigning weakness, I presume?"

Pike nodded.

"One of my favorite tactics, Granger. Perhaps war and hunting aren't as different as you presume."

"Let's hope not, for both our sakes. Help me gather all the wood you can find. I want an enormous campfire tonight."

By the time all of the preparations were finished, the light was beginning to dwindle. Pike used his flint box to ignite the absurdly large pile of dried moss, leaves, and wood before vacating the campsite. Hellion was already sitting comfortably on their little platform he had fashioned while Pike set up a campsite similar to their predecessors'. The vantage point was far enough away from the fire to be concealed in total darkness, but close enough to observe—safely, they hoped. Pike climbed up the base of the pine and joined him.

Everything but their weapons lay below, stuffed in the tents. Pike wasn't sure how good the beast's sense of smell was, but if it was like most predators', it was many times better than the two men's. Their bags and clothes and dirty cookware would permeate the air like the first breath of spoiled fish from an overripe saddle bag.

The eventide sounds had settled in for the night with the chirping of crickets and the occasional fluttering of wings from nearby roosting birds. After what seemed like ages, the fire had shrunken to a third of its size. It would, however, continue to illuminate the camp for hours to come. Pike began to wonder if he was wrong about the creature. Perhaps it had no idea they were here. Or maybe it was too far away at present to smell them.

He was staring at the edge of camp when he heard a dragging sound. He noticed his sleeping bag, stuffed with provisions, being ever so slowly pulled into the darkness away from the fire. Pike glanced beside him at Hellion, who clearly noticed the subtle movement as well. Pike notched his arrow and waited silently for his chance. What he saw next filled him with both fear and wonder. The creature stood at the edge of the darkness, with the light of the dancing flame reflecting off two goose egg–sized eyes, which were positioned at twice the height of a tall man. It had some resemblance to the form of a man, but it clearly was not human. Its face was more jaws and teeth than anything else, and they protruded forward longer than two arm lengths from where those cold eyes sat. It sniffed the air with nostrils at the end of the long snout and glanced around the camp, almost as if aware it was being watched.

The beast turned around its massive body to reveal a tail, perhaps the length of a man, when Hellion's arrow struck its back. It whirled around angrily and roared into the night, searching for the tree that harbored its assassin. The horses reared up and caught the attention of the beast from the tree line. Out of the darkness, Pike's arrow flashed to find flesh in the beast's lower neck. The arrow did not pass all the way through, as it stuck like a pin in the creature's tough skin. But the huge animal was now panicked enough to drop to all fours and race down the rock wall further west at an impossible speed.

"Great shot!" whispered Hellion, patting Pike on the shoulder. "Shall we go finish the ugly bastard off?"

"Stay put, Swash. We don't leave this tree until first light, no matter what."

Hellion shook his head and tsk tsked. "Your strategy is too defensive, hunter. In battle, you've got to finish your opponent with a swift blow. We may never see it again."

"Settle down, Hellion. There's not much more dangerous in the world than a wounded animal. It will have the advantage at night. We'll finish the job after dawn. Don't forget, tracking is what I do best."

AT FIRST LIGHT, the horses were packed and the weary pair began to follow the path of tracks and blood. The animal led them west, a far distance for the amount of blood spilled by Pike's arrow. After a short ride, the trail headed southwest into a low swampy area where the pines had given way to large willow trees. They weren't terribly far from the base of the mountain, probably a few minutes' hike. From here, the mountain still looked as impenetrable as it had everywhere else. In this area, the beast had resumed travel by standing upright, as opposed to how they had last seen it run, on all fours.

"Of all the land around us, the creature had to run into the smelliest, dampest shithole to be found west of the Mammoth," complained Hellion. "Grom says it's the driest year on record, and here's a muddy watering hole in the middle of nowhere."

Pike eyed the swampy landscape in front of him cautiously. Bubbles arose intermittently from the black backdrop of the rich bottom. Hellion was right about the smell of decay, but he definitely wasn't poetic about it. "Wounded animals always tend to go for water," he explained. "Usually, you find them dead not far away. Judging by the trail, we're going to have to do some wading."

"You're telling me you can track through privy pot water?"

"Hafta try. The animal went in here, so we gotta do the same." Pike dismounted and grabbed his spear from his horse.

"Shall I drown in the swamp with you?" mused Hellion.

"Do as you see fit. I'm used to being on my own."

Swash looked from the murky water to dry land. "I think I'll take my chances on the high ground." He dismounted and took out his bow. "I can cover you better from here anyhow."

"Fine. Tie up the horses." Pike was in no mood to argue, or to talk for that matter. He was mentally processing his surroundings. This was not the time for quips from his partner.

He jumped into the water and immediately sank into the muck. He lifted his boot to pull free. The only good news was the water itself was only knee high. He began slowly wading toward the middle of the pool. He looked back to see Hellion with his crossbow loaded, eyeing up and down the shoreline.

At least his back was covered. With the length of tail the beast had, it would undoubtedly swim much faster than Pike knew he could. *Where could the source of the water be?* After the shock of sinking into the bottom, Pike realized the water was stinging cold. The nights had been cool, but the heat of the day wouldn't allow for this chilliness. It could only mean the swamp's source came from a spring in the ground. Such was the only plausible explanation with the long drought.

He kept edging deeper until he was nearly halfway across the bog. Around him stood the weathered trunks of long dead trees, rising up only slightly taller than he, like so many skeletons in the partially buried graveyard. He was now waist deep and had to let his feet feel their way around the unseen obstacles of branches and the occasional rock below him. He did not want to go any deeper. Looking back at the shore, he knew he was nearing the end of a bow's range. Hellion claimed to be a pretty good shot, but he didn't want to stretch his companion's range. He looked down at the water to see a leaf slowly moving south, as if pushed by an unfelt current. He motioned he was heading parallel with the shore back north. Swash signaled he would stay even with him.

Ahead of him, emerging from the swamp on a small island of

rock and moss, rose an enormous tree. There were no other trees of its size alive within the water's borders. Granger made his way toward it, anxious to get a look from the higher position.

When he finally reached his destination, he grabbed onto a root and pulled himself from the water and onto the one-tree island. He waved at Swash and began surveying his surroundings. The other side of the swamp had a steeper bank than their side. He tried to see if there were any grooves in the shore from where a large animal might routinely pull itself from the water. It was too difficult to tell from his vantage point. He took a breath to relax and think before he looked down and smiled.

On the very rock on which he stood, next to his muddy, wet boot, there were a few drops of blood, semi dry. The beast had been here. He pointed to the ground and motioned to Hellion, who didn't seem to understand what he was signaling. Pike threw his hands in the air with disgust at his partner's lack of understanding.

Pike felt very silly as he mimicked an arrow going into his throat and spraying blood, which was what had fallen on the rocks he was pointing at.

"Blood!" hooted Hellion from the shore.

The outburst angered Pike as he now threw his hands in the air and put a finger to his mouth to silence his partner. Swash shrugged his shoulders in an attempt to make light of the gaff when he was hit from behind by a flash of green and knocked into the swamp.

Pike watched helplessly as the beast dragged his partner underwater and with a few quick strokes of the tail, sped toward Pike. He scrambled into a defensive position, readying himself for the upcoming clash.

Pike anchored his spear on the rocks. He would let the beast impale itself coming after him. The animal swam like a snake, with its long tail powering it forward. He braced himself for its final blow when, to his surprise, it dove below him, through the roots of the willow.

"No!" he shouted, realizing what had happened as Hellion and the animal's head had now disappeared under the tree.

He gripped his spear and drove it deep into the last visible part of the beast, about to disappear, perhaps forever, in a hole beneath the great tree. The spear drove out the other side of the powerful tail, and the momentum of the beast stopped as the head and handle of the spear caught hold of the tree roots protruding into the water. The hole from the spear tore toward the tail, and Pike heard an angry roar below him.

Chapter 13

HELLION HELD HIS breath, unable to draw his sword while gripped by the powerful claws of the swimming beast. He could feel the roots rake his body, the engulfing darkness, and the sound and sensation of the movement of cold water. Then the animal abruptly stopped, with Hellion still pitching forward. He rolled into a somersault and realized he was knee deep in an underground stream. He could breathe! The hole the beast now seemed stuck inside was surrounded by tree roots. The animal bellowed in pain. Swash drew his sword, as he had lost his bow in the attack, and stood defensively as the beast tried again and again to engulf him in its vicious jaws, an arm's length away. The monster was caught on something. Could it be Pike?

He tested his footing for a second before his battle instincts kicked in. "Attaaaaaack!" he yelled, swinging his large sword as if it were as light as the baton of a military band conductor. The beast tried to claw at him but could move no further. Swash batted each swipe away with his sword and carefully played his tactics against the predator. He swiped up to cut a forearm, then worked his way up and severed a bicep. The animal's right arm wiggled without strength. Hellion smiled. "Welcome to my world!"

The beast realized it would be dismantled piece by piece in the hole and began to back up frantically. Hellion gave it no quarter to catch its footing, for he knew space would be to the beast's advantage, and it could either break through whatever had caught it or jump through his thrusts if given too much space. He had to kill it now!

With one arm it pushed backward as he sliced at a finger and kept it off balance. He swung up, down, swirled around, and kept his blade dancing, lest the beast decide to press him.

He knew he was in trouble when its head and arms pushed the last needed shove to free itself back out the entrance of the hole. He had no choice but to press now. He emerged to see it had regained its footing and was about to thrust its jaws right back down the hole to devour him when a figure descended from the sky.

Pike had launched himself from a branch high above and landed his blade, with all his weight and momentum, through the back of the animal's neck as they both crashed into the water.

Hellion scrambled onto the tree island and was relieved to see Pike emerge from the dark water with his bloody blade hoisted in the air victoriously.

"You beautiful son of a billy goat!" yelled Hellion.

"You're alive!" yelled Pike excitedly.

Hellion brushed off his shoulders as if annoyed he'd gotten something on his coat. "I meant to tell you, I'm kinda hard to kill. It really annoys some people."

Pike smiled while still breathing heavily. "I couldn't be happier to see your face. How about you help me haul our trophy onto shore?"

Hellion laughed hysterically. "I knew there had to be a catch."

The two of them dragged the massive body closer to shore. Then, Pike tied a rope to his saddle horn and had his steed help them pull the monster from the swamp.

"If I wasn't seeing this with my own eyes, I'd never believe it," said Hellion. "I have seen that head before in my travels. I've never seen one this large, but they call it a crocodile."

Pike had no words to describe the creature that lay out before them. It was taller than Hellion standing on his shoulders, and that was not counting the tail. The head resembled a green reptilian monster with teeth longer than a man's fingers. The head and thick neck sat on a pair of shoulders that could only be described as human from the frontal view. The shoulders and chest muscles resembled a man's build, except they were also reptilian green and larger than any man's had ever been. On its back, the thick rough skin of what Hellion had called a crocodile continued the whole way until the end of the tail. It looked like a coat of armor all down the creature's back. The hands had five digits and the dexterity of a human's except they had an added razor-sharp claw at the end of each digit. The creature's legs were built much more powerfully than a human's but somehow allowed the beast to walk upright when desired.

"What was under the tree?" asked Pike as they stared at the monster before them.

"It was an underground stream. Large enough to stand up inside."

"And it led north?"

"It seemed to, but I can't be sure. Excuse me for not being more observant while that thing on the ground tried to eat me."

"I've got to see where it leads," said Pike.

Hellion looked at him as if he'd said his hair was on fire. "You're going down that hole I barely made it outta alive? Well fine, let's get our money and you can come back on your little adventure. Meanwhile, I'll buy me a boat and a crew and maybe a woman's company." He laughed giddily at the thought.

"I can't take that chance. If it starts raining, that hole might be entirely submerged by the time I get back."

"You can't be serious! You want me to waltz into town alone with the beast? What will I tell people?"

"Tell them the truth."

Hellion sneered, "I fear they'll not believe me. They might even think I killed you for the whole reward. Come back and enjoy the celebration that's about to begin. What if you travel into a whole nest of these creatures? Then what are you going to do?"

"I've got to see where it leads with my own eyes. I've never believed it possible to get to the other side. I can feel in my gut that I was meant to do this, explore this, to explain what's dead on the ground in front of us."

Swash narrowed his eyes at Pike. "You know what kind of man I am. Do you really trust me not to take the entire reward and skip town before you're back? I mean, potentially you might never come back. Then I could buy multiple ships and multiple women and never lift another finger again."

Pike patted his partner on the back. "I don't think you're as cruel as you say you are. I think somewhere along the road someone you cared for hurt you, and you won't let anyone else too close as a result. I think I might be your friend."

Hellion stared at him incredulously. "You are one naïve fool, Granger. But for the record, I hope you make it back alive, and I'll make sure you get your cut." He reached into his horse's saddlebag. "If you're going over to the other side, you might as well take this." He pulled out the thin cylindrical container protected with a cork at the end.

"What's this?"

"The only map ever recorded of what's on the other side. Use it if it helps you. I'll be wanting that back though."

"Horton Conner's map? How in the world? You've had this all along and never told me?"

"You said you didn't believe in all that."

Pike thought for a moment. "I suppose I did. Didn't believe in monsters either though. I think some things are changing. It's been a pleasure, Hellion. I'm fairly certain I couldn't have done it without you."

"The same could be said for me," Swash grinned. "But I would never admit it. Remember when you get back, the name's Lion. I've gone easy on you for using it so openly out here. But if you don't, you're gonna get me killed. And that's pretty hard to do, which means I'll be coming after your ass for blabbing." He grinned menacingly, and Pike wasn't sure it was a joke.

"You never told me what happened in the army."

"'Tis a story for another day. Now help me load up this beast before you try to get yourself killed. I'm going to be king of sheep shit town when I get back. I can't believe you're gonna miss this. Oh, and one last thing I wanted to tell you."

"What's that?"

"I think I was wrong about you, Granger. You might actually be a killer."

Pike helped fashion a wooden sled from rope and large branches for Clyde to pull their kill. Two large ends of the branches would drag behind on the ground, while the front ends were suspended and fashioned near the horse's shoulders. The large tail of the beast would drag behind on the ground but not much could be done about it. Pike had considered skinning the animal, but this monster needed to be seen on the hoof, or in this case, paw.

Next Granger packed a bag of supplies for whatever his journey might hold. His return on foot would be slow, but it was nothing he hadn't done before in the wilderness. He knew Grom would hold his horse and his money once Hellion returned. All he needed to worry about now was wherever the underground stream would take him.

Chapter 14

As Pike waded alone in the underground tunnel, his biggest fear was that his torch might wisp out. The water was not as deep as he knew it could be. He could see about ten paces in front of him, and it was as he imagined, a round tunnel carved by water over thousands of years. The ceiling had lowered considerably as he progressed, so much so that he had to stoop over to keep moving forward.

There was a familiarity to this journey that he was drawn to, like re-experiencing a verse of a wondrous song long since faded from memory. How could he explain to Hellion—or Jada, for that matter— that this was what he'd been born to do? He couldn't even explain it to himself. He was a wolf, enamored with the scent of a delicious prey. The chase, the song and dance to ensue, was merely instinct. Going back to town now would be like a wolf returning to its pack with no kill. It would not do. It would not satisfy him or the townspeople. Pike's whole life's purpose had led him to this one venture. Something of significance had to be waiting on the other side of this tunnel.

No one knew how wide the Mortapenum Mountain range was for sure. Pike hoped it could be walked in a day, although at the pace he was going, he had his doubts. He had gathered extra pine pitch, which meant as long as he didn't lose his flame, he would have an extra torch. After the first hour the tunnel began to curve, first right and then back to the left. The water was becoming shallower here, although there was no dry place to sit or rest or stretch out his hunched back.

What he did know was that he was now deep under the mountain. Time was difficult to measure without sun. He supposed it didn't matter if it was light or dark out anyhow.

With nothing else to occupy his mind, he pondered why the beast had never shown up until now. Surely other animals could have made the trip before. Maybe they had. Maybe they weren't so different from the southern side of the mountain. But why now? Was there a lack of food on the other side? A famine? There had to be a reason.

His thoughts were interrupted by something glowing at the edge of his light span. It looked like reflective eyes, hundreds of them lining the wall at the edge of his vision. Pike pulled his bow off his shoulder and squatted close to the water. The objects continued their gaze without blinking. *That rules out live animals.* He moved forward cautiously.

More reflections greeted him as he stared at the walls in disbelief. The walls were covered in amazing bedazzlement. He reached to touch the wall and grabbed one of the glowing beauties. It crumbled off with mild force. The object was clear, and yet he couldn't see through it. It was sharp and slightly smaller than the head of his arrows. He guessed it might have some value, so he stuffed a few more of the sparkling ornaments into his bag.

The glowing walls only lasted a few more paces before returning to the dull gray stone that had surrounded him this far. Pike was now entirely uncertain how much time he had been below the ground. He was still excited with anticipation of what lay ahead, but on the back of his tongue he could taste the first few notes of fear he'd experienced in a long time.

He transferred his flame to his backup torch. His back was sore, and as anxious as he was to get to the other side, he was not looking forward to the return trip home. Perhaps he could dump some of the supplies he carried before his return trip. Swash had agreed to leave him a few extra rations by the swamp. It would no doubt take him a few days or more to return back on foot to Mossport.

Pike tried to picture what the reaction in town would look like when Hellion arrived. People would no doubt follow Swash from the far fields and escort him into town like a hero. The man would savor every minute of it. And was he not a hero? There was a strong possibility Pike wouldn't have survived without him. Even so, the soldier, if left on his own, would probably never have survived, and Pike took a small amount of satisfaction in that. Hellion seemed like a good ally to have, no matter how troublesome his military career had been. He would now be famous, perhaps with a different identity, but famous nonetheless. Pike nearly felt the disappointment from the man when he hadn't guessed his true identity. The man probably craved recognition. A wisp of wind made the torch shudder.

Pike turned around and used his body to shield the precious burning flame. He'd come too far to lose it now. There was little doubt the tunnel was getting a supply of fresh air from somewhere nearby. Ahead there looked to be a trace of daylight.

He shielded the torch with his hat and moved forward into the breeze, with courage renewed and curiosity growing. Ahead of him he could hear the lazy crash of water. Pike crept forward slowly; painfully quiet, like he was sneaking up on an animal. The hair on the back of his neck stood up like a wolf's. He could smell the wildness that lay ahead.

It was a dull light compared to his torch, but it was the first natural light the man had seen in too many hours. It fell downward into the tunnel, alongside the flowing water that fed the underground stream. Pike propped the torch between two rocks and stepped forward to bathe in the airy mixture of water droplets and moonlight. Far above, he could see the moon in the night sky and nearly cried out for joy. The only way out was to climb the slippery roots that lined the underground waterfall.

Unwilling to wait for daylight, Pike pulled himself and his supplies through the opening above and into a new world.

Chapter 15

As Hellion Swash rode south, his prize in tow on Pike's horse Clyde, he felt the same sensation as victory after battle. Savoring the moment in solitude gave him time to replay the previous events over and again in his head. *Could I have slain the beast alone?* The answer he knew to be yes, but he wasn't confident he would have survived. He shrugged off his answer. The outcome was as good as he could have hoped for, so why question himself? Things looked less bleak for the first time in a coon's age. The money could give him a new chapter in life. Yet, even with a brighter future ahead, all he remained fixated on for the rest of his journey were successes from long-passed chapters.

There was the moment he signed up for the legendary mercenary army of Sisterton. The successful lie about his age pulled him from the dregs of the barefisted fighting circuit and into real battle. As much as he hated the army now, he had learned invaluable lessons during the first few months of drilling. As a boy he had never trained or practiced once in his life. His instincts were that good. But instinct and raw talent only took you so far in battle. To create the killer he would become, his skills needed perfecting to the point where he could inflict fatalities with less energy, win combat with more speed, and dissect his opponents' tendencies on the fly. He learned to push himself further than he ever would have on his own, and as a result, he got exponentially better.

Another image of himself on stage in Sisterton floated into his mind. It had been his first trip home since departing two years prior. His legendary military career was now beginning to be recognized by men who made the decisions regarding battles. General Code, the third- or fourth-highest commissioned officer at that time, placed a medal onto Hellion's uniform. His superior's rank would continue upward until he reached the top title of Supreme Commander. The medal had read, *Excellence in Commitment to Duty.* Hellion sneered thinking about it. But General Code's private words still remained with him. *I will be keeping an eye on your development, young man. Your time to rise will come, and when it does, the men will surely follow you for your bravery.* He clapped the younger Hellion on the back to expedite his exit and called the next soldier onto the stage.

At that point in Hellion's life, he was not without some ambitions of moving up from infantry. And within months, he would move up to some degree. As proud as he was at the time, he could not help but laugh at his foolishness now. To dream that a street rat like himself could rise to new heights in such a bureaucratic environment as the mercenary army was lunacy. His real job was to die before he reached his goal while pampered enlistees with family money were coddled until enough time had passed to hand them the job of a lifetime. He'd already seen numerous soft men bypass his pace by accomplishing nothing of significance. Added to that was the fact that his superiors would pocket no coin if he was pulled from the front lines. If anything, they'd lose more men. The only hiccup of his all but certain career destination was that he was amazingly hard to kill. He was a survivor.

Skipping ahead through his active but short-lived military service, he reflected on his discovery of a cache of jewels and gold that had been stolen by a barbaric tribe. Hellion alone knew the location after sparing the man who revealed its existence. Swash had accepted the realization by that point that he would never be elevated much higher than he was at present. That was when he'd made the decision. He did not report the treasure to his superiors. Instead, he devised a plan to hide the treasure until his contract was due for renewal. Then, he could walk away and never worry about money again. The only problem with his plan was that he'd need help to pull off the removal of goods in secret. That meant he needed someone he could trust. Trust would be his ultimate undoing.

Chapter 16

THE RISING SUN painted a winding pattern of rocks cutting through a dense forest of vines and colossal trees. A thick fog rose to the treetops like the growing froth from a freshly poured ale. To Pike's back loomed the gigantic mountain wall that had stopped explorer hopefuls like himself since the beginning of time. And there was something else, a faint melody in the sanctuary of his mind. Something he could swear he'd never heard before, and yet it was familiar. It was a faint whisper that he yearned to hear more clearly. As abruptly as he noticed it, the sound disappeared. *How strange,* he wondered in a whisper.

Pike decided to inventory his supplies so he could travel lighter and establish a base to return to when needed. The winding pile of rocks provided fresh flowing water and an easy route to follow to his supply cache. It also led to his route home. Being unfamiliar with the land, he decided to go on a scouting trip and would need to leave most of his food and supplies behind. His ax and spear would stay at camp. He hung his water skin on his belt and tucked his hunting blade into his belt. He stuffed some jerky into a pocket and threw his bow on his back. It was time to explore Horton Conner's world.

It was at this moment that he remembered the map that Hellion had given him. *I suppose I'm not the first to make this discovery. Hopefully my name doesn't become synonymous with crazy.* He pulled out the container and removed the cork. A brittle yellow paper slid out. Holding the document at arm's length, he recognized some of the markings. A small dot labeled Mossport's location. The mountains enabled Pike to trace where he had emerged from the tunnel. He found the marking of a small stream that led northwest. *How could Hellion have stumbled upon this?* He traced its path to find he was currently positioned on a lesser branch of the main river labeled Serpent's Gullet. Serpent's Gullet came from the west without a clear source marked other than mountains and split into the smaller portion where Pike was standing, while the main river continued on an eastern route with a slow dip south until it passed through the Mortapenums at the Serpent's Mouth.

Pike could not believe his good fortune. Grom had done well to pair him up with Hellion. Did the man know more than he let on?

He noted some other landmarks on the map before stashing it back in its protective container. Grasslands were marked to the east of the jungle he was currently in. Far to the northwest was labeled Ghenzi Village. The northeast became more mountainous. *No one will ever believe me when I tell them,* he thought to himself. *They'll all think me insane. Perhaps the animal Hellion is bringing back will give me some credibility.*

The easiest route to follow was the rocky creek bottom. It was still early morning when he set out, and although he should have been tired, his thirst for discovery would never have allowed him to relax. The sun was already intense for the hour, and the air felt warmer than normal here. Judging by the previous markings of the shore, the creek was severely impacted by the drought. As Pike carefully traveled from one large rock to another, he took note of the small fish that gathered in low pools of the creek. They did not look unlike those found on the other side of the mountain and might taste good for dinner in the near future.

The creek bank revealed just how difficult travel would be when Pike left the rock bed. Plants crowded each other for sunlight, and many vines and branches shot outward toward the creek for less competition. Here and there, Pike would spot a game trail where some small animal made a habit of drinking. Gone were the pines and rock that dwelled on the southern side of the mountain. It was as if the hunter had crossed the sea and arrived in a faraway land.

After walking about a quarter of the day, Pike noticed something out of the ordinary ahead. It looked to be smoke rising from beside the creek. It was time to slip into the thick forest to observe unnoticed. He crawled onto the bank on the opposite side of the creek.

The hunter moved slowly through the undergrowth in a quiet crawl. He was within jumping distance of the bank, but the vegetation was so thick, he had no concerns of being spotted. As he moved parallel, closer to the fire, he could hear voices but couldn't understand the language. The people he could see, clearly some type of natives, perhaps the Ghenzis, seemed jubilant at the moment. However, Pike wasn't about to stroll into their camp without a more thorough scouting. He seemed to be looking at a primitive village. The shelters were more like tents than houses, and he wagered these people might be migratory depending on the season. The men and women both had the darkest hair that Pike had ever seen. The men wore loin cloths with fringe that seemed to be made of some type of leather. The women wore only a little more with the material coming down to mid-thigh in a primitive dress with a crisscross of fabric around their shoulders and chests. All of their bodies looked hardened with muscle.

Pike had read about natives in stories, but these were the first he'd ever seen. Mossport had never been inhabited by anyone prior to its founding as far as he knew. It had always been where civilization simply ended. The natives he'd read about usually existed by large bodies of water or on islands in warmer regions of the world. *How had these people ended up in this place?*

Granger realized the natives were preparing for some type of celebratory feast. There were baskets of some type of plant gathered near one of the fires. Over perhaps the main fire, Pike noticed a large animal tied to a long spit being turned occasionally by its caretaker. The meat was charred on the outside, and the shape was long but difficult for Pike to identify. In the next few moments, the drums started banging and more natives concentrated near the fires. Many men and women began to raise their knees and dance around the fire. They began to sing out in a repetitious chant.

That's when Pike noticed a lone native, not far from the spit, sitting against a tree with a gaze fixed upon the ground. The native's knees were drawn up to the chest, and long hair concealed the rest. But the hair was of a different texture than that of everyone else in view. When the person's head finally lifted, Pike saw the face of a girl, twisted in agony and sadness. He realized her arms were tied behind her back. *How odd is this?*

The hunter thought for a moment. Then he focused his gaze back on the unfamiliar animal in time to see a front leg break out from its bindings. Granger gasped. It wasn't an animal at all. A human arm hung limp as the caretaker called for help to remove the carcass from the fire. Pike felt sick to his stomach as the natives placed the body on a crudely fashioned table and began cutting off the meat. What type of a world had he entered? He dare not leave his hiding place now. His eyes went back to the girl. Was she next on the menu? Had she known the poor soul being eaten by the laughing natives around her now?

The dancing now stopped as a tall, fierce-looking native began crying out some type of speech, yelling at the sky above. His words were received with approving yells by all who surrounded him. The chant that continued long after his speech was done rang in Pike's head over and over. "Hy-tan! Hy-tan! Hy-tan! Hy-tan! Hy-tan! Hy-tan!" The drums once again pounded the beat of the word as the people cried out the chant with joy.

Pike had never been so disgusted in his life. The girl sat with her head down, unwilling to watch what went on behind her. Perhaps she was a cannibal as well? Whether or not it was true, it was clear she knew the last person cooked. He surveyed her surroundings more closely and saw there were two piles of cut rope on the ground beside her. He understood what had happened. The girl was to be the third to be eaten. But when?

Granger sat and thought about the situation. He was very close to the Serpent's Gullet. The camp was located practically on the peninsula of land between the split waterways. He looked to the western sky. Clouds were starting to build. His instincts told him there was a good chance of rain that evening. He would have plenty of time to make it back to his base camp, even if he had to follow the creek bed in the dark. The thoughts going through his mind were the last thing one should attempt in a foreign land. Never interfere with business of the locals. He knew nothing about what was going on. Perhaps the natives only ate criminals. Who was he to thwart their justice? He sat quietly watching, thinking.

How could I return home and tell the story of watching natives cook a fellow human? Would townspeople back home not ask why I did nothing? Would I not ask the same question if I were in their place? He grimaced, knowing what he would decide to do. *I'm such a damn fool that if I end up cooked, it'll be what I deserve.* His conscience would not let him leave her to her certain fate. It seemed likely that they might not roast her until the next day. He could quietly swoop in while the natives slept. Would she cry out? He didn't know what would happen, so he continued to watch and wait.

It took a long time for the cannibals to settle down for the night. It frustrated Pike as he dutifully kept an eye on the sky. The first sprinkles he had felt in months began to fall upon his back. The breeze began gusting through the night, making anything happening across the creek inaudible. There were quick flashes of light in the night sky to the west. The storm was coming.

It had been dark long enough; he decided it was time. The girl looked to be asleep. Her body now rested against her drawn-up knees. The cannibals were quiet and seemed to be sleeping or perhaps drunk from celebrating. He hoped they all had made it back to their beds. Pike quickly crossed the creek and hunkered down below the embankment. The water was slightly higher from the rain to the west. No one could see him unless they peered over the steep bank. He crawled on all fours along the bottom ledge until he figured he was even with where the captive should be. Popping his head over the side of the creek, he saw a dwindling fire and the outline of the girl. There could be natives around her, but he couldn't see them in the darkness. But they wouldn't see him either, at least for the moment.

The hunter scaled the bank and crept close to the ground. It wasn't hard to be quiet with the growing winds and increasing drizzle. He approached the girl from behind and slowly placed a hand over her mouth as he nudged her awake. He heard a gasp and saw the whites of her eyes glimmer in the dying flame's light. She was terrified and looked ready to fight him when he put a finger to his lips. Her eyes darted back and forth, but she nodded as if she understood. Pike removed his hand from her mouth and used his hunting knife to cut her hands free. She tried to stand on her own, but she was too weak.

Pike knelt to the ground and pulled her arm over his shoulder for support.

As the two stood, the rain unleashed in a soaking pour, followed by a flash of lightening that lit up the whole village. *It's time to go!* He picked up the native girl and threw her over his shoulder. He could feel her body tense up in anticipation. Her hands latched onto Pike's jacket for added balance. Her heartbeat pounded frantically with terror against him, but she remained silent. He balanced her on his shoulder and stumbled down into the rising water. They hadn't made it far down the swelling creek when they heard screams from the village. They'd been discovered.

He set the girl down in the mid-calf water. "Can you walk?" he asked, marching in place and pointing to his legs.

She looked strangely at him and answered by taking his hand and pulling him away from the village.

"First good news all day."

She turned to him and said in an unfamiliar accent, "Thank you."

A thousand questions must have been in his eyes as he stared back at her. There was no time for any of them. "Follow me!"

They trudged downstream as the water began to rise higher. Pike's lungs burned and his feet hurt from running on the slippery and unforgiving rocks. Then he remembered the girl had no shoes on. Upon stopping, she threw her arms around his neck, indicating she would need to be carried. He picked her up, but grimaced knowing they couldn't continue long. He found one of the thicker shore areas and decided they needed to rest a little while if they were going to make it. He was beginning to have doubts that they would. He sat down, and she huddled against him. As they sat, the cold chill started to settle in quickly. She convulsed uncontrollably next to him. Pike took off his soaked jacket and covered her. It came down to her knees. They stared at the rising creek, no more able to stop their fatigue than the rise of water.

"How did you end up with them?" Pike finally asked. He wasn't sure how much she would understand.

She pointed to herself. "Unlucky." Then she pointed at him. "We've waited a long time for your return."

Return? "Unless we can get out of here in a hurry, neither of us is going to be around much longer."

Something in the now massive creek caught Pike's eye. He put a finger to his lips to silence any more talk. Moving quickly toward the two in the moonlight was a canoe, with one native searching the bank as he flew by them.

As soon as the craft was out of sight, Pike pulled the girl up and they carefully continued south, by land. The creek was becoming too much of a river.

They didn't see any more craft as they made their way slowly through the thick vegetation. Pike was very close to giving up for the night when he saw the canoe, beached ahead on the opposite shore. He slowly made his way across the river and lugged the canoe back across, where he stabilized it enough for the girl to get in. When he looked back across, he realized the native had returned to retrieve his canoe.

Without hesitation, he shoved off and told the girl to get down. A *thud* hit their canoe, and they were swept quickly away from the yelling cannibal. Pike inspected the canoe and found a crude knife stuck in its side. With the swelling river current at their back, they cruised ahead on the increasingly treacherous water. Pike used the oar to steer as best he could, but the water mostly took them where it pleased.

The ride was short compared to the walk. When Pike saw the mountain ahead, he crashed the canoe onto the shore and unloaded his companion. He ran toward the hole with the giant waterfall and fell to his knees when he saw what had happened. The hole was nearly full of water. To attempt the tunnel would be certain death.

"We're too late," he said. Like a pair of soaked muskrats, they stared at their flooded hole for a moment. The situation was too dire to panic. The internal music from that morning again raised the hunter's attention to his surroundings. He pushed it from his mind. All Pike knew for sure at the moment was that he needed to put some distance between them and the cannibals. The natives would certainly be where they stood by morning.

"Where's a safe place I can take you?" he asked the girl. She still wore his coat, which hung loosely on her small-framed body, but her former expression had now changed. No more did she have the downtrodden look of despair on her face. There was now a fire of life burning in her eyes.

"With you," she stated.

"Don't you have people who are missing you? I can take you back to wherever you're from."

"No longer," she said, shaking her head. "I am dead to them. They will kill me if I return. I was the price for peace with the Merkils. Now there will be war with my people, the Ghenzis. I will go wherever you go."

Merkils? Another tribe has moved in since Horton Conner was here. Never interfere with the locals. "But I have nowhere safe to take you. My home is on the other side of that mountain!" He pointed.

She gripped his arm tightly. "Mine will be also."

What have I gotten myself into? "What do you think about going east?" He pointed, but he realized she understood.

"East is good."

South would be better if I could get through this pile of rock. There was no more time to deliberate. More distance meant a longer life. They would need to leave the large triangle they were inside. His goal was to find a way across the Serpent's Gullet by morning. The quickest way there was to follow the mountainside.

The journey continued in the dark. Luckily, there was no carrying involved. Pike knew how far he could push his body alone, but he didn't know how far he could make it shouldering someone else. His body was just like a hunting tool. Wounds needed dressing, broken bones needed splinting, and exhaustion called for rest. They were fortunate that their principle foe for the moment was merely exhaustion. Soon they would need shelter and possibly a fire if they survived long enough.

While they marched in silence, Pike leading the way, he wondered how the girl had come to know his language. It was obvious it wasn't her native tongue. Even once a traveler left Mossport, a common language was not always a certainty. The western hunting grounds were an untamed wilderness that had attracted groups from all parts of the world. The living was tough, but the start was fresh.

The Baron had settled in Mossport under the same conditions. He was a missionary of sorts, trying to reconnect with nature when he claimed to have found Pike alone in the wilderness. No one in town knew where the boy had come from when he brought the wild toddler in to ask. The Baron was a good man to take him in and teach him. The man was Pike's only family since he could recall nothing of his past before life with the skilled woodsman.

Shaking the thoughts from his mind, Pike looked at the horizon and could see the sun would be breaking shortly. They wouldn't be able to cross the river in the dark.

The girl had remained silent all night but had kept up well with his slow pace. He would occasionally look back to find her staring intently at him. She held his jacket tightly around her as if it were the most precious article in the world. Pike silently missed his coat but knew he wouldn't be getting it back. Unfortunately, with the way his luck was running, he'd probably die from fever before the cannibals found him.

He laughed out loud thinking about it, and the girl smiled, as if she had any clue what he was thinking about.

Once they reached the river, Pike was wary about his choice. The rain had almost stopped now. However, the water was much swifter and deeper than the creek they had escaped on. The distance across wasn't so far he couldn't swim it, but he'd seen animals much more powerful than he swept away to their death. Where the river met the mountain, it turned parallel to the rocks and continued on as far as the eye could see. To be swept into those rocks would be sure death before reaching the Serpent's mouth.

Pike took out a rope from his bag. He secured one end around his waist and tied the other to a tree trunk.

"I'm going to try to swim it. If I don't make it, you'll have to pull me back over. Once I reach the other side, you need to tie yourself like this." He showed her how to loop the rope around her thighs and waist. "You'll hold on to our supply bag, and I'll pull you to the other side."

The girl nodded in understanding. Pike walked up the river as far as the long rope would allow. *The only thing dumber than this is waiting here for the Merkils. I wish we would have brought that canoe.* He ran and jumped in before he could change his mind.

Immediately he was carried downstream as he kicked and stroked for the opposite bank. His rope was extra-long, but it would be moments before he'd be at its end. He swam with all his strength and realized he wouldn't make the shore. He fought as if he had a chance until he felt a hard blow to his side. He instinctively grabbed a hold of the object to find himself clinging to an uprooted tree that had fallen in the river. He held on, gasping for air. Slowly, he pulled himself closer to shore until he was able to scramble onto the bank. He fell to the ground, soaked and exhausted. When he looked up, he could see the native girl tying herself with the rope like he'd shown her.

"Go further upstream!" he tried to yell, waving her in the right direction. He couldn't breathe right, which he knew was a very bad thing right now. The girl ran upstream as he had directed and waited with her eyes fixed on him. He crawled to a sturdy tree and tied a knot, double checking its strength. He held onto the rope and walked to the water's edge. He still couldn't yell, so he motioned her to start.

She swam better than he did, but the river was ruthless. Too quickly, the rope began to straighten out. He dragged the rope toward shore, hand over hand with his back muscles on fire. He couldn't see her as she was buried underwater, but he felt her fighting to help him. *Please hold your breath just a little longer.* He tugged harder. *I'm not losing you here!*

Then he saw a head and arm emerge on the shore. He ran to her, following the rope in case the current took her again. He laid her on her back, her chest heaving, trying to suck in all the air in the world. The light descended upon her dark hair, and for the first time he got a truly good look at the girl in the morning light. She was beautiful. Her skin was tanned with teeth glowing like ivory exposed by a smile of relief. Her eyes remained closed. Granger momentarily forgot both his pain and his manners as he openly gawked at the site before him.

"Who are you?" he asked in a whisper.

She looked up to catch his gaze and, smiling, pulled his arm to her chest. "I'm Khawna."

He untied the girl and saw the gashes the rope had left in her sides.

"I'm sorry," he said.

She raised a hand to his bleeding side. "You're hurt worse."

It was true, though he probably wouldn't admit it to her. A part of Pike wanted to stay on the riverbank staring at the girl until he could no longer keep his eyes open. He didn't know how long it had been since he'd slept. But it was the beautiful girl who took his hand and helped pull him to his feet. She donned her new jacket, and they grabbed their supply bag. Ahead they stumbled into an open prairie of tall grass. They had survived the night.

Chapter 17

AFTER A NONSTOP journey through rain and treacherous ground, a very damp Hellion Swash rode into town. With his dark glasses and unique hat back on to resume his disguise, all of the townspeople present stared at the rider from a distance, in awe of the monster now being hauled behind Pike's horse. A few braver civilians eventually approached the curious sight to fall in line behind the procession. Some people cheered, but most just stared quietly in disbelief. Word must have reached Grom ahead of him because he was waiting for Swash outside his shop with a solemn look on his face.

"I'm glad to see you alive, son. What's become of Pike?"

"Granger found the passage the animal used to come through the mountain," replied Hellion from his mount. There was a collective gasp of air by the townspeople. "He decided to explore it. Should return in a week or two. I tried to tell him his idea would make me look like a lily-livered lion for not going too. Lucky enough for me, I don't really care. You can't get in a barnyard argument with a goat-brained fool; otherwise, people take you for the jackass. Anyhow, I'm not good at this public speaking stuff. He asked me to bring back his trophy, and so here I am."

Grom walked over and clapped Hellion on the back. "Good work by the both of ya. I knew if anyone could get it done, it'd be Pike Granger. I suspect you'll be wanting your cut?"

Swash flashed his cruel grin. "Let's just say for the record, the beast made me earn it."

"Har har!" roared Grom. "I'm happy to give it to you. I just hope Pike doesn't find more of these animals to hunt!"

The crowd transformed into a jovial mood as they crept closer, first venturing a touch of the tough green skin, then pulling open an eyelid, then sneaking a look at the giant teeth. Then a young boy made his way to the front of the crowd.

"Did you find my pa?" the boy asked, looking up at Swash.

Hellion looked around, biting his lip. Then he got off his horse and put a hand on the boy's shoulder. "We found their last camp. Beast attacked while they slept. Nothing much left to find, I'm afraid."

The boy ran back and buried his face in the bosom of his crying mother. More questions were shouted at Hellion.

"Where did you find it? How did Pike kill it? Are we safe now? What if Pike doesn't come back?" He started to attempt to answer the questions before it became too much. Then he just pushed his way through the crowd into Grom's shop and shut everyone else outside. He wanted to be alone. But first he wanted his money, which Grom happily paid him. He left the horses and beast to Grom, and with money in his pocket for the first time in a long while, he headed to the Mammoth Inn for the comforts of a bath and a warm meal.

It was past midday and the inn was largely empty, which suited Hellion fine. The barmaid was the same one who had given him the evil eye before he had left. She continued to stare at him suspiciously as she served him bread and ale. Hellion, for his part, made no attempt to start a conversation. He was tired and hungry. He drank his first beer quickly and slammed it down, only to replace it with another. Enjoying the effect, he repeated it. He had made an honest small fortune, and it felt good. Now he could travel the world and recover the stash of wealth he'd acquired less than honestly. His tale would be told and perhaps written about for years and years to come. So why was he drinking alone?

"I knew he wouldn't come back," said the girl after a few mugs.

"He will when he's ready," replied Hellion from behind his mug.

"I don't think we'll ever see the man again," she said with a sigh. "My guess is, he might even be dead." He could sense her studying his face carefully for a reaction.

Swash chewed his bread and swallowed the mouthful with a gulp of ale. "Nobody can best that man in the woods. He'll be back, but he needed to see the other side first."

"Why didn't you go with him?"

Hellion hiccupped and belched loudly at the suggestion. "Probably because I have a brain. I tried to talk him out of it, if you want to know. I wouldn't be concerned about that one coming back though. He's smart and tough. When he's ready, he'll come strolling in, and he'll tell us all what's on the other side."

The girl put her hands on her hips. "He tell you anything of his plans when he does return? You spent a good deal of time with him. He'll have all the money he'll ever need, like you. Will he stay in town or travel back to the civilized world?"

Hellion eyed her suspiciously. "He didn't mention what he was going to do with all the money. Maybe he'll sail back across this fresh-water ocean and write a book. Maybe he'll find himself a proper woman there and settle down."

The girl blushed when he said it.

"You sure seem deeply interested in Pike."

The girl snorted. "You mistake my intent. I think the man's a fool for going on the trip, and I told him so before he left."

"Aye, maybe you did, but you didn't count on us killing the beast either now, did ya?"

"You act as if you know anything about it!" With that she slammed his refilled mug in front of him and stormed into the kitchen.

"Hey! What about my bath!" shouted Hellion to the swinging kitchen doors.

Swash eventually tired of his own company and staggered out of the inn. Some women simply had no manners. Speaking of such, it occurred to him that it had been a long time since he'd had a woman. He took the familiar walk through town until he found what he was looking for.

The red light now lit the single window of the old building as the sun had fallen for the day. Sailors were known to have a large appetite for a woman's company, and every town with a port generally provided its own harbor for lonely men. He knew not to have too-high expectations for his visit, but at least for a price he would have some companionship.

Swash knocked on the weathered back door that had served as the main entrance for many a morally depleted man. He was shown the warm inside with carpet and soft cloth covering the windows and the walls. Silk was draped from place to place and felt relaxing as it tickled his skin while the young woman led him to the choosing room. The room was heavily scented and contained numerous lit candles while the half-dozen girls working that evening reclined in their revealing gowns.

He sat on a velvet chair to observe them as they came to him one by one, to sit briefly in his lap and whisper something in his ear about how much pleasure they would give him. This was the normal formality he was accustomed with. Finally, he chose a girl. She had bright red hair and warm, swollen lips. She instantly grabbed his groin and softly led him into a dark room with a single candle burning. As she dropped her gown and began caressing him, Hellion forgot for a short time how truly lonely he was.

Chapter 18

THE OUTRAGED MERKIL chief paced back and forth in his leather-covered shelter. His teeth ground together as he pictured the scrawny girl sneaking past his sleeping guards. Adding to the mystery of the Ghenzi girl's disappearance was the account of his scout whose canoe had been stolen, along with the two sets of tracks, which corroborated his story. The man's tracks were large bulky prints and unlike any moccasin prints the chief had ever seen. It was clear the pair had forded the Serpent's Gullet and escaped for now. He scowled at the thought, knowing all too well that the escape would reflect poorly on him by the elders' council. Perhaps another warrior would even be emboldened enough to challenge his leadership in the ring of combat. He would need to make a gruesome example of any such man who'd try.

A greeting was shouted from his shelter's entrance flap, to which he responded with permission to enter. The elderly man with froth-colored, stringy hair whose head poked under the flap was Clivegon. He had once been a strong warrior, but those days had long since passed. He now looked feeble with his head bowed and a sag in the skin of his neck where strong muscles had once bulged with intimidation.

"What news from the council do you bring me, old man?"

I bring you wisdom, from seven men with enough years combined to total fourteen of your lifespan. I urge you to listen. We must demand another sacrifice from the Ghenzis and restore our strength."

"This cannot happen. To expose our weakness to our enemy will mark the beginning of our people's end. They must not know she escaped."

"They will know soon if they don't already. Who else could have helped the girl unless someone from our own camp? She will return to them. She will tell them what becomes of their tributes each moon."

The tall, chiseled leader shook his head fiercely. "She will not because they would hand her back over to us to save their own hides. The girl had help from someone from a different tribe. The footprint is different. It is a large man. We need to find him too, so we can kill him to avenge the gods. Then we must eat them both to regain our power."

"The council foresees ill signs following this girl." The old man now started pacing around his leader, as if instructing a youngling how to lead. "It is not wise to take up this hunt, especially while we are in need of feeding. Every day the moon gets smaller, and so does our strength without proper sacrifice. We need a replacement soon, at all costs."

"You speak to me as if I were a child, Clivegon." He pointed a finger at the old man's chest as he stepped closer to him. "You and the other fools act wise, but you're really just old, weak, and scared. If I had heeded your advice on the war with the Ghenzis, we would still be sacrificing our own people on the spit every full moon. I have brought us to where we are today. I brought the rain only a night ago by providing us with a sacrifice. I am the reason our numbers have grown. I fill people's mouths with food and put children in our women's bellies. I am the chief the gods demand, and you would do well not to forget that."

The old man grimaced at his leader's words. Slowly the lines in the old warrior's face transformed into what could almost be described as a smile. "I foresaw your death if you continue the hunt for your lost sacrifice. How does that help our people?"

"Your foolish visions might scare others in the tribe, but not me. You can tell the council of halfwits I've already made up my mind. I will lead the hunting party. I will make us stronger than ever before. I will not lose to a Ghenzi girl."

Clivegon tried to argue his opinion civilly while absorbing the scorn of his chief. The man's arrogance had always been a concern to the elders, but lately their leader's power had gone to his head worse than usual. The chief was drunk on his own supremacy. There was not a warrior around who could match him, and he knew it. Success and victories had changed their leader, and probably not for the better.

The old man left disgusted but not surprised. The chief respected no living man, whether friend or enemy. Not that there weren't both sitting on the council, but his disregard for advice would ultimately be Chief Hytan's downfall. Clivegon's job was to make sure it did not become the whole tribe's downfall. The former chief had seen many a chief rise only to fall in his eighty years, but the current one was the most headstrong of them all. There may not be generations to come if he became too reckless.

When Clivegon reached the shelter with the remaining six white-haired tribesmen, he told them the plans must be prepared for the hunt. Hytan had no interest in their visions. There was grumbling and head shaking as they rose from their circle around the fire and prepared to spread the word to the camp. The fifty best warriors would accompany Hytan. Preparations included packing for the hunt and securing the camp in the chief's absence.

While Hytan stewed in his bone-fashioned chair, the old man's smile lingered in his memory when foretelling his death. He did not like Clivegon's expression at all. The man definitely seemed pleased with himself. The truth remained that more of the council's prophecies never materialized than actually occurred. The council was jealous of his power. No leader in the history of the Merkils had dared dream of all he had accomplished. He would not let his authority be challenged by a group of weak cowards. The girl would be caught, the same as whoever had helped her. His mind was set.

"Leader, may I come in?" It was the voice of his favorite wife, Latella.

"Come in," he said, trying not to sound annoyed, although he was.

She entered with her head bowed, her long hair covering her face. It also covered the scar on her cheek that he had put there to mark her as his own.

"The word is spreading that you are leading the hunt to recover our sacrifice."

"Good. We plan to leave at first light tomorrow. How is my son?"

Latella raised her head upright now that the formality had passed. "He is strong like his father. The fever has passed. I think he would like to see his father."

Hytan had no stomach for squealing children, which was only part of the reason why he kept private lodging from his wives. He also had found that keeping a steady rotation of bed warmers kept him and his women happier. Sure he had his favorites, but he kept these matters to himself. He had missed Latella as of late, but her duty for now was to his young son. He needed to be fed at all hours of the day to ensure he grew strong.

"Perhaps I shall visit him when I return. And I will bring back two sacrifices to make up for the one that escaped. My son will have the first drink of their blood."

His wife smiled with excitement. "Our people will rejoice to see you return."

"Some will, others may not, but they will all be reminded why I lead."

"Do the elders not wish you to pursue the sacrifice?" she asked, surprised.

"They do not. They say it will be bad for our people. But they only wish to undermine me and make me look weak. I have no appetite for their war of words and deception. I'd rather like to gut them all like boars. They are weak, scared old men who were once content to eat their own people. Not one among them was ever fit to lead on his best day. The reason they have so many years is because they were never brave."

"No man was ever brave compared to you, my husband. All men fear you for good reason. When you are victorious, the whitehairs will once again look foolish."

He looked into the angry eyes of his favorite wife as she scorned the wise men further. She had a temper to rival his own, and she was fiercely loyal. This was why she was his favorite. He rarely had to strike her because as strong as she was, she rarely forgot her place. But as strong as they both were, it would not be enough unless their gods were appeased with the sacrifice he would provide. This was his lone concern.

Chapter 19

PIKE AND KHAWNA walked all day through the prairie. The grasses were nearly taller than Pike as he pushed through to make a trail. The previous night's rain on the warm ground had created a hazy fog, giving the landscape a mystical look. More than once the pair overtook a small crest in the prairie to gaze down upon herds of animals from a distance. There were grazers with long twisting horns that grew skyward as long as a man's arm. Pike's best guess was that they were a type of large antelope. He also saw the tallest animal he'd ever seen as it reached to the tops of the few scarce trees to pluck off leaves that the rain had just revived. Pike had heard tales about such massive creatures from across the seas but had never seen anything to compare to them. How could they be here?

Khawna's stomach would growl from time to time, and Pike was famished as well, but he'd already decided they dared not stop until dark. They had to assume they were being hunted, and Pike didn't have the strength to put up resistance if it came to a fight. For the time being, other than heading in a general direction, they had no plan, no destination, and no certainty of the future. Pike had seemingly endless questions that had formed in his mind since he'd rescued the girl. It had been a dangerous night, and although the threat was not over, it seemed a good time for answers.

"How is it that you speak my language?" Pike finally asked.

She looked at him quizzically. "From a man described just like you."

"Horton Conner?"

She smiled and nodded her head. "My namesake. He taught our people many things besides language. He came from beyond the mountains with much wisdom about building and planting food and growing our tribe. He taught us everything we needed to thrive, except how to fight." She paused. "But now you're here."

"I'm just a hunter. I know how to survive, but I don't know how to fight." He ran a hand through his hair, unnerved by Khawna's belief in him. "How did your people thrive with the Merkils as neighbors?"

"They have only come from the west recently. They believe they gain their strength from eating humans. Whenever the moon turns whole, they need human meat or they become weak."

"And your people are afraid to fight?"

"We tried and failed in the beginning. The Merkils are experts at war. They killed many good warriors. Now we must pay them tribute of everything they ask. To resist is impossible. My people suspect that tributes are eaten, but it is not discussed. We know that no tributes are ever seen again."

Pike pondered that silently for awhile. His strength was beginning to fade as they continued on a northeast heading, judging by the sun. Khawna noticed and began to break trail for the pair, allowing him to follow her lead while holding his chest with his right arm. He believed he had a broken rib from the river crossing. Khawna had felt his chest and was certain he would be fine once they got some rest. When he coughed up blood later in the day, both of their expressions became worried, but neither said anything.

The sun was going down when they found a group of trees on the prairie to rest under for the night. Pike decided they'd traveled far enough to risk a fire and went about gathering whatever branches and burnable plants he could find. He took out his supplies and cooked a satisfying meal of canned beans with bacon. His companion could not get enough of the exotic combination.

"Khawna, what do your people normally eat?"

"We grow gardens like the paleface taught us. We raise our own animals near town for when the hunting is no good. We store excess grains for in-between harvests. It is not bad food, but I like your food better." She smiled as she shoveled more beans into her mouth, and Pike laughed.

"These food stores, is that how your people survive the winter snow?"

Her eyes narrowed at him. "What's that?"

"Snow? It's the white flakes that pile on the ground. You know, when it's cold?"

The girl clearly had no idea what he was talking about. "It doesn't snow here?" he asked.

Khawna shrugged her shoulders with a confused look.

Very interesting.

"Do your rivers ever freeze with ice? It was a mild winter, but surely it was much colder before I arrived?"

She crossed her arms. "I do not understand why you worry about the cold. It gets cool at night and warm in the day. Is that different than your side?"

Pike rubbed his chin with his thumb in thought. "Quite a bit different," he replied. "Speaking of different, what do your people call the animal that stands as tall as two grown men?" he asked.

"Many animals stand that tall. We saw a giraffe today, and there's also the elephant with a long nose." She held out her arm from her nose and grabbed a piece of jerky from Pike, showing how an elephant puts things in its mouth. They both laughed at her antics.

"But this animal had a mouth like this," he snapped his arms together like a crocodile. "And it walks on two feet, like a man."

Khawna stopped laughing. "Where have you seen this animal?"

"It's what led me through the mountain. It was attacking my village on the other side."

"This is a bad animal."

"I know. That's why I hunted it down."

Her eyes were white with disbelief. "You tracked the Tarmigan?"

"Me and another man. I killed it the same day I rescued you. Are there any more around here?"

"Killed? More? There is only one Tarmigan, and it cannot be killed."

"I've seen enough dead animals to tell you it was definitely expired when Hel...er...Lion hitched its carcass to my horse and dragged it back to town."

"This animal cannot die. It is a very old creature that our people have avoided since the beginning of time. We do not bother it, and it does not kill us."

Pike shrugged his shoulders. "It wouldn't leave our town alone."

Khawna scooted a little further away from him as her eyes shone with fear. "If this is true, something very bad will happen to you."

"It already has. I'm stuck here, I'm injured, and people want to eat us."

She continued to stare at him. "The elders have always warned to stay away from the Tarmigan. The creature is cursed. Somehow you have survived. There is great fortune in that, but you cannot escape the curse. Unless you were chosen..." She cut off there and stared in the distance in thought.

Pike scoffed. "I don't believe in such things. We all make our own choices. If you believe it, you'd best rid yourself of my company. Maybe you should run back to those elders that handed you over to be eaten."

Khawna continued to stare into the night for a moment. Then she sighed and moved back closer to Pike. "I will not leave you. You are not afraid like them. My fate will be yours."

"You sound like it's a death sentence. If I can heal up, I can survive almost anywhere on my own. Especially where others cannot."

The girl's eyebrows rose. "There is a place where it is said that wounds heal quicker…" she began. "No one I know has been there because it's been forbidden. But the stories of its power are true, just like the stories of the paleface and where you come from. If we can find it, we will stay there until you are better."

Pike frowned. "Where is this place?"

Khawna hesitated. "No one has gone for a long time. Our people are not allowed to leave our territory. I know it exists in the mountains."

"Hmmm." Pike pulled out his map. The corked cylinder was amazingly still dry on the inside. "I can see we're here," he referenced on the paper. Khawna crept to his shoulder. "Any idea what the place is called?"

"Serpent's Spittle," she said.

Pike traced the map eastward to see only grasslands noted. To the north a lesser mountain range was labeled. He looked closely at the drawing until he saw what appeared to be a drawing of a snake's head, spitting drops of venom in the air.

He pointed to the picture. "Could this be it?"

"I would not know until we see it. It should be a dead area. Nothing grows near these mountains."

"Do the Merkils know about this place?"

She shook her head. "They are foreigners to our land. They know no stories about the history of our ground."

Pike sat, resting his chin on his hand. "Whether it helps or not, and I clearly am a skeptic, it might be a good hiding place for awhile."

Khawna grinned happily.

Pike noticed. "What aren't you telling me?"

"There's nothing to tell. You doubt its powers. Lay your head in my lap and rest."

Pike complied and felt her hands gently rub his hair. He allowed his body to relax under her spell. He was beyond exhaustion, and her company was comforting. What he couldn't understand was why the girl was now staring off into the night sky grinning from ear to ear.

Chapter 20

THE CURIOSITY OF Mossport had been quenched for the day as darkness descended upon the town. Nearly every inhabitant had come to Grom's shop to see the remarkable creature. The animal's corpse was stored in a horse stall below the store, and the town would decide what was to be done with it in the morning. Its body was chained to two of the support beams to prevent any thieves from dragging off what was surely a newly discovered species. Grom had sent letters to Sisterton to get the newspapers to document and publicize the events of the little town. He would sleep well tonight above his shop, knowing he had done his part to save his little outpost of civilization from destruction.

There was loud, joyous music to be heard from the Mammoth Inn tonight. The townspeople were likely to celebrate until morning. The air was clear, and the music traveled well. Grom almost wished he could join them in their carefree celebration, but there was too much to be done tomorrow. He was already behind in his work from the excitement today. As glad as he was for the occasion to be behind, he couldn't let his procrastination carry over further.

The shopkeeper felt proud knowing he had recruited and outfitted the right man to hunt down the beast. Sending Lion with Pike had also been one of his better decisions. Certainly no other two men in town or perhaps even Sisterton could have gotten the job done. The money invested in the venture was worth every penny for the security of his business and the town. Once the news spread across the lake and perhaps even across the world, it was likely that more settlers and adventurers might be lured to grow the small port and increase his business. Perhaps if business was good, he could sell it in the future and even run for mayor, if they ever created the position.

With all the positive visions of the future floating around in his mind, another thought began to gnaw at his fanciful future. What if this was just the beginning of worse things to come? As Grom lay next to his snoring wife, he couldn't shake the worry that if Pike had now been able to cross the Mortapenums, what else might find passage? After all, what they had just killed was the only known animal to make its way through. This monster could be the drip before the oncoming flood. Perhaps they should destroy the tunnel. Of course, he'd have to wait for Pike to return…if he ever did.

He sat up with worry. Horton Conner had warned in his book that the combining of the two worlds could cause irreversible damage. *To our side or the other?* He had also hinted that the two worlds had not always been separated. Something was believed to have caused the rise of the Mortapenums. Either way, come tomorrow, Grom would be writing another letter to Fort Tuttle, the lonely military presence on Mammoth Lake. It was situated on the south shore of the lake, approximately halfway to Sisterton. Thus far, the commander had ignored his pleas for help to kill the beast. Now, however, the man might realize that Grom was not the boy who cried wolf. He was the man who got things done.

Both the bed and room suddenly shook with a violent snap.

Landquake?

His wife, Hilga, sat up and smacked him.

"Why'd you do that?" he asked in surprise, rubbing his shoulder.

"Fer wakin' me up. I don't feed you cabbage for good reason. You shook me awake."

"It weren't me! I think it was a quake."

He braced himself for another hit as the grouchy woman reached her arm back; then the whole building shook even harder. There was a loud *snap* somewhere below them.

Grom scrambled out of bed and lit a candle. Some picture frames had fallen off the wall.

"See, I told ya! The only thing big enough to make that racket would be another one of those monsters below us!"

Before his wife could answer him, Grom threw on his clothes and raced down the two flights of stairs. No one was in the shop, so he continued into the stable below. When he reached the beast's stall, he found one chain had snapped and the other had broken through the wooden support beam! The beast was gone!

Grom ran back upstairs to street level and out the front door of his shop.

"The beast has escaped!" he yelled. The few drunken people staggering in the street laughed at him like he was a madman. He ran back to his shop to arm himself with an old sword and a lantern before returning to the street.

"The beast is loose! See his prints here!" This time a woman came to Grom's yells. She saw the giant footprints in the lantern light and screamed. More people took notice.

Grom followed the path as it headed for the loudest place in town, the Mammoth Inn. A string of people were following him now. The music played on, with no evidence of any commotion. Grom fought the urge to run and followed the trail. The path went around the gigantic building and stopped at the corner. Claw marks had gouged up the wooden sides of the building. The monster was inside!

Grom ran around to the front entrance and up to the stage. He grabbed the piper's hand and the instrument stopped, followed by the young man singing and the customers clapping.

"The beast has escaped! It's in this building now!" The stirred-up citizens who had entered behind him gave him more credibility this time, and he saw the terror in the crowd's eyes.

"What should we do?" asked a man with eyes half-closed by ale.

"Arm yourselves, friends. I'm going upstairs to flush it out. Where's Jada at?"

"She's gone up to Room 36 to tend to Lion, our passed-out hero," said the young girl behind the bar.

Grom led a group of men up the stairs as the rest of the crowd in the great hall murmured worriedly amongst themselves. The whole lot was paralyzed with fear.

When the hastily gathered group turned the corner on the third floor, Grom realized that Room 36 was exactly where the claw marks had been heading. He signaled for silence as he slowly turned the knob and pushed the door inward.

The candle still burned in the room, but they would not find a trace of Jada or their hero that night. They were gone.

Chapter 21

THE MORNING AIR was already warm, even though light had not
yet broken on Chief Hytan's village. His wives had dressed
him in spectacular fashion with his favorite blood-red leather
leggings, moon-shaped bone earrings, and red war paint on his face
and chest. On top of these he added his favorite ankle bracelets of
human teeth and his bone mail necklace fashioned from human ribs.
The imposition of fear on all those around him was a never-ending
duty.

Hytan looked over the fifty warriors who now stood before him,
awaiting his command. They were all good fighters, but none were on
his level. He would often scream at them, his eyes burning through
them, just inches from their face, in an effort to harden their nerves.
They were all young and strong. The Ghenzi girl and her helper
would not be able to outrun them long. In the hours since the rain
had stopped, the river had crested and was now returning back to
its normal flow. Hytan's scout had already found where the pair had
crossed. The path would undoubtedly lead them out of the jungle and
into the open plains. From there it would be anyone's guess. The fact
that they were going in the opposite direction of the village made him

think his intuition was right. The man helping her was no Ghenzi tribe member.

The warriors continued their brisk jog as they found the remnants of a trail through the grassy plain. Every so often, Hytan would stop to examine the ground. It gave his warriors a chance to rest and allowed him to make sure they were still only tracking two sets of footprints. If the man and woman had met up with others, he had to be careful not to lead his best warriors into a trap. It was unlikely, but a chief must always be aware of such things, especially when they traveled far from their village.

When the war party did stop, there was mostly silence among his men. They were well trained and knew better than to upset their leader. They hunched low to the ground and studied their surroundings. The men were ever keen to Hytan's reaction to the trail and remained alert for the next order he would assuredly bark at them. The chosen title for his best warriors was *dearth*. Each of the dearths had proven themselves worthy of his elite force through years of training. Hytan himself had been a dearth prior to his rise to chieftain. All of his peers were just as deadly in those days, but none was as crafty as he. It was the crafty ones that a chief must keep a close eye on. His predecessor had failed to do an adequate job of that. To show weakness would embolden a challenger. While having too many challengers was bad for the tribe, an occasional rival was a necessary part of leadership. A wise chief used these fools to serve as a reminder to the rest of the clan not to test him. Challengers who lost to the chief in the circular battle pit or *Quill* were eaten by the tribe, thus increasing their strength as a whole.

Hytan located a spot where his prey had clearly sat down to rest. Where were they going? They were getting further away from the Ghenzi village with every step. They were exposed in the open grasslands, and he was sure his men would close in on them in little more than a day's time.

It all seemed a little too easy for the Merkil chief. Aside from the trouble the escaped sacrifice had caused, Hytan did enjoy a good hunt. He would almost be sad when they found and slaughtered the two leaving this trail. However, he surely would enjoy roasting them on his fire shortly afterwards. After all, the gods must be appeased, and his tribe had already let them down once.

He recalled the terrible days of his youth. At the time, the elders had followed the old tradition of sacrificing one of their own every full moon. He remembered the terror of finding out who was chosen every time. Some chosen had died bravely, but most fell into despair and begged until they finally met their death. And for all those years, the Merkils' numbers had remained small. They would never be able to grow into the tribe that he envisioned they would become. As Hytan got older, his skill had increased to one of the best in the tribe with a spear, making him too valuable for sacrifice, unlike his younger sister. It was after he'd been forced to eat his own sibling, alongside the rest of his tribe, that he'd decided the old way was no way to live. He wasn't ready to challenge yet, but he would hone his skills until the day he was ready for the Quill. Hytan would go on to be a camp defender or *shyra* before his rise to dearth. Being a dearth was one of the highest privileges of the tribe, second only to chief or council, which were supposedly equal in the eyes of the gods. The difference was, most dearths were eventually killed or maimed in war or hunting if they stayed too long in the role. Hytan had survived for ten years. He had become ruthless, but more importantly, crafty. He had envisioned a new way to grow his people and make them stronger than ever. He would offer three sacrifices each full moon to triple his people's strength. The first victims would be the chief, his son, and his wife after Hytan won his challenge in the Quill. From there, he overruled the council and waged war upon the more numerous Ghenzi. In one swift strike with his dearths, he attacked their village, killing nearly all their young men of fighting age before they knew the Merkils were a threat. The women, along with old men and young boys, had a choice to make. They could ensure peace by sending three tributes each full moon to the Merkils, or they could be completely annihilated. What they weren't told was what became of their tributes. This was yet another reason the girl could not escape.

From that day on, the Ghenzis were easily manipulated by keeping the young male population to a minimum for farming needs and harvesting the rest to be eaten.

With all his power came privileges. He enacted a law allowing him to take any woman in the tribe he wanted, even if she belonged to another warrior. It became his right as chief, and to the council's horror, he used it freely. It created a fear in his men, and he could manipulate them easier if they worried that any wrong step could cost them their woman. The best food was given to Hytan, his clothes were the most ornate, and his weapons were superior to all others in the land. In short, he lived like a god among men—a cruel, vengeful god.

Naturally, the only thing that could frighten a man of his stature was to lose his vast power. He knew sometime down the road his time as chief would come to an end. But that would be many years from now. If he could secure his post long enough, he could hand his position down to his son someday. That was his exit strategy. He had no intent to step down to join the council fools. It would be a test against time, but it would keep him in power and not end with him getting eaten. He would burn himself to ashes before he gave his strength to anyone else.

In the back of Hytan's mind was the old council adage: *As it is in nature, so it is with man.* Often if one breed of an animal became numerous, a calamity occurred and brought the population down. It could be sickness, it could be fire, it could be drought, it could be a lack of a food source, or it could be the introduction of a new predator. It was the last that Hytan had to be constantly looking out for. His rise could spawn another to take him and his people down. It was just one more reason to be as ruthless as possible, as far as he was concerned. Never, ever, should a chief show weakness.

Chapter 22

Captain Gordon sat tiredly in his cabin. *The Rose Tattoo* bobbed gently beneath him as she awaited work while tied down at the port of Sisterton. The port was more like a large river that connected Mammoth Lake to the sea. She was the envy of the world, one of the biggest as far as port cities went, and yet the port was in its infancy compared to the other large ports that lay across the Gridlock Sea. She had grown quickly and hastily with more wood than stone, whereas the older ports had evolved slowly over the centuries. Of course, while the other ports were still young and evolving, the lands of Sisterton and the Mammoth were uninhabited. It was only a few generations before the present that the first explorers had arrived in this bleak land. While the immediate area surrounding the port city was hospitable to civilization, the steep Mortapenums of the north and the vast Deadlund desert to the south prevented the region from sprawling with human life.

Gordon was tired because sleep was difficult with his present worries. He needed work to pay his crew and to continue the payments on his ship. Having lost her once before and starting over with nothing for the second time in his life, the mere thought of financial hardship kept him up at night. He had sent his first mate, Linden, to the transportation authority to offer his ship's services for freight transportation. His once-a-month contract to deliver to and from Mossport was hardly enough to keep his head above water. Side jobs were a must, and the better the pay, the fewer questions Gordon would ask.

It would not be true to say that the thought of collecting the fugitive reward had not crossed his mind once during his idle time at port. For unknown reason, the Governor and Mercenary Army of Sisterton were offering a small fortune for the whereabouts of Hellion Swash. It would be enough money to pay off his boat for good and possibly retire. The vile man had threatened the captain's life upon his discovery during his last run to Mossport, and yet, he had also spared it. Moreover, the man had taken his beloved map. At the time, the captain had decided the paper was not worth his life. Could the man truly find him to enact revenge after he collected the reward? And what about Swash's promise to return and pay handsomely for the retrieval of a pile of treasure he had hidden? Could his story be true? Gordon really couldn't know for sure, but he did know the man had scared him enough to keep his mouth shut.

Then there was the stigma of being the rat. Captain Gordon was no friend of Hellion Swash's, but he had given him his word. Reputation was important in the shipping world. The captain dealt quite often with unlawful citizens, and more often than not, he profited most from ventures with them. To be a snitch would forever end a large part of his business as well as his honor among smugglers. He shook the idea from his head once again. Swash would return. He, too, had given his word.

A knock on his door had the captain jumping up from his chair. Could Linden have an offer? He ran to the door to find Orson, one of the youngest members of his crew, waiting with a smile.

That smile gives away too much. The boy would need to grow out of that if he ever wanted to become a captain.

"What's the grin about, Orr?"

The boy bit his lip, trying to suppress his excitement. "There's a man at the dock. Says he's looking for some special cargo to be hauled."

What have we here? Showing up at a ship outside of the transportation authority likely meant a person was desperate or nonconforming to legal regulations. The term "special cargo" led Gordon to believe the latter.

"Check him for weapons and send him to my cabin. I have a feeling he won't elaborate on the docks."

"Yes sir, Captain."

Orson ran back down to the docks. When he returned with the man seeking voyage, he found the captain sitting in the corner, with full captain attire on, including hat. His face looked hardened. The man was ready to drive a hard bargain.

"Do you have money?" asked Captain Gordon.

The man held up a small pouch and jingled it in his palm to show it was full.

"Where do you seek passage?"

The man stared back at him without emotion. This was not his first time.

"I need special cargo delivered to the city. It is only a few days' voyage to the island of Guanhaila."

Gordon knew the island well. It was a popular smuggling port to the south. Its location put it in proximity for so many shipping routes one could never tell what smugglers were bringing in from there.

"I assume your special cargo will need extra care while going through port inspection?"

"That is why I am here."

"How large?"

"Nine barrels."

"You will need to ship more supplies. I have to have something to show port officials when they board."

The man cursed. "I only have so much to pay."

"Then your money must be turned into additional cargo, which I will keep as payment. In addition, for my troubles, I will request one barrel of whatever it is you're shipping. As far as the rest of your payment, I can sell rum easily. Fruit is cheaper, but it doesn't keep like rum."

"Your price is steep. You do not know what you're hauling for me, and yet you're requesting it as payment. I caution you, it is extremely dangerous if not properly cared for." The man shook his head in disgust. "I need this done now. I agree to your offer, and you will have your rum. I can get you dried nuts as well. They will keep better."

Gordon tipped his hat. "You're a smart businessman. One barrel of mystery with five cases of rum and five carts of mixed nuts and you have a deal."

"I can handle that. I want to leave tomorrow if possible. I was told you were good; that is the only reason I'm here."

"You heard right. I'll prepare the paperwork for inspection and handle the supplies. Will you be coming with us?"

The man nodded his head. "The barrels will not leave my sight."

The captain shrugged. "Whatever makes you happy."

Chapter 23

Jada was surprised to still be breathing. She'd been bringing Lion a pail of water only to find him passed out on his bed. The fool had drunk too much and had sent word that he needed to talk to her. Some talk it would have been, as he was clearly incapable of speech. His clothes were disheveled, his eyes glazed over, and he smelled like a wine wagon had wrecked into a whorehouse. In fact, she was the real fool for even coming up to his room. However, beyond general pity for the tramp of a man, she had also hoped to keep him from coming down from his room and irritating her good customers.

While she had stood, pail in hand and scowl on her face, staring at the helpless pile of a scoundrel on her fine sheets, she had felt a slow, warm pressure enclose her throat. All she saw before spilling onto Lion were the long scaly fingers that encompassed her throat and her mouth, quietly choking her into silence and ultimately, unconscious submission.

Now she was awakened to the jostling of a steady gait carrying her like a sack of potatoes. She was entangled with a man. By the smell of him, it had to be Lion. They were moving, as if riding a horse, and yet they were suspended rather than heaped on the back of a steed. The fabric holding them felt like burlap, possibly one of the enormous bags that brought supplies to Mossport. She was scared and could remain quiet no longer. Her muscles were cramping, and she had no idea how long she'd been unconscious.

"Let me out!" she yelled as loud as she could.

The bundle she was entwined inside didn't slow down.

"Stop, please! I need air!" She tried again, the result the same.

"Please keep it down; I have a terrible headache," complained a voice belonging to Lion.

"Lion! We're trapped, you fool! Get us out of here!"

She felt a hand roam from underneath her to feel her face and hair.

"Stop it, you goat-brained oaf! It's me, Jada. Keep your filthy hands to yourself!"

There was a groan. "Good morning, barkeep. You know, you weren't saying that last night. I feel like a drowned rat. I hate to complain, but these are the roughest hotel sheets I've ever slept on. Can you get off me so I can go back to sleep?"

"If you were in my bed last night, I'd have put a few extra holes in your head with my blade. Can't you feel us moving, you obtuse ovine? We've been captured!"

"I simply love a girl with an imagination. Pull these covers off us. Who has us?"

Jada was so aggravated she reached underneath her, found some skin and pinched hard.

Lion's cursing startled even her. The bag stopped moving and was lowered onto the ground.

"Nice work, you ale-guzzling oaf!" she whispered.

Lion said nothing to address the insult while massaging his side where Jada had pinched him. The reality of the situation may have finally started settling in. She was only mildly surprised it had taken him this long.

When Jada emerged from her cloth prison, she realized how bad their situation was. Towering over her and Lion was the previously slain monster he'd brought back to Mossport.

"Well, I'll be a billy goat's uncle! There's another beast, barkeep! Run for it!" Hellion bolted for the bushes like a rabbit for a briar patch. Jada stood still, frozen with terror. The giant reptile plucked Lion out of the bushes as if he were a mouse dangled in the air by its tail. Jada waited in horror for that enormous set of jaws to flash open and bite the man in half. The beast raised him to its muzzle and inhaled a large sniff. Its eyes and nose wrinkled in disgust at the man's odor.

"Set me down!" yelled Lion angrily. To his surprise, the beast slowly lowered him onto the ground. "Toss me a stone," he said very calmly to Jada. Instead, the monster reached into the sack and threw Lion's duffel at his feet. Did the animal know it contained his concealed sword? He stared back in amazement for what felt like ages to Jada. The beast did the same.

It brought my weapon on purpose. Lion let the bundle lie on the ground. "I'm not sure what happens from here, Jada," he admitted uncertainly. "The animal's been dead for days." The beast lowered itself to all fours and revealed the wound from Pike's sword.

"How is this possible?"

The beast smoothed out some dirt on the ground with a paw. With a claw, it sketched two figures with weapons then perhaps a picture of itself. It connected each figure to form a triangle.

Lion did not comprehend. "Barkeep, it's trying to communicate, but it's too primitive to make out."

"It probably thinks the same about you."

By now, the beast was growing impatient as it kept pointing at Lion, then itself, and then the painting. Lion and Jada looked at each other. It seemed to give up and pointed north, motioning them to follow. Jada began to follow.

"What are you doing?" asked Lion, astonished.

"Clearly it wants us to follow, or we'd already be dead. Shut up and follow it."

Lion mumbled something she couldn't hear but picked up his duffel and began walking behind her. The beast turned back, and though it was impossible, Hellion could swear there was a grin along the face of that giant crocodile head.

And so they walked. They were far from town with no supplies and led by an animal that could kill them without a moment's notice. The same animal had already been killed by Pike once and yet, here it was, leading them through the hot springs of the north.

"Where is it taking us, Lion?"

"I'm guessing to its home. The way Pike went in was much further west than this. I just wish we had our horses because if this thing doesn't kill us, the walk might."

The beast stopped in front of them as if it understood. It knelt down on all fours in front of them.

"I think it's offering us a ride," said Jada. "Should we climb on?"

Lion was already pulling himself on before she finished. He reached down and grabbed Jada's hand to swing her on behind him.

"I'm not trying to be forward, barkeep, but I think you better hold on tight. This ain't no horse." She wrapped her arms around his torso, as he leaned forward with his arms and legs wrapped around the beast's neck. The smell of ale was starting to air off the man at least. Although, at this point, she really wasn't concerned about the smell. This would be the greatest tale she'd ever be able to tell, as long as she survived.

"Yaaaah!" yelled Lion. As the word left his mouth, the creature bolted forward like a sturgeon downstream.

Chapter 24

THE DAY HAD been bad for Pike. The pain in his side was getting worse, and he was slowing down. What he really needed was a few days of rest. The landscape had begun to change over the last few hours. The prairie grasses and enormous animals were behind them. They were traveling up a slow incline where the weather was cooler and the vegetation grew sparser. The ground became harder with every step they took, jarring Pike's bones. It was obvious to see why the place would be avoided by natives.

Khawna pushed onward forcefully in her bare feet, which made Pike feel like the burden of the two. She would surely fare better if she left him behind. Another advantage, if she could be convinced to abandon him, was that it would take longer to track them if they split up. Pike had mentioned it earlier in the day, and she had been insulted at the thought of abandoning him. "I was not born without honor," she had said angrily before she took his hand, only to pull him forward more quickly. Then, after some thought, she remarked, "I would be no better than our cowardly chief to leave you for the cannibals."

The rocks sloped even steeper from here. Looking at the map, Pike judged it would be another full day before they reached their destination. As he marched forward with teeth clenched in pain, little white flakes began falling around them.

"Snow?" asked Khawna, catching some in her hand in wonder.

"Ash," said Pike, nudging a buildup of gray on the ground with his foot. "With as weak as I'm getting, I won't last long if we have to fight off Merkils."

"You are plenty strong, hunter. Just slow. It is the cold that makes you lag. It will get warmer the higher we climb."

"I hope you're right. From all I've ever heard or seen, the big mountains always have snow on top."

She turned around and reached up to pat him on the head. "This is a special place. Do you not believe me yet? You will see soon. I have heard stories since I was a child about its powers."

"I'd rather see it sooner than later. I might not make it if it's too much further."

Khawna again turned around and looked fiercely into his eyes. "You will make it because you must. You survived the Tarmigan for a reason. You came into our land for a reason. You rescued me for a reason. You are here to bring balance, to be the song in our people's long silence, which means you cannot die."

Pike stared at her in thought for a moment. "I wish I knew what that meant," he eventually replied.

Now she grinned at him. "As I said, you will see soon. I am here for a reason too. I must help you until you're ready."

What crazy notion had gotten into the girl's head? "I'm not used to needing anyone's help. I've lived alone for many years in the western hunting grounds. I don't even come in contact with other people but two days a year. The other people are different than me. They depend on others in town. I can't be like that. I only know how to take care of myself."

Khawna looked at him as if she pitied his life. "Do you have a woman?"

He shook his head. "There are few women in the hunting grounds."

She began to nod her head, thinking. "You have no tribe, no wife, and no young to care for. You're not an old man yet. All great warriors need help at times. I am with you because you chose to help me. We are now connected in song. I am entwined with you now, no matter how weak you become. You have no woman to forbid it, so I will be your woman. I will be what it is you need."

Pike sighed. *What have I gotten myself into?* "Khawna, that's not what I'm asking for."

The look she returned made him hold his tongue from saying anything else that might be hurtful. But then her expression turned back to business. "Is there another woman you wish to have? I will help you get her."

He gripped her hand tighter as she led him forward. "No. There is no other girl. You would be a perfect woman. You're beautiful. I can't take my eyes off you. I don't want you as some sort of slave or payment of debt. I want you to enjoy your life, which hopefully will be longer than the next few days. That's why I asked you to leave me behind."

Now she smiled again, the hurt gone from her face. "I would very much enjoy life as your woman…even if only for a night."

Pike swallowed at her bluntness but couldn't deny his feelings. "Here's how this works where I come from. We still don't really know each other. If we both somehow survive, I will ask you if you still want to be my woman. But I plan on going back across the mountain someday, so think carefully if the time comes. My world is very different from yours. You can say no if you want. I'll understand."

"You tell me you live alone far in the woods. How is this different from here?"

Pike didn't have a good comeback, so again he held his tongue.

"We live very much like your people. The paleface taught us your ways. If you were to see my village, you would see that we are the same."

"I doubt it, but I won't argue with my woman-to-be," said Pike with a painful chuckle.

Khawna laughed. "You make funny words, but it is never good for a man to anger his woman."

"Maybe our people aren't so different after all."

She raised her hand up as if to jokingly hit him. "It's what I've been telling you!"

Then, as she held his hand tightly, her other arm pointed far out in front of them. "Do you see the glowing from the cloud far above?"

Pike squinted and looked to the top of a small mountain ahead. He could not see the very top due to the haze, but there was a faint glowing as she had said. "That's a steep climb."

"We will make it. It has been climbed before."

"How do you know all this?"

"From stories, hunter. We will get there tomorrow."

"Are you still going to want to be with me tomorrow?" he joked.

Khawna smiled and rubbed his arm. "Yes, very much, hunter."

Chapter 25

THE TOWN WAS engulfed in panic. Various accounts of sightings of the beast circulated the streets and became so embellished the truth was difficult to sort out. An emergency council had been appointed to put a curfew in effect. Everyone was in fear of a second ambush. People were posted on rooftops to provide a warning system for when the beast returned. Grom supported the efforts fully, especially since he was appointed head of the council. All that anyone knew for certain was that two citizens were gone without a trace, and the monster was back for blood, not sheep. Jada and Lion were presumed dead, although there was no evidence to confirm the suspicion. Speculation ran rampant. They had all seen the animal dead with their own eyes. No breathing, no pulse, no life. Children had walked up to the carcass to pet it during the celebration in the street. It could have snapped them like so many twigs had it awakened at that moment. And it had broken free from chains to boot!

Grom had furiously penned another letter to Fort Tuttle and sent it off with a costly carrier pigeon that morning. The request was no longer just an investment in the little frontier town; it was life or death. For now, they needed to do what was necessary to survive until the army came with reinforcements. He told himself they would have to come now. From there, the word would spread east to the small eastern seaports and ultimately to Sisterton. His carefully planned news press sensation would now become a horror story.

Aside from taking defensive measures, all the town could do now was wait. They stood no chance of tracking and confronting the beast on their own without Pike. And where was the man now? For all Grom knew, he, Lion, and Jada were all dead. Of course, Pike was not an ordinary man. Should Pike still live, if he could get the hunter word about the danger he was in, perhaps he'd have a chance against the beast. But how could the man expect an animal to return from the grave?

Grom stood outside his store, gazing blankly at all the happenings out in the street. There had to be something else he could do. A familiar, wiry man wearing circular spectacles approached him.

"Grom, I've finished with the inn. I'd like for you to show me where the beast was held until its…escape." The man was dressed in a business suit that had once been quite fashionable in the coastal cities. Age and overuse had left it faded and dated. The man had once been a reporter for a real newspaper back in Sisterton. Something had to have gone wrong in his life for him to end up in Mossport, yet he was willing to help, and the council had decided everything must be documented. He stood ready with a notepad and pen in hand.

"Briley, this might could be the story that puts you on the map. Course, might wipe our town off that same map." Grom opened the door to his store and called to the girl in the stockroom. "Dora! Please come out and watch the front store fer me. I have an interview to give to Briley."

The teenage girl eagerly ran from where she'd been organizing supplies in the back room. She smoothed her hair in an effort to make herself more presentable to any would-be customers. She often had an aloof look to her, but the girl was a hard worker and Grom trusted her with the store.

"Yes, Mr. Grom. I'll take care of everything. Don't worry about a thing, I've got it all covered."

"Thank you, Dora." He turned to Briley. "Follow me around back."

The back stables were partially built into the ground. The giant beams that were sunken into the ground supported the store and upper living quarters above that. There were a dozen stalls in all, although only three were occupied presently. Grom was grateful for this since there were a lot of horses that might have needed to be put down after witnessing the beast break free. He stopped in front of the last empty stall in the corner to present Briley with the scene.

"For the record, how did you get it here, Grom?"

"You saw yourself, didn't ya? Pulled it behind Pike's big horse o'er there. I hope he comes back soon to get the iron-willed animal." The black stallion watched the two men suspiciously as he ate his hay. "I chained both arms to the main beams of my shop, and you see what remains. I thought I was preventing someone from stealing it, not it from escaping." The remnants of the chains lay upon the bedding, where a large indentation served as a reminder of the size of the previously captured animal.

Briley bent down to examine the broken chain. "I see it broke one of your supports. The other chain almost looks as if it was cut. Take a look." The chain was worn down by large groove marks, almost as if it'd been smashed with an ax.

"I would have heard a tool working on the chain all night. The only things I heard were the shaking of my store and the great snap of the support beam." Briley was quiet for a moment and started making a sketch of the stall in his notebook. Grom held the lone broken chain in his hands in disbelief. Then a funny thought crossed his mind, and he started picking through the straw. After finding nothing, he sat in the indentation of the beast and felt on either side. His finger nudged something, and he plucked it out of the bedding for closer examination. Briley gasped, but Grom smiled.

"Now we have something to prove what we're up against." In his hand was a bloody tooth, the size of a spearhead.

"I guess there was no ax," said Briley, as he crossed off some of his former notes. "May I make an outline of that for my story?"

"Sure can," said Grom. "Whatever it takes to get us some help out here. Don't know fer sure how much good it'll do though. This animal is strong, fast, smart, and apparently can't be killed. We all may have been better off leaving and hoping it can't find its way to Sisterton. Please don't write that down, Briley."

"We'll keep that off the record, Grom."

"Appreciate it. As long as we're off the record, how'd you end up in Mossport, anyhow?"

The man was silent for a moment. Then he glanced upward, licking his lips in a painful smile.

"I needed a new start, you might say. Got let go from the job of my dreams."

Grom scratched his head. "I hate to pry, Briley, but were it budget cuts or performance?"

"Neither, if you can believe it. I investigated the wrong story. A man I'd never met said he was onto me, told me not to publish it. When I tried to move forward, I was let go without cause. By the time I got home, my apartment had caught fire. I got the message."

"Must have been a damning story."

"Let's just say it would have been very bad publicity for a very important person in Sisterton."

Grom knew he was probably pushing too far. Oh well. "Business tycoon or political person?"

Briley adjusted his glasses with resolve. "I've said too much already. If I told you any more, you'd be in danger."

Chapter 26

SWASH WOULD HAVE gladly walked for a spell if the beast would have stopped. The creature acted as if everything depended upon how fast they moved. Needless to say, all Hellion and Jada could do was hold on for their lives. On the north side of the hot springs, the beast threw aside a massive boulder to open up an underground tunnel. It was a huge and ancient opening that made for an absolutely terrifying ride in the dark. As the ride continued in the tunnel, Hellion knew they were passing other openings from time to time by listening to the echo of their breaths and the beast's claws tearing into the cold stone and clay ground.

"I'm scared, Lion. Can you ask it to stop?" Jada's voice sounded worried, breathless, and very much unlike her.

"I'd like to stop too, but I would rather get out of this rabbit hole. Won't do any good to communicate, we'll probably only anger the animal."

"I should be in my room sleeping. Thanks to you, I'm trying not to fall off an animal that might eat me before the night is over."

"You act as if it's my fault you're here."

"Because it *is* your fault! What part wasn't your doing? It was *you* that helped Pike track the beast. It was *you* that brought it, still alive, back to town. It was *you* that got so sick I had to come up to make sure you hadn't drowned yourself in ale last night. Lastly, it was *you* that the beast came after. I was a bystander! I shouldn't be here!" Her voice echoed into the darkness as they surged onward.

"Well, it's not like I brought you here on my own!"

"Of course not. I would have had more sense than to skip town with a wool-headed city boy!"

"Maybe if you conserved some energy from your unending scrutiny of me, you might be of some assistance in helping us survive."

"Oh, you're doing a real crack job. Now it's my fault we're stuck in this unending hole? And don't tell me what to do! All I've done is point out the facts!"

"Barkeep, I'm not who you think I am. I've killed men for lesser arguments."

"Oh, are you trying to intimidate me? Please tell me how many women you've killed."

"You have no idea…" And that's when the beast finally stopped.

Hellion took the unexpected opportunity to slide off quickly and stretch out his wobbly legs. Jada did the same. They heard some rustling and saw light enter from above as the beast pushed the rock-slab roof off their tunnel. The animal was breathing heavily. It was clear that the hours had taken a toll on it.

Swash wasted no time in grabbing onto roots and pulling himself into the daylight above. They were beyond the mountains. He turned around to see the great wall to the south now. The land had a different feel to it than Mossport. The air was humid, and the plants seemed lush and greener than the other side.

"Hey, Mr. Chivalrous! You were supposed to help the lady up first!"

"Sorry, I forgot my manners while making sure it was safe up here." He reached down to grab the hand that had emerged from below. Upon pulling her above, the look on her face changed from anger to wonder. She forgot to insult him for a moment.

Next emerged the beast from the earth. The gigantic animal pushed the rock back into place, sealing the tunnel. Then it sat down for the first time, almost like a real human.

"Looks like our escape has been sealed. Guess we're not going home anytime soon," said Jada.

"I'm afraid I can't let that happen," said a deep voice.

Hellion's eyes went so white with terror that Jada would have laughed had the voice not rendered her dumb.

"You can talk?" she finally managed.

"You will find many things are different in this world, young lady. Your first lesson is looks can be deceiving. Yes, I know what you've been saying about me, what you've called me. Don't look so astonished. If I could have spoken to you on the other side, I would have. I don't make the rules. The longer I'm outside this world, the more power I lose."

"What are you?" asked Hellion.

"To the natives, I am the Tarmigan. To your people, I am the beast or monster. What am I really? I think of myself as a guardian of the land. I've lived here for many human lives. Many, like your friend, have tried to kill me. None has ever come as close as you. There is a reason I couldn't kill you and your friend."

"Why have you brought us here?" asked Jada. "You can certainly do more than this scallywag ever could."

"I can do very little myself," the Tarmigan replied. "I am what you would call a force of nature. Can a tree build a house? Can the sun plant and harvest a field? Can the wind inspire people to follow it? No. This land, and one man in particular, needs the help of both of you. That is what I can facilitate."

"Why were you attacking our town? Why did you kill innocent people!" Jada blurted out.

"I was drawn to your town by my duty as protector of this land. There was an energy given off there that I sought. A canticle that called to me. The sheep I apologize for, but must I not eat? My loyalty is to this land that we are now in. Anyone trying to kill me is in essence trying to kill the land. As a result, they must die."

"So you're here to kill Pike?"

The Tarmigan looked abashed. "I am not here to kill your friend. He is the song that my land needs. His melody becomes stronger with you two near. You were wrong earlier to blame this man with you for being here now."

Hellion immediately pointed at the Tarmigan while looking at Jada. "See! I was right! His words."

"You could blame the man you call Pike, but it is not his fault either. It is his song. The melody of prophecy and destiny. This land has been shrouded in silence too long. The land chose him, but it also chose both of you."

Jada seemingly ignored Hellion's taunt. "What is so special about Pike? I never heard the man sing, but I doubt it's his strong suit. I guarantee he has no idea what you're talking about. Besides, we all have real lives on the other side. At least I do." She narrowed her eyes at Hellion. "How long will we be gone?"

"Your inn will continue without you, young lady. This world may not. Don't believe that this world isn't connected to your own. Everything here will eventually matter to you, either now or in the future. If the one you call Pike prevails, you may return to your lives if you wish, but I suspect you won't."

"Can you predict the future, Tarmigan?" asked Hellion with sudden interest.

"Better than any human ever has."

Hellion scratched at his raven tattoo. "Well then, tell us what we need to do."

"Heed carefully, swordsman, I cannot just tell you what to do. Things will soon begin to unfold, and even I cannot say how. You will do what needs to be done on your own when the time is right. For now, I just need to get you to your friend."

Chapter 27

COMMANDER BURIN SAT in his tower room overlooking Mammoth Lake. The wind was relentless in its clash with the giant sandstones that protected him from the elements. He had one of the few windows in the fortress, but he couldn't care less. The fort was the equivalent of prison for someone who craved war. He and his men guarded a massive lake that required no guarding. The lake was bordered on the north and south by mountain ranges, making accessibility impossible from the north and improbable from the south. On the other side of the southern mountains lay a wasteland desert, uninhabitable and nearly impassable for man. To the east was the great modern city of Sisterton, so named for its resemblance to the old empire's capital of Altanica across the sea. The lake was mainly used for fishing vessels and the occasional cargo ship to and from Mossport at its western shore. He was babysitting sheep that couldn't leave the pasture. His time was wasted drilling his soldiers daily for no purpose other than to keep them from getting bored and undisciplined. He couldn't wait for his next placement.

When he did dare dream, it was of nothing but rejoining the unending wars across the sea. He had been there briefly and savored every minute of it. In a short time he had been engaged in tremendous battles on ships, on beaches, and in jungles. And while his career was set to blossom in promotion, he was disgraced by one of his best soldiers. The monster had turned on his own men, gotten caught and sentenced to hang, and then escaped again. Burin suspected he'd had help from other sympathetic soldiers. Nothing, of course, was ever proven. The other men had loved Private Swash much more than any would ever care for their commander. This was one of many reasons why Burin had paid off a man to kill him in battle. All had not gone according to plan. Hellion Swash was difficult to kill. After his escape, the man left piles of dead soldiers everywhere he fled. Needless to say, Burin's failure to catch him had reflected poorly upon his superiors and also the mercenary army in general. This instance, along with several others in his past, had also led to some suspicion about his practice of weeding out his men. Too often, he was told, good soldiers in his rank met with unfortunate ends. *It was never personal,* he thought to himself.

So the commander was stuck here for now, in what he considered and most definitely was meant to be punishment. He could win no fame here. He had no challenges to overcome. The last commander stationed here had died a year prior in his sleep of old age. The man had been stationed at Fort Tuttle for twenty years! To have to look forward to that type of sentence pained Commander Burin. But he would apply for another position in a year's time. The army could not keep him bridled forever.

There was a knock on the heavy door leading to the stairway.

"Yes? Who is it?"

"It's Pippendale, sir. We've received a note by carrier pigeon. It's an urgent message from Mossport," replied the squeaky voice.

"Come in, Pippendale. Let us see what could be so urgent on the frontier. Someone probably stole another man's goat again. Would you care to wager on it, son?"

The skinny young man entered the room with eyes lowered to the floor. Pippendale knew better than to joke with his superior. He could laugh with you one moment, then order you whipped in the next breath for not calling him sir.

"No, sir, I would not care to wager. Shall I read it to you?"

"Yes, yes, Pippendale. By all means please read it slowly this time. When you carry on too quickly, it sounds more like defecation from your mouth than words."

"Very…well…sir. The letter is addressed to the Commander of Fort Tuttle, two days past.

Dear Commander,

It is with regret that I inform you of an attack on our settlement in Mossport. It began with the slaughter of sheep some weeks past. We sent out a six-man hunting party fer the vile creature and they never returned. I outfitted our best tracker along with another drifter and they succeeded in killing a new species of animal, or so we had thought. The animal returned to life and escaped after claiming two more victims. The town is not safe. We need your protection. We believe the beast is from beyond the Mortapenums. It stands as tall as two men and has teeth the size of a man's hand. I'm sure you had doubts about past letters I've sent, but now everyone in town can corroborate. Please come at once!

Signed,

Grom Liller

Commander Burin sat silently contemplating the message. He'd already thrown away a few recent messages from this Grom Liller. Could this account be true? Earlier pigeons had been too vague for him to take seriously. But if it was true, he could be the hero that saved the little outpost. If it was false, he'd be the goat that would never be promoted again. It had been months since he'd had to make a decision more important than what uniform to wear for the day.

"Gather me up twenty men, Pippendale. We'll at least investigate this threat to the good citizens of Mossport. Leave word that Jennings will stay behind in my place. I mean to leave by tomorrow morning, so be quick and get us supplies."

"Sir, yes sir. Will I be accompanying you, sir?"

"Yes, Pippendale, I will need someone to be my messenger."

Pippendale didn't know whether to celebrate or despair. He was finally getting off this pile of rocks, but he still had to deal with the commander. In the very least it would be a change in his routine. He saluted the commander and ran off to make preparations. There would be very little sleep for him tonight. If everything wasn't perfect for their departure, he would feel the wrath of his superior.

Commander Burin watched the lanterns scurry about in the night below his tower. Men were shouting and cursing as they hauled crates out to the docked ship. It would be a few days' journey to Mossport, and times could change depending on the weather. Twenty-two men, counting himself and Pippendale, were more of an exploratory force than a defending force, but he could not move four hundred men without more details. To move larger numbers of men would require him to inform his superiors back east of his troop movements, and he wasn't interested in garnering more ridicule.

A newly discovered frontier species would make for a great tale when he returned with the carcass to Sisterton. A successful trip might be his best chance at a ticket off Fort Tuttle. The voyage would only mark his second visit to the frontier colony. Anytime he had leave, he always sailed east.

Yes, a change of scenery would suit the commander well. Being with the same men every day made time crawl. Every one of them would probably like to see him gutted for being the asshole he was on a daily basis. But he didn't care. He knew he was exactly what those men needed. The subordinates rarely realized the value he had brought to the fort. Without him they'd grow careless, sloppy, and unlawful, which is how they were before he arrived. His job was not to be a nice guy. Not now, not ever.

Chapter 28

THE SUN WAS dipping below the horizon by the time Pike and Khawna reached the base of Serpent's Spittle. The rise was not as tall as a mountain, but it was terribly steep. Ancient steps had been chiseled into the rock to make the climb manageable, but one slip of a foot or hand, and the climber would tumble down a height nearly three times the height of the Mammoth Inn. Khawna tied their long rope around Pike's waist and carefully climbed to the top herself. Pike was tired, but as Khawna had said, it felt warmer now that they had neared their destination. He heard her yell down to him and felt the rope tighten around his torso.

Every reach of his arm to the next step shot pain signals through his chest. He began to perspire so heavily he feared losing his grip on the grooved rock. He felt the flakes of ash falling weightless upon him as he concentrated on his climb.

"Hurry, hunter!" he heard called from above. He felt two quick tugs that nearly took his breath away. He wanted to yell at her to stop, but he couldn't find the air he needed. He looked down quickly and then back up to realize he was a quarter of the way up. *Reach up with left arm, pick up right leg. Right arm up, drag up left leg. Repeat, repeat, repeat.* Pike was a shell of his normal self. It had only taken a few moments for Khawna to scale the same cliff. He would be lucky to get up by morning at his current pace. *Faster!* he screamed in his head. *Left, right, left again, right, left…*

Pike's hand slipped from a grooved stone. He heard what could only be translated as a curse in native tongue above him as the rope jerked upward and he slammed back into the rock. His hand caught another hold. He hung on, unmoving for a moment.

Khawna poked her head over the ledge above. "Can you move, hunter?"

"Yes…just have to catch…my breath. Please don't pull the rope so tight."

"You're halfway up. It would be bad to fall."

"I'm aware. I can't…go any faster. I'm sorry." He heard more muttering in native tongue above him.

Finally, he became courageous enough to continue. The rope slackened some, allowing him to breathe easier now. The process was slow, but after what felt like a week's worth of effort, Khawna took his hand and pulled him over the ledge where he collapsed to the ground.

They were both saturated with sweat and labored in their breathing. Pike offered his canteen to her first before he took a sip. It would be best to conserve supplies since he could not climb down anytime soon.

When Pike finally was able to push himself off the ground, he beheld a curious sight. There was a glow of orange illuminating piles and piles of human bones, strewn about in various positions. To his left lay an intact skeleton with jaw gaping open, giving an impression that it was screaming out in agony. Beside it was another skeleton curled up with knee bones touching jaw, enclosed with a hug of skeletal arms.

"Where have you brought me, Khawna?" he asked in fear.

"These are the skeletons of fools. They came to steal the power the Serpent's Spittle holds. You are not a fool; you will be safe. I told you this place holds power for our people. The stories say it is only the greedy that never leave. You will heal quickly here. Come, take my hand, and I will show you."

She led him through the bone piles toward the pool of orange glowing light. The pool was large and lay against a steep rock wall that continued higher to the tip of the towering rock structure they were on. The closer they got, the thicker the piles of bones grew under their feet. Many were so old they compressed to dust when stepped on, but not all were so ancient. Pike initially tried to avoid them, but it became pointless.

As the pair approached the pool, Pike noticed something glowing red embedded in the rock wall, high above the pit of fire. Its color changed from red to green, then to blue. It was shaped like an ornate spear, but clearly it was not wood and stone.

"What you are looking at has killed all these men," said Khawna, now appearing to glow in the strange light. "Do not let it trouble you. Sit here with me and rest your head in my lap. I will tell you about the Spear of Song. Take off your coat. Breathe in the warmth. It will heal you.

"The elders say the Spear of Song once belonged to our people," she continued. "Its power was unmatched, and our people prospered while our chief wielded it. We lived in a beautiful village, much better than where we live now. It is said that we cannot even imagine such a place as Joventin. As years passed, our people changed. We took our prosperity for granted. We were ungrateful for our lives of ease and believed ourselves above our duty to be protectors of the lands. At some point, we lost the spear. We don't know how. And yet here it rests to this day, close but unreachable. I do not tell you this to make you desire the spear. You say you don't believe. Your doubt protects you. You would die like so many that surround us if you sought it. Only the one spoken of in prophecy may take the spear. The one of same song as the spear." Khawna stared blankly into the distance silently, while stroking Pike's hair.

Pike felt very tired. He could feel the confidence Khawna had in her story and in this place. It was clearly a place of reverence to her people. As he sat thinking about her words, he was thankful to her for allowing him to avoid resting his head on a pile of bones. Within moments, Pike forgot where he was. He could see himself sleeping under his warm furs in his cabin as the days and nights rolled on. Khawna was there keeping logs on his fire and spoon feeding him meals as he lay in his bed, recovering. His breathing became less labored, but he was still so very tired. He saw himself drift off to sleep with a concerned Khawna watching over his weak body as she held a hand to his forehead.

Pike saw himself roll over in his sleep and nearly fall to the ground, but she was there to stop him. She gently rolled him back into place and climbed into his bed with him. She put her arms around his sleeping body, and the whole world turned light and then dark. He could see hungry animals circling the warm cabin, searching for a way in. He knew he was safe. The days started going by quicker, and he saw his eyes open.

The snows of winter began to melt away, and he was able to get out of bed. Khawna helped him limp around the cabin, and they both smiled and laughed joyfully. Before long he was picking her up in his arms and twirling her about in the cabin. They walked outside into the purest pine-scented forest and hiked for hours together.

He saw himself working on the house in between his hunting trips. Land was cleared, and Khawna started a small garden. Little green sprouts became noticeable in the dark soil. Soon he was building what appeared to be a small wooden crib, and he noticed himself holding Khawna's belly with affection. She began singing a song that was familiar to him, though he couldn't recall where he'd heard it.

> *When are you coming home, my dear,*
> *the time has been so long.*
> *I've been waiting for you, my sweetest,*
> *I'd never do you wrong.*
> *Please hurry home, my only,*
> *I long for you in my arms,*
> *There's never been one like you, my love,*
> *none could resist your charms.*
> *And if this world should steal from me*
> *the only that I'll ever love,*

I'll follow you into the next world,
whether below us or above.

PIKE SAT UP and heard Khawna finish the last line of the song. "Did the paleface teach your people that song as well?" she asked.

"It sounds so familiar. I must have heard it as a child. I can't remember who sang it." He paused. "You have a beautiful voice."

Khawna smiled happily. "I am glad it pleases you. You have slept all night. How do you feel?"

Pike stood up and helped her to her feet. He raised both arms above his head and took a deep breath. There was no longer any pain. Khawna was smiling even bigger now, as he looked at her, puzzled.

"You are healed, Pike the hunter. It was as I told you."

Pike stretched his legs and arms and back and felt like his old self again. He picked Khawna up and twirled her in his arms while she giggled like a little girl.

"I had the craziest dream while I slept," he started. "We were back in my cabin, and you were taking care of me…"

"I know."

"Wait. You were actually in my dream?"

"Yes, hunter. I saw everything. I did everything." She put a hand on his shoulder. "This is what could be."

Pike stared at her in disbelief. He reached his hand out to her and she took it, placing it upon her chest. He pulled her close to him and their bodies collided with a thud, but neither one cared. They could have a future yet. Each one looked into the other's eyes, and they both knew what the other was thinking. Before they could turn thoughts into action, they heard the sound of someone pulling himself over the ledge.

Pike pulled away from Khawna, grabbed his knife, and ran at the assailant.

Chapter 29

THE CLIMBER WAS spent from the ascent, allowing Pike to easily pin the person down with a knife to the throat. His hand muffled a familiar voice.

"Etttt mmmffff!"

Pike pulled his hand back in astonishment.

"Get off, you brute! What is the matter with you?"

"Jada? How on earth?"

"We came to help you. It's a long story." She looked deeply into his eyes, as if she was searching for something within him. But at present, he was only able to convey the astonishment that she had come for him. She and did she say...

"We?" he asked.

"Yes. Lion is climbing up now. What kind of mess have you gotten yourself into? You should have come back with Lion." She paused. "No, you shouldn't have even gone after the beast in the first place. You just couldn't listen. All you men are the same." Her hands flew up in motion with every word she yelled. Pike instinctively threw up his hands to protect himself. He heard a laugh from behind him.

Jada picked up on the amusement instantly. "Is there a half-naked girl up here with you, Pike? What exactly is going on? Women back home aren't good enough for you? How could you stoop to this level? Can she even talk? Lion! Get up here! You aren't going to believe what's been going on up here!"

A voice from below called up, "I'm almost there. Please don't throw Granger off the cliff before I'm up."

"Well, you better hurry then, you slow oaf!"

Khawna walked up to Jada with arms crossed. She was no longer laughing. "Who is this angry woman, hunter? You told me you had no woman. If this is true, why does she act like angry viper?"

"Khawna, this is Jada. Jada, this is Khawna. I would go further in details, but right now we have a cannibalistic tribe hunting us."

"They eat people?" asked Jada with eyes bulging.

"Yes...well no, Khawna doesn't. I helped her escape from them, but we could be trapped here if we don't go. How did you get by them? How exactly did you get here?"

"We had help. There's an underground tunnel that runs all throughout this land. This is going to sound crazy, but the Tarmigan brought us to help you."

"Crazy sounds fitting. Wait, how do you know what they call it?"

"Pike, it came back to life."

Pike glanced at Khawna, who shrugged as if to say, *I told you so.* "But I saw it dead with my own eyes."

"It's okay," said Jada, putting a hand on his shoulder. "I saw it too."

The look on Khawna's face now that Jada was touching Pike was anything but friendly. He quickly pulled away when he saw Hellion reaching an arm over the crest of the climb. He grabbed his arm to pull him over and caught a glimpse over his shoulder.

"Tell me that thing isn't here to kill me."

Hellion for once didn't have his usual sly grin. "It's safe, Granger, I swear. He was the one that knew you'd come here. He keeps talking about prophecy, songs, and a restoration of balance to the land..."

"It talks?"

A deep voice called up from the steps. "Yes, hunter, I speak many languages. Don't look so astonished. You need to accept a lot of facts in a short amount of time if you are to survive."

Pike looked at his friends gathered around him. He wasn't sure if he was replying to them or actually to the beast that was talking to him. "Why should I trust that thing now when it was trying to kill us, Hellion?"

Jada looked at Swash and mouthed *Hellion?*

"Thanks a lot, Pike." He shook his head in disgust.

"Because, hunter," replied the Tarmigan. "You managed to do the one thing that has never been done before. You killed me."

"Well, apparently not," replied Pike. "You attacked our town, killed our livestock, and killed six good men. I had to protect people. I know nothing of prophecy."

Now the Tarmigan pulled itself over the ledge and rose to full height. "I have been searching for you for a long time. You cannot comprehend how long. I regret the deaths of those men, but they died because they were not you. The prophecy states that only the gifted man shall not die by my hand. You did not die. Unfortunately for them, they attacked me and were not gifted. If you were not this man, you would have perished and I would have kept searching.

"Is the Ghenzi girl alright?" asked the Tarmigan, pointing at Khawna. She had backed up to the bubbling lava and looked dangerously close to taking the last step back.

"Khawna, stop!" yelled Pike. "It's safe!"

"It is a bad creature, Pike. It cannot be trusted. It will try to attach itself to you! My people know!"

The Tarmigan sighed. "Yes, your people know to leave me alone, because I will not bother them this way. But your people have been waiting a long time for Pike, young girl. He is the one that they have longed for. You know what I speak of. Why else have you brought him here? He will need your help if he is to succeed."

Khawna took a step forward. "I know he needs my help. I have pledged my life to him, yet he does not want to accept it. He does not know our ways, but I can help him with that. You must give me a token if I am to trust you."

"I'm sorry," replied the Tarmigan. "I cannot give anyone anything but words. To do more than that would end my existence. It is the price I pay. What you do with my words is your choice. Your people were once great, but selfishness destroyed them. You would do well to remember those words; they will have significance in your future if you survive."

Hellion and Jada stood watching the discussion take place without them until Jada couldn't stand it anymore. "So why have you brought us here? The native girl clearly knows something we don't. How can we help him if you will not tell us? I didn't come here to get eaten!"

"I do not know how you are needed," the deep voice countered. "I just set the table. I gather the ingredients. I give you a chance. Pike may need your help today or ten years from today, but either way he needs you very much. I can tell you this. His song has never been clearer. The most probable way Pike survives is if he holds the spear at the end of this day."

Khawna ran to Pike. "Hastiness killed all these around us. There could be another way."

"You know I'm right, native woman. Why else did you bring him here? You know he could lead you to Joventin. Clearly, you feel the same energy from him that I do."

"I do, but I will not let him die. We came here to heal."

Finally, Hellion spoke up. "I'm here to help, Pike. The beast brought us this far; I see no reason not to trust it. You've got us mixed up in something much bigger than ourselves, it seems." He looked around at the piles of bones. "It looks like a lot of people have come after this spear, which means it must be one heck of a weapon. I believe I'd like to see it in your hands." His wicked smile was back. "What's the game to get our hands on the spear?"

"There must be true need and a pure heart to wield the Spear of

Song. That is all that is known. It can be seen, but getting to it has always proven fatal," said the beast.

"The pure heart talk obviously rules me out," said Hellion.

"So you've brought us all this way to stand around and watch us perish while trying to get the spear?" demanded Jada angrily. "We can make our own spear a whole lot easier."

"No. I will not be staying. I will return though, hopefully in time." With that, the Tarmigan made its way back to the steps and began descending the ledge. The group stood in shocked silence for a few moments.

Pike stared off into the distance thinking, trying to sort out everything that had just happened. He knew he had to be quick and decisive. *There was a solution to all of this.*

Khawna was a ball of nerves. She wanted to protect Pike from the spear, but she also had a duty to help him obtain it. Pike was indeed the chosen one to save her people. She had figured it out quickly. They didn't deserve him after what they'd done to her. They were weak and spineless. Why should Pike risk his life for them? She also did not trust the Tarmigan. It was said that the beast had an influence on the downfall of her people in the old days. As far as they had fallen from their height of power, it was said they had never been as lowly as they were now because of the Merkils. Perhaps that was why Pike had come to her. It was time for balance. Regardless of everything else, the Tarmigan was right about one thing. The hunter definitely needed her help most of all.

Chapter 30

HYTAN WAS NEARLY giddy with excitement. His fugitives were definitely hurt or fatigued as their progress had slowed between resting points. He and his men approached the mini mountain that he had seen glowing from a distance. Now the girl and her rescuer would be trapped. His people would be picking the pair from their teeth very soon. The warriors were hungry and angry, ready to exact their revenge. The prize was now within reach.

Hytan sent scouts to make sure there was no other way to scale up or down the high rise of rock. He could hear distant voices at times but could not make out the words. The accent was different than he was accustomed to hearing, and he wondered if it could be from another tribe further north. Why another tribe would entangle themselves with the Ghenzis' fate was beyond him, but they too must be punished for their involvement.

The chief did not believe his prey was aware that they'd arrived just as the sun was lifting above the horizon. He hoped to keep the element of surprise by sending a few dearths up quickly to protect the top of the climb for the rest of his men. He would send a group of five to go quickly, with a reserve group twice that size to scale up the steep steps once it was safe. The rest would wait below with him.

The time was right. He tapped his five men on their shoulders and they began their ascent quickly. There was no sound to be heard. The only equipment they carried was their hungry knives that sparkled in the morning rays while swinging from their hip sheaths.

There was still dialogue exchange up above, which was a good sign. Within a few moments his first dearth was at the top, peeking over the ledge. He signaled to the man below him, who, in like manner, passed the signal down until the fifth man held up his fingers. The chief squinted, staring intently up to the sky. It looked like four fingers. *Four? How could he not have noticed four distinct tracks?* The Merkil leader did not like surprises, nor odds not entirely in his favor. He tapped five more dearths and practically shoved them into the climbing grooves. *Quickly!* he urged them silently. The men clamored up the steep climb.

The warrior nearest the ledge must have seen a weakness. Instead of waiting for reinforcements, he crawled over the ledge silently, and the second man was pulled half over before there was a scream above.

Hytan could now make out more than two voices shouting. His third dearth pulled himself up, gave a cry, and ran out of view. *One more to even the odds,* thought the chief. He readied another five warriors at the base. Their order was to wait for the signal that the entrance was secured before starting.

The fourth warrior was pulling his leg over the cliff, but in the next instant, a boot came into view, crushing the man's hand beneath it. It was followed by a kick to the head, which ushered the fourth brave into descent.

"Clear the way!" yelled Hytan as the body sped toward his assembled warriors at the base. They jumped away quickly before their comrade exploded onto the rocks.

"Climb halfway, then wait for the signal!" snarled the chief in anger. He needed them above quickly, or the situation could get out of hand before they were in place.

Now it was the fifth dearth's turn to climb over. Someone was waiting for him above, and he knew it. He waited out of reach patiently for the other warriors above to secure the summit.

Hytan paced back and forth. The craven at the top was stalling his attack! In the very least the man could attempt the assault and pull the guardian down with him to his death. He began yelling at the man. "Climb over! I'll kill you myself if you stay there!"

The dearth remained frozen. He looked below at the remains of number four and clung to the ledge with bloodless fingers. Hytan was furious. He ran to the groove in the mountain and began pulling himself up. He knew the men above him would flee upwards to get out of his way. No one wanted the chief's wrath. His skeleton jewelry banged against the hard rock as he pulled himself quickly skyward. The men above him looked down, and he could see the white terror in their eyes as he scaled toward them quicker than they were moving.

Now the fifth climber had gotten the message. He was holding onto the rock with one hand and had his knife raised in the other. He lashed and tried pulling himself over at the same time. *Yes,* thought Hytan. *Instill fear in their hearts. They will surrender soon enough.*

That's when a smaller defender became visible above. The presumed woman had a large-handled object in her hand. She tossed its contents onto climber number five, and he screamed and fell. The men above and Hytan clung closely to the rock as the frantic body fell, clinging for something to hold on to. The coward grabbed another unlucky dearth, and the two sped toward Hytan. He brandished his knife because he knew they would try to take him down with them. When the panicked warrior tried to grab him, he swung his body sideways, almost losing his one-handed grip before burying his blade into the mountain and securing himself. The two dearths crashed below.

What sorcery were the defenders above using? The men ahead of him were now discovering it firsthand as the girl tossed a second helping of agony to draw out their screams. They retreated down the ledge in terror, and Hytan knew he'd be trampled if he didn't get out of their way.

There was another pour from the girl, and suddenly Hytan knew their terror. A liquid struck half his face and burned uncontrollably. His face sizzled and his hair began to burn. The pain was unimaginable. A warrior above him jumped to his death screaming. Hytan bore the pain as he climbed down quickly. The temptation to touch his face was indescribable. A small drop landed on his arm, and he saw its damage as it melted into his muscle.

Down he climbed as more of the burning liquid flung from above narrowly missed him. By the time he and his men reached the bottom, it was just him and three others of the original ten sent up.

Chapter 31

ALL BUT ONE of the four above panicked when the first native surprised them. Jada let off a blood-curdling scream while Hellion had never felt more alive. He actually smiled when the Merkil appeared out of nowhere. The ex-soldier missed the feel of hand-to-hand combat with men on the battlefield. He was tired of living in the shadows. Dealing with hostile natives was almost second nature for the grinning man who now held a sword. The cannibal was only able to occupy Swash long enough to let his partner up before Hellion's dancing blade opened him up.

As he pulled his blade from the man's chest, the second warrior charged toward Pike. Hellion cursed and rushed to the hunter's aide. To Hellion's dismay, Pike stood squarely with his hunting blade in hand on flat feet. *You must be evasive, Granger! Use his energy against him!* The native raised his arm, about to collide with Pike and run his blade home, when Pike caught his thrusting forearm. The other hand dropped his own knife and enclosed on the warrior's throat. There was a sickening crunch and a moan from the assassin as Pike had apparently broken the man's arm. The native's knife dropped, useless, to the ground. A third native appeared, and Hellion ran to protect the two girls with his sword. Pike seemed to have the situation in hand.

As Swash started his deadly dance with his new victim, Jada ran to cut off the next native trying to pull himself up. She began stomping on his hands when Khawna grabbed a handled pan and ran in the opposite direction to the pit of lava. She came to Jada's aid and flung the contents at climber number four, who, with a yell, let go of the ledge. Khawna ran back to the lava pool to refill her new weapon.

Hellion wasn't able to end his fight as quickly as he'd have liked. The native, upon seeing the results of one of his partners and Pike squeezing the life out of another, chose not to assault him directly. Rather, the warrior danced around, faking advances and withdrawing. Finally, Swash turned on the offensive, and he wasn't feigning. The native was no match for his sword and could only backpedal so far before he was sliced up and down.

Hellion turned around to see Khawna drop more lava below. Although her pot was glowing red with heat, she had wrapped cloth around the handle and held on long enough to dump more doom upon their attackers. The retreat began back down the steps.

Pike held his attacker down, as the group walked over.

"Kill him, Granger," advised Hellion. "He won't hesitate to do the same if he gets loose."

"I've never killed a man," said Pike. "Maybe he can help us. We need information about these people."

Khawna picked up her pan as she walked closer with a look of retribution in her eye. She might kill the man herself.

"Khawna, ask him how many more are down there."

"He will lie, hunter. They are bad people. Better to kill him quickly."

Pike looked at the man, still writhing in pain from his broken wrist. He did not doubt the man would take little thought in slitting all of their throats, given the chance. He also could not stop staring at the man's yellow teeth, thinking those were literally going to chew and eat Khawna and perhaps himself. The man began speaking in an unfamiliar tongue.

"What's he saying, Khawna?"

"He says we are doomed. That his people will eat us after we die from thirst up here. He says they will never let us escape." The man started talking more softly now, and Khawna craned closer to hear. In that instant, the man twisted his head around and took a wild bite as Khawna screamed, trying to pull away. With a mouthful of Khawna's hair, his eyes glazed over as Pike ran his blade through the crown of the cannibal's head. Pike stared wide-eyed at the man he had killed.

Khawna sobbed in shock at what had just happened. Jada tried to console her as she pulled what was left of the tangle of hair from the dead man's mouth. The man disgusted her so much she didn't want to touch him, but she had to be strong if only for the rest of the group.

"That takes care of one problem," said Hellion. "But we have a lot more to kill below us. The savage was right; they won't give up until we're dead."

"Then it's time to take a look at that spear," replied Pike with a new look in his eye. He glanced at each in his company, his eyes lingering on Khawna slightly longer. "Jada, I need you to watch the climb in case there's any more sneak attacks."

For once, she didn't argue. Pike was the voice in charge. He led the other two to the burning pit. The spear hung out of reach against the cliff wall, its colors dazzling in the daylight. Even if he could somehow reach the spear, Pike was worried he might not be able to detach it from the rock. He could tell a few of the skeletons had reached it, but they had been unable to pry it loose or get back out of the ledge next to the cliff wall. As they got closer, he observed there were even the remnants of a hand still on the spear. The body had long since burned and melted into the rock. So how was he possibly going to reach it?

Khawna stood watching Pike, her eyes conveying her worry about the man she'd sworn to protect. She stood with arms crossed while the now forgotten chewed piece of her hair waved gently in the breeze.

"We could tie a rope to you and see if you could climb the rock wall to it," suggested Hellion. "Course there wouldn't be much left to pull in if you fall. Or maybe we could throw these bones at it to see if we can knock it loose. I guess if it falls in, we're done for though."

"The Tarmigan seemed to think that only I could do it. I have to reach it to find out." He started to attempt a climb on the cliff wall to see if it would be possible. If he could get high enough, he might be able to anchor a rope and swing to the spear and back. The rock wall was even more vertical than the climb up, but with no footholds. He could only manage to pull himself up half his height before his fingers slipped and he fell back to the ground.

Jada sat at the edge of the climb. The natives below howled with anger from time to time and would look up to glare at her. How could these people eat a person? What kind of monsters were they? Apparently, she'd taken up with monsters recently. She'd had no idea that Lion was actually the fugitive Hellion Swash. His ridiculous disguise now made sense. Even his idle threats earlier… She shivered. Her only option was him and Pike now. If things went bad with the natives, she decided they'd never take her alive. She wouldn't let Pike fail though. The next attack was likely to come at night. To wait for them to die of thirst or hunger was not what was done with livestock. And that's exactly how the cannibals viewed them.

Perhaps the Tarmigan could hunt them at night. But no, it had said it wouldn't interfere unless attacked. How inconvenient. What a worthless creature to have on your side. All that power, all those teeth, and unable to do a darn thing but lead her and Hellion here to be a part of the butchery. It was clear Pike had now fallen for Khawna. The way they looked at each other left no doubt. So what purpose did she now serve, sitting, watching the natives below? She was no fighter, no hunter. She was skilled in hospitality, which would come in completely useless with the barbarian tribe below. The only other skill set she had was building things in her mind. Oh, how dreadful the Mammoth common room had looked before she'd redone the whole thing. Previously, there'd been no stage. The ceiling had been lower, leaving the room too loud and cramped until she raised the roof three times as high. The inside walls had never been finished and properly insulated. And how about the center feature fireplace? It had originally been a plain cast-iron stove with a timid round chimney pipe crawling unceremoniously into the ceiling in the corner. She and everyone else loved the way it was done now. A huge, warming fireplace, accessible from all sides, in the middle of the room called everyone to gather around it and be merry on the cold winter nights. Rocks lined the gigantic chimney rising to the third-floor ceiling like a mini mountain that was glorious to behold. It was perfect for their setting, just a stone's throw away from complete wilderness.

The man she had hired to complete her vision was very secretive about his methods. He was from the east and wouldn't tell what he used in his mixture. Whatever it was, it stuck those rocks permanently in place once it hardened. The man boasted he could build almost anything with it. He'd even gone so far as to say he could build a house with it if anyone could afford it. She didn't doubt the house might stand longer than most around. If only that man were here now with his materials. He could build a bridge straight across the death pit that would stand for a thousand years.

Jada looked over to see Pike fall back to the ground from his short climb. Hellion was shaking his head, saying it would never work. She glanced over the cliff to make sure there was no new threat. There wasn't. She noticed a drip from Khawna's scalding pan and nudged it with her foot. She began thinking.

"What have you come up with, Pike?" she asked, walking over.

He wiped his brow. "I need to climb about halfway up this cliff to attach a rope. Then I can drop down and swing out to the spear and safely back."

"How are you going to attach the rope?"

"I'm going to have to get lucky and find a hole or jagged edge up there to tie to."

"What makes you think you can climb it?"

"Because there is no other way to do this with what we've brought."

Jada looked around and smiled. "I think I have a way to get you up higher."

Pike and Hellion exchanged glances. Khawna's brow narrowed even further.

"You must have figured out how to grow wings then!" taunted Hellion. "I don't like it either, but we've inventoried all the supplies we have."

"I don't think you're counting what we didn't bring. It's time to build some stairs, you sheep-witted warriors. I'll get you as high as you want to go. From there, it's up to you." She smiled with satisfaction as the two men scratched their heads in bewilderment.

Chapter 32

PIKE STARED BACK at Jada with a repulsive look of approval while Hellion absolutely loved the idea. It was undeniably both sick and twisted. Unfortunately, Pike had to admit he'd never have thought of it by himself. "It's a morbid idea, but it just might work. Everyone gather the bones."

And so they had their building material for stairs. Luckily, there was no shortage of skeletons. There may have been enough bones to build a house and then some. They built a wide base for the first step. Once the bones were arranged in a sturdy position, Pike poured the lava from the pan over them to hold them in place. While it was cooling, they began stacking for the next step. Each step was as high as Pike's length from knee to foot, making it ideal for him to climb. The steps were kept short, allowing Pike to get the ball of his foot firmly planted. It took some time for the lava to cool, but the cooler it got, the sturdier the stairway became. The four worked for hours, rotating lookouts for the climb entrance. The Merkils were undoubtedly planning something below, but for now they waited.

By the time they had constructed the necessary height, it was nearing dark. It was probable another sneak attack would be attempted, so Pike wasted little time taking the rope and climbing to the top of his platform. He studied the wall closely, looking for any surface that he could anchor his rope from. The rock was mostly smooth as he felt around above his head until his hand brushed a soft area in the rock. He pushed his hand hard into the mossy indentation, and his hand pushed through it. It was a large indentation in the wall that allowed his hand a sturdy grip. When he shifted his weight onto the hold to pull himself up higher, he was alarmed to feel his handhold move.

He cautiously let go and landed back on his platform. There would be virtually no sunlight within moments, making him frantic to see what had happened. He called down for the pan, which was handed up to him still very warm. He set it upside down and stood on it to get a little more height.

He reached a hand up into the groove again; this time instead of pulling down, he pulled outward, away from the cliff. To his delight the stone began to move. It was heavy, but it could be pulled out in little increments by wiggling each time.

"What's going on up there, Pike?" asked Hellion.

"I think I've found something in the wall. There's a piece of rock that was cut out." He reached up with both arms pulling outward and felt the full weight of the rock teetering above his head. The rock was circular with a hole drilled through the center and wide enough that he could grip it firmly from the inside. He set it on the platform gently, as it weighed nearly as much as he could hold; then, he placed the pan on top of the rock to see an opening in the cliff.

"It's a tunnel. Hellion, I need you up here to give me a boost. It looks like it goes in pretty deep."

"Why would there be a tunnel all the way up there?" asked Jada.

Swash climbed up to Pike's perch. "Are you sure you can fit? It looks pretty tight. Maybe one of the girls should try."

"Don't look at me," said Jada. "Ask your tribal girlfriend."

"No. I think it should be me," said Pike, ignoring Jada's cold glare. "I'm going to tie the rope around my foot. If I start yelling, yank me back out."

Pike got the push he needed from Hellion and pulled himself into the tunnel past his waist. The passage was narrow and led downward. He was glad he had Hellion there to pull him back out if needed. "I'm crawling down, guys."

He barely had room to move his arms, but it was enough to reach out and help pull and wiggle further down. After covering his own body length twice, the tunnel turned to his left. It was a good sign since that was the direction of the spear. Now even more excited, he pulled himself quickly along. The confined space of dark, cold stone should have terrified him, but he felt abnormally calm for the situation. Life-crushing weight surrounded him above and below, and yet he felt a peaceful determination to reach the tunnel's end. He knew it couldn't go too much further. With his next outreach, his finger brushed against something in the tunnel ahead of him. He heard a brief high-pitched sound and then…nothing. After waiting a second to collect his focus, he carefully allowed his fingers to brush back over the object. The high frequency from before hummed in his ear, this time less alarming. There was something familiar about it. Pike focused on what he now held, noting the feel of a wooden stick. He wrapped his fingers around it and pulled it closer for examination. Oddly enough, the hum slowly pulsed with more strength in his head as he now held what appeared to perhaps be an old spear.

He used the long handle to poke further down the tunnel and realized it came to an end just ahead. Was it really a spear he now held in his hand? *If only I had some light.*

Immediately the spear in his hand began glowing with white light, illuminating the rock hole he was now in. He gasped at the pulse of energy he now felt surge through him and then again when he saw the drawings on the tunnel walls. A chief was drawn holding the spear pointed skyward with one hand while another man, dressed not like a native but more like Hellion, stood beside him. The frequency was increasing in intensity. Pike could feel tingling in his arms and legs as the hairs were starting to stand on end from both the sound and what he saw next. Two females were drawn on either side of the second man, and the rest of the people drawn were natives on their knees. *Can it be true?* His eyes lingered over the pulsing light emitted from its shaft.

The far end with a spearhead now glowed red. For the first time in many years, Pike was afraid. What had he discovered? Why had it been hidden here? Was the other spear a decoy? He had more questions than before on top of a feeling of uncontrollable energy that needed to be released.

"Pull me out, Swash!" he yelled as his words echoed off the end of the tunnel. He winced from the power of his own voice. To him, it almost felt as if the tunnel shook. He called again, but Hellion didn't pull him out. Pike yanked on the rope with a foot but felt no pressure. That was when he thought he heard Khawna scream. Growing frantic, he pushed against the stone, trying to force himself back out the way he had come. The downward slope made it nearly impossible. It would take hours to inch back. He was trapped.

The realization made him angry. The sound in his head was growing unbearable. He was too close to whatever he was supposed to do to fail now. He gritted his teeth in pain and rage. If something happened to his friends, he would be broken. He *had* to get out of this rock-laden crypt. In desperation, with tears beginning to run down his face, he took the spear and jabbed the red end into the tunnel's end, screaming words—no, sounds—he had never heard or spoken prior. The frequency in his head was no longer inside. It was coming from him or perhaps the spear, but he couldn't distinguish the object from himself as all at once there was a deafening *crack* and a burst of red light pulsed from the spear's end. The frequency returned to its previous low hum with its former glow of light. Pike opened his eyes to peer through the dust. The tunnel end had been blown completely out! He crawled to the edge to see eyes watching from the shadows of the plain. There were more sets of eyes than there should be.

He glanced to his side and saw the decoy spear still dangling above the lava. It no longer glowed. The illusion had been powered by the object he now held in his hands. It was a trap that had claimed countless lives. He alone now possessed the actual Spear of Song. Why? Because he could hear the hum of a song in his head? What had caused the melody to reveal itself? In that instant, a sense of understanding washed over him. The drawings in the tunnel meant that this was not happenstance. He had been drawn together with Hellion purposefully. The girls too. Everything had been set up for this moment. It was a moment of need for the spear. It was supposed to happen this way, which also meant…he had to save his friends. The song washed over him, and he processed possibilities of multiple actions. The scenes of all the outcomes played simultaneously in his head. He could visualize what would happen before it occurred.

A spear was hurled at him, and he batted it away at the last second only to hear it bounce off the rock wall and disappear into the melted rock.

"Light!" he roared. Immediately the whole mountaintop was illuminated by the spear. The canticle was growing stronger, hovering in the back of his mind, but Pike held it back, trying to control himself. All the people on top of the small mountain, Merkils and friends alike, now shielded their eyes in disbelief. He pointed the spear outward and began twisting his mental picture of what he wanted to happen. The frequency in his head began to rise and fall and bend in loops. It was awkward at first, but he fought it with everything he had, and it quickly began to fall into a harmony in his mind. He felt as if he'd known the powerful harmony his entire life. It was the same faint melody he'd heard the morning he passed into this land, only stronger. It was a song he could sing, a language he could speak. Before him, the remaining skulls and bones rose into the air and began to form a bridge over the pit of lava. He could feel himself smile as sweat ran down his face from the concentration to single out the melody. The warriors had seen enough. They flung down their weapons and narrowly avoided pushing one another to their deaths in their haste to climb back to ground level, leaving Hellion and the girls confused but unharmed.

Pike passed over the lava without so much as an ember touching his feet. Swash swore aloud in astonishment while Jada hid behind him. It was Khawna that ran to him, unafraid, and held his face to hers. When she touched him, he could feel all the emotions she felt for him surge across his synapses. He cringed when he realized her loyalty was stronger than her own will to survive.

He kissed her on her forehead, now hearing…experiencing…a

different, lighter frequency than before. He pulled away, leaving her standing alone, and walked past the other two to the edge of the cliff where the Merkils were yelling and descending as fast as their arms and legs would allow. The ones at the bottom were yelling angrily at the scared men fleeing the mountaintop. They needed a sign.

Pike focused his mind on the familiar frequency once again and raised the now pulsing spear into the night, and the sky split open with lightning. The spectacle illuminated the mountain and all of the surrounding areas. He felt totally in control of the spear, of the night itself. For a brief second, he saw the gargantuan Tarmigan and what stood behind it. It was another tribe of armed warriors to the west, looking up at him holding the spear. He already knew they were Khawna's people, and they were there to help him.

"Attack!" he yelled over the deafening tone in his head, while waving his illuminated spear. Bolts of lightning erupted from the skies and rained down upon the Merkils below. The night gave way to his new people's cries as they ran toward the cannibals who began to scatter.

Chapter 33

THE NIGHT WAS lost, and Hytan knew it. The bolts of lightning rained down upon his men, summoned by the man with the glowing spear above them. The ground shuddered with each jolt of power, and the chief saw more than one of his men struck down and burned with unstoppable force. The air smelled unusual with a burnt tinge and something unrecognizable. During the flashes, Hytan glimpsed the distant mass of Ghenzis assembled, and for the first time in a long while, he felt afraid.

"Disperse north!" he screamed at his terrified dearths, as some cowered and others scattered in all directions. They would be slaughtered if they stayed put. It was his destiny to live to fight another day. As far as winning went, today would not be that day. Around the mountain the cannibals ran in the dark, hoping their enemies would not pursue their overmatched force. The land north was largely barren and uninhabited. He did his best to conceal his fear and turned it into anger as he yelled at his dearths to hurry.

While they ran silently, blindly into the night like so many spooked antelope, he thought of the implications of the power the Ghenzis now appeared to hold. He had enjoyed his time as the alpha of the land, but now nature had turned its course. The sacrificial livestock were now emboldened. *Why had they fled to this mountain? Was it a trap all along?* He thought of his wives and the rest of the tribe he was now cut off from. They would surely be enslaved or worse if he could not get back to them.

Then the chief recalled the words and smile of Clivegon. Could the old man have really seen this coming? The leader of the elders had also said he'd foreseen Hytan's death, but that had not come to pass. The Merkil leader didn't know if he could change what was already set in motion to happen, but he knew he would never submit to anyone as long as he breathed. No man was better in combat than he. No man had ever had his passion or the vision he possessed. The fate of his people relied on what would happen next. He brushed his hand over the raw flesh on his cheek. The Ghenzis would pay dearly for this night.

What remained of the Merkils' once proud force stopped running when daylight broke. They had not eaten or rested since the morning they departed their camp. They were weak and demoralized. But they were still alive, and it appeared the Ghenzis had not been able to find them as of yet. Now they could travel slower and regain their strength while Hytan figured out their next move.

The terrain consisted of hills with thick shrubbery and rock-covered ground. There could be no planting of crops in this region, and with scant hunting game, there was little reason for any tribe to settle the area. However, the hard ground would also make tracking his men difficult for the other tribe. They would have to scavenge thoroughly to find whatever meat they could harvest to regain their strength. There would be no more human sacrifice for this moon. Hytan knew the importance of it to his men, but he could not spare any fighting men. It was an unspoken law that obedient dearths were not to be eaten. They were too valuable to the strength of the tribe.

In another important matter, how could he regain control of the southern lands? The fact remained, although armed and emboldened, the Ghenzis were by no means good warriors. His dearths were worth four Ghenzis apiece, even on their worst day. However, the man that held the spear had temporarily broken their spirit. Hytan tried to push the images of lightning from his mind. Perhaps even worse was what he had glimpsed standing on the hill, seemingly leading the Ghenzis. The Tarmigan. It was supposed to be hostile toward all humans, but that didn't seem to be the case on that night. Hytan had seen the animal before while hunting and withdrawn immediately, unwilling to provoke its wrath. Naturally, there had been headstrong warriors in the past who attempted an attack on the ancient animal. Most of their bodies were never found.

A Merkil scout came running toward the chief excitedly.

"What have you found, Sytus?" The man was his fastest dearth, which also made him an excellent vanguard.

"I have found shelter. A hidden cave with one entrance, big enough to fit an entire tribe."

"The gods may favor us yet. We will move the men inside. Once we're hidden, I want you to take three more dearths and scout the perimeter. We may still be hunted for days to come. For now, we must remain hidden."

The lean scout nodded in obedience and led the rest of the dearths onward. They headed northwest, in between two large mountain peaks. Hytan liked the approach. There could not be an assault except by their current path. If the cave could provide reliable water, he would be very happy. He scanned the ledges of the mountainous terrain for green patches of growth. It was near some of these patches he spied goats laying in the sun and nibbling at the ground. He allowed himself to smile, encouraged by the new land.

The entrance of the cave was concealed, making it virtually impossible to know what lay behind the shrubs they had to push through to get inside. Once through the entrance, they felt their way down a long tunnel. This could be his stronghold. From here he could stage future attacks on smaller forces, while remaining hidden. His next step would be finding a way to get the rest of his tribe to their new home. He had to assume the Ghenzis would move quickly upon the vulnerable village. His enemies could be moving in on his people this very night. He knew what he would do in their place, but the Ghenzis were a different tribe than the Merkils.

The chief decided his next move would be leading a very small scout force to try to rescue his people. Small numbers were less likely to be found and would move quickly. If only he could reach them, he could preserve his people. His dearths would need women, and Hytan needed his women as well.

The Merkil leader spoke of his plans to no one while his force entered the hole in the earth. He needed to check his surroundings more thoroughly before committing to his plan. There were also more logistics to consider, such as assigning hunters and guards and who would command in his absence. He hated giving any warrior a taste of his power, but someone had to hold the others accountable to his plans while he was away.

The small entrance to the cave had been deceiving. As soon as he and his men had walked through a long, narrow tunnel, the cavern opened up immensely. It was only after they'd made fires inside that they began to appreciate the size of the cave. Hytan could hide his entire village inside and not be crowded.

He strutted around his men, proclaiming the gods were giving them just what they needed. This was a test, and as long as they stayed the course, revenge would be theirs and the rewards would be plentiful. The dearths' sullen and forlorn expressions were starting to lift with their leader's words of encouragement. Their courage was exactly what Hytan needed. The chief was about to unveil his plans to Sytus when one of his men approached with excitement in his voice.

"Chief Hytan! We've found something in the cave!"

Hytan motioned for Sytus to hold his thought. "What is it that is important enough to interrupt your chief?"

"There is a passage, and something else!"

"Stay away from any passages! I can't afford to have any dearths get lost or fall to their deaths in an underground cavern!"

"But leader, the way is marked."

"How so?"

"There are carvings at the entrance. They tell of ancient trails underground. They say the tunnel will take us south!"

"Take me to the tunnel. We may have a change in plans," said the Merkil chief.

Chapter 34

FTER A TWO-DAY march, Pike and company were welcomed into the Ghenzi village like royalty. He could not believe the elation he brought to the faces of the natives as they followed his procession into the center of the large village. Khawna had tried to describe her home to him on their journey, but he had not expected such a civilized people. The houses were quite permanent, fashioned from a skeleton of heavy wood and filled in with smaller branches and soil with moss that grew right on the houses. It was a stark contrast to the tents in the Merkil village. There were even ditches designed to lead excess surface water away from the buildings and back into the Serpent's Gullet.

The center of the village, perhaps more accurately described as a town, had a building for storing excess grains and other harvests, not so much unlike Mossport. Pike marveled at the sights and people around him until the journey stopped in front of the largest building in the settlement. It looked to him like an attempt to build a castle. There was a fence surrounding the building with multiple levels, including watchtowers. Unlike the rest of the village, it was made of stone and clay.

"Your village is quite different from the Merkils', Khawna," Pike commented.

"Yes, the paleface taught us much about your ways. He helped us preserve our food and set up a village where everyone helps each other. He designed all that you see, many lifetimes before us."

"What is the significance of this building?"

"This is where the chief lives. You will live here now."

Pike glanced at Hellion and Jada in astonishment. "What about the chief that lives here now?"

"He may leave at once or choose combat with you." She smiled, patting her hand on his shoulder.

Pike tried to ignore the comment about combat. "Maybe he could stay and help me. I know nothing about your people and customs. How can I be fit to lead without help?"

Khawna shook her head angrily. "His time is done! It was he who sentenced me to sacrifice. He will not be pleased to see me. He will suggest they return me to avoid war. He is weak, hunter. He is not strong and fit to rule, as you are. And now you have the spear."

Pike looked in his right hand and then out into the crowd. After the initial astonishment of seeing three foreigners in their land, the natives' eyes were all on the spear. Word had spread quickly about what Pike had done with the weapon. It was to be their salvation. Pike was the chosen one who had delivered it to them. Never mind the fact that he had never been in a real battle or led any group of people on anything other than a hunt. He heard a chant begin to be repeated louder and louder. *Ny-tel! Ny-tel! Ny-tel!*

"What does Nytel mean?" asked Jada.

"It means wise one or favored one," replied Khawna. "It was what we called our chiefs back when they were strong."

Jada rolled her eyes. "They clearly have no idea how much of a fool he is."

Khawna stepped up to Jada's face. "You should not talk of the Nytel like that. To do so in public would require a public nude whipping." She smiled as the words came out.

Jada's face reddened. "That seems a bit harsh for speaking the truth. Pike, you wouldn't let that happen, would you?"

Pike pushed his palms toward the ground to gesture her to take it easy. "Jada, we are in a totally new world. We had best all tread carefully and listen to Khawna."

Jada's death glare was broken up by one of the warriors ushering everyone into place.

"Hyrechee loe vasa se quano," the warrior shouted at the top of his lungs.

"We come to dedicate a new chief to our people," whispered Khawna.

A man emerged from the balcony of the castle above them. He was easily the most well-nourished man in the village from what Pike could see. He answered in the same tongue that the hunter could not comprehend. "On what grounds do you bring this foreigner to our camp to oust me, your chosen representative," whispered Khwana.

"He has the Spear of Song!" shouted the warrior back to the man on the balcony.

"Has he slain Hytan then?"

"No."

"Has he provided you with food to cover all the seasons?"

"No."

"Has he managed to keep you from war and certain death?"

"Not yet."

The man smiled. "Then you will seal your doom by choosing this man. He is not one of us! He is an outsider from the lands of destruction and will take advantage of our people!"

After translating, the next words came from Khawna'a lips in a language Pike could understand. "Will he send his people to be sacrificed? Yes, that is what happens to our people who are traded for your peace. They are eaten! Will he give a share of our food to the Merkils as well? Will he never leave his walled fortress to lead his warriors into battle? This is all you have given us. It is a life of never-ending debt to the Merkils. You sent me to be eaten by savages, but it was this man who rescued me. It was he who brought the rain with him that we so desperately needed in our land. It was he the Tarmigan revealed was the next Nytel. Lastly, it was he who took the spear, without fear, and drove the Merkils into the north lands screaming. Leave now, or he will cut you down!"

The chief glared at her with contempt. "You, woman, have started a war." He continued in the language handed down from Horton Conner. "You, who were barren and of no benefit to our tribe, could have kept our village from certain destruction. I order my warriors to send you back and beg for mercy from the Merkils!"

Barren? Pike raised his spear, instantly feeling its hum in his ear, in his mind. Its tip once again radiated red with his emotion. "She will not be sent back. No one will ever be sent for sacrifice again. Your people will no longer live as livestock for the Merkils under my rule."

The warriors shouted loudly again, "Ny-tel! Ny-tel! Ny-tel!"

"I will not leave!" shouted the man angrily. Before Pike could respond, the warriors rushed upon the stone fortress and climbed up the balcony to lay their hands on the now blubbering fool. They took his headwear; they took his necklace and left him with nothing but a loin cloth. Then they threw him bodily from the confines of the village as he kicked and screamed at them like a madman.

"He should be killed," said Hellion, with a hand on his sword.

"He will be, if the Merkils find him," replied Pike. "I don't wish for our stay here to start with bloodshed."

"This is not just your stay, hunter," said Khawna. "This will be your life. We are your people now. Your song is within all of us now. You will not be able to leave."

Whatever else Pike wanted to say in that instant was washed away when he felt a small pulse from the spear. He realized quickly to argue would not go well. With a sigh he tried to think of what someone wiser than himself would do in this situation. "Shall I appoint some type of council to advise me?"

Khawna shook her head. "It is your wife that is your first advisor. This is who you must pick first."

"We already agreed on that."

She shook her head again. "The tribe will not allow it. I was barren before." Her gaze drifted downward.

"Whatever happened before no longer matters. I saw you with a child in my dream. It must be you." Pike surprised himself with his insistence.

Khawna nodded her head but looked concerned. They led their small group into the mini-castle and up the stairs to where the old chief had stood shortly before. Khawna made the announcement to the tribe, who were now all gathered within the walls.

"He must produce a son!" the shouts started. "This cannot be!" Khawna looked at him with sorrowful eyes.

"I can't do this without you," he whispered. "There must be a way around it."

Khawna chewed on her knuckle. The words were not what she wanted to say. "The only option would be to take a second wife…"

Pike's eyes went to Jada immediately.

The prickly barmaid looked up, astonished. "Now that it's convenient, you want me? I don't think so, Nytel. I don't share my men. The only way I would consider it is if she's out." She glared hostilely at Khawna.

"That's not a possibility," he said firmly. "I'll have to find someone else."

Jada's jaw dropped, to the delight of Hellion. "Just like that, you're moving on? One obstacle and you give up? Some chief you're going to make. Apparently, you don't have much taste since you refused my counteroffer. I don't know how you don't see it, especially since I'm twice the woman that girl will ever be."

Khawna did not take the insult well and proceeded to shove Jada aside. "I have a sister that will be a much better choice, hunter. This woman does not belong here."

The effect of the shove and insult led to a slap on Khawna's face, which in turn led to an all-out fight between the two women. Swash burst out laughing, noticeably not doing a thing to break up the commotion. The rest of the village cheered while the two women wrestled, screamed, and cursed for everyone to see.

Finally, Pike had enough. He embraced the rhythm now humming in his head, pointed his spear to the sky, and yelled "Stop!" Thunder echoed from the blue sky, and the ground shook from the reverberation. The two, now frightened more than angry, stopped their fight.

"I need you both, so therefore you must help me. Call yourselves what you want. You heard the Tarmigan. I need your help."

Hellion interjected, "He said you need me too, but don't even try it."

Pike waived off the remark. "If either of you two is unhappy with my decision, you are free to leave the castle now. I have a lot to do, and I need people I can trust. This is just a formality anyhow. He looked at Jada, waiting for her to burst into tears and run off. She didn't. She had tightened her lips and narrowed her brow. He could tell she was determined to go through with it.

Jada walked over to whisper in his ear so that none could hear. "I'll do this just to help you. Don't even think for a second there will ever be any physical contact between us. You're lucky I'm not wool-headed enough to let you try to rule alone."

"It's settled," said Pike. "Now on to our next order of business. Swash, I need you in my council. We'll have to find a few trustworthy people for more guidance. Khawna will help with that. Please tell the people to disperse while we make our plans. I will address them again later."

Khawna obeyed, as Pike knew she would, and the rule of Pike Granger began. To say Pike was surprised at the words and decisions that had just left his mouth would be an understatement. *How is the whole village listening to me already? Who am I to be barking out orders and plans?*

He looked at Hellion, who just shook his head at him. "Really, two wives? I was going to try to talk you out of one. Your life's about to be miserable."

Chapter 35

LATER THAT EVENING, after an exhausting day of reports ranging from current food stores to defense of the village to plans for the Merkils, Pike reclined in his new home with Hellion. The girls were not permitted to stay in the new chief's residence until a formal ceremony was complete. The arrangements had already begun and had been another time-taxing chore, but the ceremony would be completed in a fortnight. The absence of Pike's future wives was a welcome break from the tense situation he had now created.

Pike was surprised to learn that this village was only the base village of multiple locations that he would now oversee as chief. The speeches and planning were finally completed for the day, and it was nice to speak plainly with Hellion in the plush quarters.

"Are you sure this village can spare the extra food for this wedding, Swash? We don't know how many will come from neighboring villages."

"Yes, Pike," he replied as if annoyed. His eyes were bloodshot. "I told you the granaries are quite full. I've overseen supplies before, you know. Well, I guess you probably wouldn't know. Even if the stores weren't full, it would be necessary to empty them. Chain of command is all about appearances. You can't afford to make bad impressions or these people might turn on you."

"Have some patience with me, Hellion. I didn't ask for this job. I'm not used to worrying about the welfare of so many lives. I'm used to just looking out for me. I'm going to need a lot of your help, friend."

Hellion chuckled. "There's that dirty word again. When are you going to learn I'm not cut out to be that kind of person, Granger? I'm a mercenary. A bad apple. Sure I'll try to help you, but only because it benefits me while I'm here. This whole open-tab deal you have is top notch, by the way." He raised his cup in the air. "Listen to me when I tell you the truth, please. In the meantime, just try to act like you know what you're doing. No one here is your friend. Especially those two snakes you've chosen for wives."

Pike pondered over his words. He was a bitter, bitter man to be sure. But why? "Tell me what happened, Hellion. If you were such a great soldier, how'd you end up in Mossport? You said you were being honest with me, so tell me. Who could I tell here? Who would care?"

Hellion sighed. "You're probably right. We'll probably be trapped here for the rest of our lives." He shook his head at himself. "Course, that might be a better thing for me. With all that reward money out there for me, there's scant chance of me ever being able to stay in one place very long." He paused again. "Listen well. You'll be the first to ever hear the full shitty story.

"After some successful years as a bareknuckle fighter on the streets of Sisterton, I enlisted in the army at age fifteen. Thought I needed to see the world. Had to lie about my age, of course. They overlooked it, and my training began. I was instinctive with the sword, spear, and bow, and with training, I quickly became one of the fastest. I drilled against the most experienced soldiers and learned enough tricks to keep myself alive by the time I first saw action. The most important trick to becoming the best is to stay alive. I was good at that, and then I got even better. I started keeping track of the lives I took in each conflict, and soldiers began to notice I was worth four or five of a regular soldier. Naturally, men gravitated toward me and wanted to follow me in battle. But you see, I couldn't give orders, because everything follows a chain of command. My superiors began to realize I should rise in rank, and yet my turn to advance never came. Like most things in civilization, it's more about who you know if you want to move up the ladder. I was a low-class orphan. Big deal, whatever, once you're in hand-to-hand combat, titles mean nothing anyway. Then we got a new commander who had ascended the ranks quickly. He came from another company, so no one knew much about him at first. But stories follow wherever one goes. He was a man who didn't like to be challenged, and it appeared whenever he encountered competition, something unfortunate would happen to the soul at odds with him."

"Let me guess, you challenged his authority."

"You would think so, right? But no, I just did what I did best—created bloodshed. This certain commander advanced my rank to just below him to help lead our men. I never asked for the advancement, but naturally I did a fine job and made him look good, until the final battle. In the middle of an attack that I was leading, one of my own men drove a spear through my back. I had called this man a friend, Pike." He shook his head. "No such thing. Before I killed him on the battlefield, I made him talk. He screamed who had paid him for the deed. My men heard his cries. They saw his weapon in my back. After our enemy was vanquished, I skipped the medical tent and went to the next in authority above the treacherous commander. I was greeted, instead, by my own commander who had already reached the man, and perhaps bought or persuaded him. They put me in chains and were going to try me for killing my own soldier. I thought my men would save me in the trial, but as it turned out, a few had been bought and the rest were murdered before they made it back to camp that day. As you can tell, I was cooked.

"That night I escaped my chains and murdered ten guards before escaping on the commander's own white horse. I'm not proud of any of that, but I had no choice. I would have been hanged the next day. After all the killing I had done for the army, they were going to put me down like a rabid dog. I made my way from port to port. I had to kill more soldiers here and there because my picture was immediately plastered everywhere. I don't know how many I killed. My reward kept growing. After months of running I decided to head to the edge of nowhere, and that just happened to be Mossport."

"I'm sorry," said Pike. "I had no idea. But at least you're innocent."

"I was, until I killed my own people to save my neck."

Both men were quiet for a few moments. Finally it was Pike who spoke up.

"Well, you'll always be safe here at least. The Tarmigan brought you for a reason. This whole song he mentioned includes you. Maybe it's because of what you've been through. You've seen the famous coastal cities across the Gridlock Sea, I imagine, and you know the corruption and pitfalls that we need to avoid. With your help, perhaps we can do great things for these people. They don't care about your past here. Look how much they've already learned from a man that visited them over a hundred years ago. These people will thrive once we eliminate the Merkil threat and end the practices of the last chief."

"If there's a reason I'm here, it's because of what I can do with a weapon in my hand. That and maybe the map I lent you…speaking of which, I need to get that back eventually. But with you holding that magical spear in your hand, I don't see how much I can add to the equation. What's it feel like to hold that thing, anyway?"

Pike looked up to the ceiling. "It's almost like a melody that starts in my head. I think that's why they call it the Spear of Song. It gets louder and louder, and I think it feeds off my emotion. But the power it uses, that's already out there. For instance, I'll tell you about the lightning. I could feel the electricity in the air above us. I couldn't create it, but I could channel it with the spear, and that's exactly what I did. If the weather was different, I'm not sure I could do it as well. But the spear intensifies everything for me when I'm holding it. That night on the mountain, I could feel fear as an energy rising from the Merkils. I could feel how exhausted you were from the long day and night. I could feel love and other emotions from Khawna. I don't know what to do with it all yet, though. It's hard to explain. Do you want to hold it?"

"No," Hellion said quickly and backed away with his hands up. "Best to keep something like that away from a killer like me. I wouldn't want that type of responsibility for all the gold in Sisterton. Just give me a normal spear or sword, and I'll be just fine."

"Suit yourself," said Pike.

"Where does this all lead, Granger? Can you see anything in the future when you hold it?"

Pike didn't want to tell everything about the weapon, but it did feel good to reveal some of it. "I can see hints and possibilities, but nothing long term. It's just enough to give me an advantage in battle, I think."

"I guess I better not pick a fight with you then, huh?" Swash slapped him on the arm. "Damn it. You probably saw that coming, didn't you? I'd like to know if we'll ever be able to leave this land. Not that I'm in a hurry to get turned in for a reward, but it would just be nice to know."

"I'd tell you if I knew."

Hellion leaned back on his pillow with his arms behind his head. "Of course you would. So where do you think the Tarmigan went?"

"It never said. Just said it would be back. The last thing it growled to me was *these people are in good hands now*. Do you believe that? I'm about to get married to two women I hardly know. How in the hell could I possibly know what I'm doing?"

Hellion roared with laughter. "When you put it like that, you might be the unluckiest guy in the world. Say, Granger, could you have one of your serving women bring me some more wine, please?" The ex-soldier's posture told the tale best. He was half on and half off his pile of plush pillows, with a reddened face and a glossy smile.

"You know, you're not going to be worth much as a counselor if you stay in the cups all the time."

Hellion objected with his tongue hanging idly outside his mouth. "I'm a philosopher when I drink, my friend. In fact, the night I decided to accompany you, I drank quite heavily. In fact..." He stuck his index finger in the air to assert the importance of his point. "It might be more dangerous if I weren't drinking this wine. You should be thanking me."

Pike rolled his eyes. The two had been through a lot together in a short amount of time. Why not let the man enjoy his vice? And so he counseled himself silently as Hellion slowly drifted into unconsciousness.

How was he going to manage two women at once? Jada was more than enough trouble by herself. Since he needed them both, he was going to have to make it work. Khawna knew this land and its people. But what of the revelation that she had been barren before? And with whom? He had so many new questions. Yet, with her by his side, he would feel much more secure. Jada was crafty, but he felt loyalty from her when he held the spear. She would speak her mind, and she also wouldn't let him go through with a bad decision. It wasn't in her nature to give in to him or keep quiet to please him. She had survived quite well in the frontier town as a young woman on her own. The inn owner had adapted once and would do so again. She was strong and independent, but she would be there when Pike needed her.

Now it was Pike who took a cup from the servant girl and sipped silently as he stared at the colorful tapestry, deep in thought.

Chapter 36

THE DAY OF the wedding arrived. Pike had not been permitted to speak to either bride for days. He had started to become quite unsettled in his solitude with his drunkard companion. As chief, he had taken to carrying the spear with him everywhere he went. His reasoning was twofold: to practice with it and to protect it. Whenever it pulsed in his grip, he felt the tone within reach and his senses heightened. He was trying to control it with more precision and proper understanding. With it, he felt like the chief he was supposed to be. Without it, he felt like the lone fur trader he had always been. The man he had been was not fit to rule, not fit to protect, and definitely not fit for one wife, let alone two.

His quarters were opened up to the village for the day of the ceremony. Tapestries adorned every wall, even the ceilings. It was as if he'd been transported out of his new stone home and into the likes of some rainbow-blasted hotel in the coastal cities. He'd heard stories about fancy hotels but had never been east to confirm the hearsay.

There were drums and chanting as he was ushered down the aisle of his courtyard, adorned in his colorful robes, where his throne of gold and precious gems awaited him. The cheering of his new people was deafening in the open air. They had been under oppression from the

Merkils and their own chief for so long; they echoed an undertone that Pike could feel even when his spear wasn't in hand. It was an uplifting song of hope. He didn't know if it was the power of the gathering of natives or the power of the spear, but whatever it was, the feeling that rushed over him was beginning to quell the anxiety he had been feeling for days. He had all the confidence in the world when he raised his spear into the air and pointed at the cloudy, drizzly sky above them. Almost instantaneously, the clouds began to separate and beams of sunlight poured down upon the gathered people. The crowd became hysterical with joy and amazement.

When Pike took his seat upon the throne, complete silence fell upon the ceremony. From beyond the gathered people came the call of a high-pitched flute. All eyes turned away from their Nytel and to the back of the center aisle to see a large platform carrying both Khawna and Jada. Eight men, clad in warrior breeches with bright paint upon their faces and chests, carried the women down the same path that Pike had just walked. The cheering began again as Khawna waved to her people with a smile that couldn't be faked. Jada sat with arms crossed and knees drawn upward, clearly uncomfortable and unhappy. The girls were dressed identically and were both stunning in their own way. Bright purple silk hung over their right shoulders and continued flowing past their feet. Their hair was braided upward and towered above their heads in an intricate linear design. The contrast in their beauty could not be more evident. Khawna's jet black hair glistened in the sun's rays, and her dark features were offset by the pearls peering through her smile. Jada's fair skin and light brown hair made her seem like a delicate beautiful flower blossoming in the sun. Both were beautiful. A man would be most fortunate just to have dinner with either one. Both would be Pike Granger's.

The closer the procession approached, the louder the murmur of the crowd grew. Pike felt the time was appropriate to stand while waiting for his wives to arrive. He breathed in fully, feeling stronger in that moment than any other in his life to date. The spear in his hand vibrated with power—whether from him, the girls, or the crowd, he could not discern. All who were previously seated followed their chief's lead and took to their feet. The warriors finally reached their Nytel, and Pike could smell the mix of sweet fragrances that covered his women.

Upon the lowering of the platform, the girls were ushered off and escorted to their places, which were a step below Pike's right side for Khawna and a step below his left for Jada. Their gaze moved from Pike and fixed on each other, like cats daring one another to look away first. Pike cleared his throat and motioned for the head of the ceremonies to come forward.

An elderly robed man emerged from the audience. Everyone's attention should have been drawn to Pike and his brides-to-be in that moment, but something had a few turned around. More and more noticed the unusual behavior and followed suit. There was a low roar of murmuring that started to grow. Pike peered to the east, over the wall of the courtyard, and saw a large object running their way. There was only one thing it could be. The Tarmigan.

Many of the villagers began to scatter as it approached, screaming with fright. Many had not been in the village when it came to lead the warriors to the Serpent's Spittle. The situation was quickly turning into chaos. Pike yelled angrily and slammed the butt of the spear into the ground. The village shook, and all the people, including the brides-to-be and even Hellion, fell to a knee.

"Nobody run! It is an ally!" yelled Pike.

The Tarmigan ran on all fours up the aisle until it stopped in front of Pike, huffing from exertion.

"What news do you bring, friend?" asked Pike. "We've missed you these last two weeks."

The animal's eyes were frantic with terror. "It is the Merkils! They attack your town as we speak!"

Jada jumped to her feet. "We must go, Pike. They have no defense against warriors!"

Khawna got up more slowly. "The ceremony must be completed. The chief needs his wife first!"

"There is no time," growled the deep voice of the Tarmigan. "The village won't last long without your help."

Pike caught the devious cat-eye of Hellion, whose crooked smile told him more than any exchange of words could.

"The wedding is postponed! Warriors, gather your weapons. Your Nytel needs you. We leave immediately!"

The crowd returned to chaos as men scrambled to get to their huts for their weapons.

Khawna looked angrily at Pike. "Why must you go? You can't reach them in time. They are dead already."

"Maybe so, but it's my fault the Merkils are on the run. It's my job to use this spear to help people. You, my bride-to-be, will be in charge while I'm away. Use our reserve warriors to protect the village. I'm going to find the fastest way to the other side of the mountain."

"How's that?" asked Jada.

"Straight through it," he replied coldly.

Everyone around him gasped.

Chapter 37

WHAT HYTAN SAW before him was a new future. An entire town of farmers and traders was his for the taking. There were women to be had, livestock to be taken, and people to be sacrificed. The Merkils may have been defeated by the man with the spear, but through the secret tunnel they could conquer a new world. His scouts had found a few dead ends in the passages, but the furthest tunnel south had not disappointed. He had spied the unsuspecting village from afar. The townspeople had no warriors, just laborers that his superior dearths could overpower in one swift attack.

He did regret leaving behind his Latella and their son, but he had no magic with which to defeat the man with the spear. To try and rescue his village was quite possibly to deliver himself to the chopping block. His village would become the spoils of war. Perhaps the Ghenzis would go easy on his favorite wife and child. Perhaps not. Hytan knew what he would do if he was in their place. He turned his mind from the thought.

"Leader, we have not been spotted yet," said Sytus. "Shall we attack now?"

The chief shook his head. "We announce ourselves in the night.

That way we overtake them before they realize our lack of warriors. They will be frightened and give up without much of a fight."

"We are not afraid to fight, Chief Hytan."

Hytan put his arm around the younger warrior, excited for battle. "This I know. But slaves are no good to us dead. We are rebuilding our future. Besides, these people resemble the man that held the spear. Should he find our tunnel, we will need hostages to stop him from calling the sky fire down upon us."

"What bargain can be struck with a man that has the power of the gods?"

"Our people for his, if he hasn't slit their throats yet."

"You are wise, great leader."

"Our people must hope so, if we are to survive in this new world."

THEY SAT AND watched the villagers' movements all day. The beasts that some rode upon fascinated the Merkil chief. He watched the children running in the streets and angry mothers chasing after them. Men stumbled out the door of the large building by the enormous lake. They walked without balance—drunk on some type of fermented fruit or grain, no doubt. The women wore clothes concealing everything that Hytan had interest in looking upon. He would change that soon.

Something caught the villagers' attention from the gigantic body of water midafternoon. The Merkils strained to see, but they were too far away. Half the town seemed to have made their way to the shore for a better look.

"What is happening?" demanded Hytan from his scout. "Get closer and report back to me. Do not be seen or caught!"

Soon enough he looked upon the water and saw a sea vessel approaching. He had never seen a canoe of such size, but then again, he had never witnessed such a body of water. By the time Sytus came back, it was nearing dark.

"What has arrived from the sea?"

The young man tried to catch his breath. "It's more men…fighting men."

Hytan punched the air with anger. He should have already attacked! "How many men?"

"Over twenty. They carry weapons and come in matching dress."

"It is another tribe that must rule these people," said Hytan, scratching his chin. "These warriors we may have to kill first."

"They stay in the large building that men stumble out of," said the scout.

"That's where we attack first."

The odds weren't as heavily in Hytan's favor now, but he still maintained the element of surprise, as well as the dark, assuming he could force surrender before morning. The plan would resume, and he and his warriors would have even more glory as there would most certainly be a fight. His stomach groaned with hunger. He craved human flesh. It was always that way before battle. It was how he preferred it now. Better to be hungry and angry rather than full and satisfied. Satiety was the enemy of power. A leader should never feel satisfied. When one did, his enemy gained advantage on him; and if not the enemy, perhaps his own warriors. Better to keep them hungry too.

WHEN PIKE AND his army reached the southern border, his men all rested their eyes on their chief. After all, he had said they would go through the mountainous wall, but even he was unsure how to do it.

"Tarmigan! Come up here!"

The great beast approached slowly.

"How shall we get through?"

"It is beyond me to see," replied the deep voice. "But if it is done, it may not be undone quite so easily."

"What choice do I have?"

The Tarmigan crossed its bulging, human-like arms. "The same choice every leader has. The risk is great, and so is the reward. The two worlds have already begun to blend into one song. Your power could balance the worlds or destroy them. It all lies on you."

"What do you think, Swash?"

"The world may never be the same," he snarled. "Which might be good since I never cared for it much before."

"Pike, please hurry!" said a worried Jada.

With that he raised his great spear above his head. Everyone behind him took two steps back, even the Tarmigan.

Pike Granger reached into his mind and was startled to find multiple hums pulsing with different melodies at once. *Which one do I need?* The songs blended together. He strained to concentrate. He could hear someone yelling now, asking if he was alright. He yelled out in pain and threw his free hand out to keep them away from him. He could barely hear his familiar tone among the confusion in his head, and he reached mentally for the tone while squeezing the spear as if the band of sound was before him. He had it! He steadied the spear, now grabbing it with his other hand, and slammed the red-hot head into the earth in front of him. The world itself shook, and everyone but Pike fell to their knees. Rocks began tumbling down the great mountain wall. Trees shook violently along with the ground, where a tiny crack grew from the tip of the spear. It was miniscule when it started toward the mountain, but the further it reached, the wider it became. The shaking grew more violent, and Pike thought he heard Jada scream. He could feel the heat radiating from the power of the spear, but it was too late to stop now. The mountain broke with such a sound, there was no doubt in Pike's mind that the town would hear it.

The shaking continued, with Pike's arms rippling from the frequencies being unleashed. He could feel the mountains beginning to part further and further. Finally, he lifted the spear from the ground. The noise, the shaking, and the shear energy release immediately stopped. There was dust everywhere in front of them. No one spoke for a moment.

Granger lifted his spear into the air, and with little effort, produced a light wind that blew the dust out of their way. Everyone gasped. The mountain had been broken. Directly ahead was a gap in the mountain that extended deep into the earth. On the side of the gap was a ledge wide enough to walk upon without falling to one's doom.

"As you said," said Pike, motioning to Jada, "time is short." He raised his spear and ran through the newly created mountain pass. His warriors followed, energized by the echoes of their cries against the ripped apart mountain. The race was on.

Chapter 38

PIPPENDALE WAS HAPPY to be on solid ground again. The rolling waves of the choppy lake had drained him of his energy. The commander was so angry at the young man's sour stomach, he had sent him away from the cabins to surrender his meals to the frothy water. He was afraid Pippendale's weak intestines might spread to the other men if not quarantined to the upper deck. The only good part about the unfortunate ordeal was that it became his escape from Burin. But now that was over. The soldiers had taken free refuge in the Mammoth Inn.

"These inbreeds couldn't protect a chicken hut!" exclaimed Commander Burin. "The only immediate natural barrier is the lake, which cuts off their escape since they hardly own any boats. In a hundred years they haven't put up a fence, tree line, a hill, or anything to fortify this piss pot of a town. The only thing they've had going for them is there's never been anything out here, until now."

"Sir," replied Pippendale. "We have just twenty men with no fortification. Shall we send for reinforcements?"

Commander Burin would have loved to slap the little twit for even dreaming of making a suggestion. His messenger boy thought to give him counsel? What would be next? Perhaps the cook could be his navigator? Maybe his chamber pot attendant could be his engineer? He could see his counterparts in Sisterton making jokes at his expense for years. They would say Commander Burin needed a full army to kill one scary overgrown bear that was eating the villagers' sheep. Oh, how brave and resourceful he must be! He could kiss his career goodbye after that.

"Pippendale, please engage your brain prior to your tongue. We have one animal to kill and twenty-one-and-a-half men capable of carrying out said action. You, my messenger, are the half, as you are half a man with half a brain. Luckily enough for you, I was born with brains and enough other manful parts to make up for what you and the rest of the men lack. I will protect this town as promised. Now, listen carefully while I give you *my* orders. I'm not in the mood for screw-ups or suggestions. Got it?" He didn't wait for an answer. "I want ten men posted at all times. Twelve-hour shifts will be swapped. I need viewing platforms built and finished today for said sentries to be on lookout. The rest of the men will be on twelve-hour standby should there be any sighting."

"Yes, sir!" replied Pippendale, with his usual enthusiasm. He scuttled about to relay the orders. As he was walking out of the Mammoth, Grom was walking in.

Grom had already come to the realization that he wasn't going to like the commander of Fort Tuttle. The previous fort commander was much more of a gentleman than this arrogant jerk had been upon his arrival. This man, wearing his pompous large brimmed hat with a ridiculously large plume, was in fact, an asshole. But, since Grom was accustomed to a more political life of getting along with everyone, he bit his tongue and continued to try to get things done for his town.

"I trust you've made yourself at home, Commander?"

The man seemed surprised to be approached again by the store owner. "I've done the best I can, despite the environment. This place is a filthy disaster, Mr. Grom. I'm half tempted to take up your own bed so you could suffer what I now must endure in this neglected establishment."

Grom chuckled. "That means you got to take my wife too. Har! I might just hold you to that deal!"

The commander stared back at him blankly. Did he dislike Grom or did he not understand jokes?

Grom cleared his throat. "But in all seriousness, we've been doing the best we can. The owner, Miss Jada, was taken by the beast and I'm treading water keeping it going along with my own shop til she's found."

"What makes you think she's not dead like the others? You've told me this animal is a vicious killer. And how exactly does an animal of such a size that you've described sneak into a crowded place of business and "steal" someone? Was the whole town inebriated? I'm fairly certain someone would see a bear walk into a bar."

"I told ya, Commander. It weren't no bear. That tooth I showed you was real. Everyone in town saw its green scaly head and jaws when we thought it was dead. It's smarter and stronger than any animal ever discovered. And if it wanted her and Lion dead, it could have done it there in the room. Plus if it was going to just eat them, we'd have found something by now."

"Yes, yes, I'm sure if the beast was not as clever as you claim, your good townsmen would have no doubt discovered every clue left by now, right? And you said there was a man named Lion? Tell me more about this man."

"Well… Lion was a drifter. New to town. Probably some type of ex-soldier, I'd have to guess. He was quiet, always wore a cap and dark glasses over his eyes. Very secretive, that one. Him and Pike were the two men that killed the beast the first time."

"If the beast took this…Lion, what happened to the other man? I would very much like to talk to him."

"That's the other thing, Commander. He never came back with Lion. He decided to stay adventuring once they killed the beast. Thought he mighta found a way through the Mortapenum Mountains."

Commander Burin smiled. "Did it ever occur to you that this Lion may have killed the other man to claim your reward?"

"Why would he make it up? He only took his half of the reward anyway. He could have said the beast killed Pike, and we'd have all believed him. I admit I don't know him well, but I don't think Lion's that kind of man."

"With all due respect, shopkeeper, you're in over your head. If this Lion is who I suspect he might be, he's more dangerous than any animal out here. You may even be right about him being alive. In fact, I wouldn't be surprised if it was him that kidnapped the woman and stole the carcass of the beast. You're very fortunate we showed up when we did."

Grom winced at the evil smile now growing on the commander's face.

Chapter 39

THE SUN HAD slipped beneath the horizon quite some time ago. The villagers were now all asleep. There were oddly garbed warriors posted in hastily built platforms on three sides of the village. They wore dark, arm-length coats and pants, as if they were trying to look identical. Fires had been built to illuminate the field of vision for these scouts. How could they have known about the imminent attack? Hytan knew his men had not been seen. The villagers may have increased their odds against his men, but their fate would be no different. The lookout towers did put a snag in the chief's original plan. His small group of warriors could ill afford to lose the element of surprise, and so, they swam.

The dearths kept their weapons on their backs and eagerly followed their leader into the cool waters of the Mammoth, north of town. It was by far the largest body of water they had ever seen. The new plan was to attack the largest hut first, as it seemed to be where the fighting men were staying. After the executions there, the watchmen would be the only ones left to attack. They would be killed one by one as they were already trapped upon their wooden platforms. The rest of the village would surrender without a fight.

Hytan swam toward the shore until he felt smooth stones under his feet. He could hear his men's labored breathing, but with the gentle breeze and waves breaking against the shore, he knew they wouldn't be heard. The Mammoth Inn was a stone's throw away and did not have a single candle lit at this late hour. The first scream would surely cause mass confusion and panic, so they would need to work quickly.

The entrance from the lakeside had been barricaded. Rather than risk a noisy entrance, he led his wet group around to the front of the establishment. They walked through the front door without incident. The room was large and empty. A dying fire in the center of the room provided enough light for Hytan to realize that everyone was asleep on the upper levels of the building.

The chief took the bulk of his force, leaving just three below to finish off any attempted escapees. The dry wooden stairs creaked with the weight of him and his warriors. The further they climbed, the darker their surroundings became. Hytan crawled slowly, on his hands and knees like a cat, lurched low to the ground. His men followed in imitative fashion. They reached the second-level corridor with closed doors. One lone window at the end of the hallway provided a weak glow of moonlight in the hallway. He motioned a few warriors to each doorway. On his signal, they would simultaneously open four doors, quickly and quietly before dispatching the inhabitants. If all went well, the others wouldn't wake until it was their turn to have their throats slit. If it didn't happen as planned, they would have a real battle.

The leader clicked his fingers, effectively giving the audible signals. They all pushed on the doors, but nothing happened. They were bolted shut from the inside. He could smell the frustration of his dearths. He'd put them through much in the last few moons. They once again looked to him for an answer, for leadership. How could he keep the element of surprise now? He needed a distraction to draw them out, but not a full-scale attack alarm. They couldn't knock down the doors, and they couldn't spout war cries to announce their presence. What could cause panic?

He clenched his hands angrily as no answer came to him. The wooden floor squeaked under him as he punched the air with his fist. This enormous wooden hut frustrated him to no end. He wanted to watch it burn to the ground when he was done. And then, with that thought lingering, he smiled to himself.

Back down the stairs they crept. His men gathered everything burnable and made a pile of aprons, firewood, and straw from the stable. They took a glowing piece of log from the dwindling fire and watched the little flames start to grow on the dry, dusty straw.

Hytan and his men waited eagerly on the ground floor as the fire spread to the wooden floor. The old building was like a hundred-year-old tinderbox. The flames began to light up the stairs and hallway above. Still, no one stirred from their rooms. Perhaps they'd all just burn to death in their beds. It really didn't matter to the chief at this point. As long as they were eliminated, he would have little resistance.

PIPPENDALE WAS FINISHING up recording the reports of the platform sentries. It was still about three hours until daylight, and no one had seen any sign of the beast. In all fairness, at least three sentries had been asleep when he checked on them. Commander Burin was going to be furious. It was such a peaceful evening, it was hard to believe any creature would show up now. The only excitement they ever got at the fort was when Commander Burin wanted to make an example out of a soldier. Oh, how he seemed to enjoy every minute of it. Public whippings, public brandings, and dropping soldiers far offshore and making them swim back were a few of the favorites of his sadistic boss.

As the young messenger walked through the deserted street, there was only one building with any illumination currently. Through the cloths covering the window was a low red glow from the house of ill repute. Pippendale had heard stories about such places but had never been himself. He wondered if the commander would have them stay long enough for him to have a chance. He checked his pocket and found that he probably had coin enough for the total experience. What time had the commander expected him back? Before sunrise, he'd said. Perhaps the Mammoth Inn could wait just a little longer…

He walked up to the heavy, wooden door and found it locked. With more determination, he knocked harder. He heard someone walking to the door. The door opened slightly inward.

"What are you after so late, little man?" an elderly woman cackled. She was wrinkly and pale, with yellowed teeth and eyes glazed over with drink. In short, she physically embodied everything that witches were said to look like. The young man was almost unnerved.

"I've got coin," confessed Pippendale. "Are you still open?"

"The only one available right now is me, Private Moneybags. But don't worry, I'll give you a good price." She flashed the yellow teeth with some ivory missing and the door opened wide. Pippendale saw at least four soldiers' jackets on the coatrack. "My girls are already booked for the fortnight, in case you were looking for something a little younger. But don't rule out my experience."

Pippendale backed away from the door just in time. The old hag made a grab for his pants before he could get off the porch. Her claws ripped a piece of fabric off his trousers, but he didn't care. He ran for the Mammoth Inn as fast as his legs would take him.

When he got there, he knew something was wrong. The lone window for the great hall danced with light while all the bedroom windows were dark. Pippendale burst into the vast, open room to find natives eagerly watching the fire above. His eyes lit up with terror when the biggest one of them all, wearing bones as some type of apron, turned around and pointed him out to the others. He gave a harsh, restrained shout that Pippendale couldn't understand. At once, two of the natives ran after him! He slammed the door shut and ran for the one man in town who seemed to run everything. Grom.

Pippendale had very little physical appearance that would suggest he was a soldier. But, if there was one thing the small man could do better than anyone else in uniform, it was running with speed. He easily increased the gap between him and the warriors. When he reached the general store, he was not surprised to find the doors locked. It was wishful thinking on his part to try. He ran around the back and found the wooden stairway that led him up to Grom's living quarters. He knocked first, then, upon getting no answer, let himself inside, locking the door behind him.

He turned around to find a hairy, large, naked man holding something menacing above his head.

"Grom, stop! It's Pippendale! The town's under attack!"

Grom rubbed his eyes and lowered what appeared to be an iron. "I knew that beast would be back. Why are you telling me? Where are the soldiers?"

"They're trapped, sir. The natives have set the Mammoth on fire!"

"Natives! What?!" Grom pulled on his pants while his wife, still on her side in bed, began grumbling about the commotion he was making. "There's no time for subtlety, woman! Where's my war ax?"

She huffed angrily. "The same place it always is. Hanging on our wall like some ridiculous decoration."

Grom grabbed what must have been the ax from the far side of the room; then he opened a chest and pulled out something else. A shiny bugle.

They opened the door to find the two warriors below, panting heavily.

"Natives!" cried Grom. He raised the bugle to his lips and blew so hard, there was no doubt the entire town was now awake.

Chapter 40

HYTAN WAS TIRED of waiting. His two men hadn't returned yet. Fortunately, there'd been no noise thus far and the soldiers were still in their rooms. He was beginning to sense something was wrong with his plan. Someone should have been awake by now. The smoke was becoming so thick, he and his dearths had to evacuate the building and wait outside in the dark. He hated not knowing what was happening. If their presence was discovered now, they'd be exposed in the moonlight with little cover.

Just then he heard a high-pitched, piercing sound in the night air. It echoed through the village and was unlike anything the chief had ever heard before. There was no way anyone in earshot could still be asleep now. As the wind carried the drawn-out sound across the land, it carried Hytan's advantage away with it. He pulled his men under the overhang of the Mammoth Inn, against its wall.

Hytan heard the unmistakable sound of metal as six men stumbled out the door and into the street, coughing while trying to hold their weapons high in their hands. When they huddled together, like some type of trained fighting force, the Merkil leader realized it was past time to spring his number advantage on the men. He stepped out from the shadows.

The six fools didn't have the look of men who would surrender. Five surrounded a man in a large hat who seemed to be in charge. His words seemed angry as he snarled commands and his men obeyed, forming their defense.

Hytan approached the group openly, spear in hand as if not attacking. The men weren't fooled. In one quick motion, he raised the head of his spear and hurled it at the man in charge. Unfortunately, one of his men dove in front of him, his chest engulfing the deadly spear. He let out a scream, and the other men unexpectedly charged the larger group of natives.

It was close-quarters combat with knives, swords, spears, and fists. The swords were more effective against knives, but the few spears the natives had managed to swim with evened the field. Hytan grabbed an arm as its knife was thrust at him. He raised his knee into the attacker's chest. The soldier went down, and the chief buried his own knife in the back of the man's skull. His men were winning the numbers game, but the man in the large hat had already put down two of his warriors. Hytan couldn't afford to lose any more, so he stepped in front of the dearth about to engage the man.

The man had one of the large swords of the group and had hacked off arms of his first two victims before dealing the final blow. Hytan called for a spear, which a dearth immediately tossed to him. He gave a test thrust toward the man, which he easily knocked aside with that vile, long blade. The man showed none of the fear the other men displayed, betrayed by the terror in their eyes. His experience with the large weapon was obvious. The directional parlay with his blade to the spear wasted little, if any, of the man's energy.

Hytan pushed a harder jab. Again, the man stood his ground and easily batted it away. The followers of the man with the sword were getting cut up quickly by the dearths. It wouldn't be long before they were finished off at the current pace. Hytan took his time wearing down the man in the hat. A little showmanship would go a long way in building his men's respect.

The Merkil chief could feel the eyes of the town upon all of them now. They were weak, scared, watching from what they thought was a safe vantage point. Behind windows, cracked doors, and from dark alleys they lurked, hoping their soldiers could somehow fend off the dearths. They were waiting to become his slaves.

Then, in an instant, everything changed. A blinding explosion of light struck one of the dearths and he glowed like the sun. Immediately, a deafening roar knocked everyone from their feet. They stared in disbelief at the now burning man, crumpled lifeless on the ground. Hytan knew who was near.

"Take hostages!" he yelled to his men. "It's the Ghenzis!" He was terrified but not yet beaten. His men rushed to grab the commander from behind, along with his last two men. They were still in shock from the explosion. Overpowered, their weapons were ripped from their grasps while so many hands held their arms behind them as they were tied up.

"Regroup to the south!" yelled the Merkil leader. They wearily pushed the three prisoners along with them.

Chapter 41

THE REFLECTION OF the burning inn scorched in her eyes from her distant vantage point. That bright reflection might well have been a window into the rage that boiled within Jada upon her discovery. Without a word to anyone in their party, she bolted from their position straight into the town.

"Stop!" yelled Pike. He would have had more luck telling a fish not to swim. The wrathful woman kept her head down, running straight for her livelihood.

"Keep her alive!" Pike commanded Hellion. The man complied with a nod and started after her.

Pike knew there couldn't be many warriors in the Merkil force. One thing he'd promised himself this time was to not allow any escapees. His previous failure to finish them with one blow had caused this mess in the first place. He should have hunted them all down that very night. Hellion had been right.

He split his warriors into three units to surround the town against the sea. Commanding an army was mentally exhausting. Pike had deeply wanted to chase down Jada, his future wife, himself, but a chief couldn't desert his warriors. They needed one leader with one purpose. Should the Merkils see him with the spear, they would scatter like cockroaches in every direction, leaving little doubt some would escape. Patience was needed to tighten the noose around the town. He and his men needed to remain hidden until the right moment.

Swash bounded after Jada. The woman had no weapons, which, aside from being a brainless move, also made her faster than him. Did she honestly think the Merkils would stand by while she poured buckets of water onto her flaming inn? Was she going to tongue lash them so severely that they'd lay down their weapons and beg for mercy? What did she possibly believe she could accomplish other than getting herself killed?

He followed her past farmhouses, over and under fences, and down into the little town, which was beginning to glow in the light of the flames of her once glorious inn.

She finally stopped in the alley across from her inn to see actual soldiers fighting the Merkils. But their numbers were too few. Hellion put his hand on Jada's shoulder, if only to make sure she didn't dart into the street to join what looked like certain death for the soldiers.

In that moment of trying to catch both their breaths and figure out a plan, a bolt of lightning exploded on one of the Merkils. There was instantaneous chaos and commotion as everyone jumped away from the charred warrior now on the ground, unmoving. *Pike's learning quickly.*

The Merkil leader took little time to assess what had happened. He used the surprise to take three hostages. Hellion figured he was hoping for a snack if he made it out alive. It was doubtful he would.

"Stay here," growled Hellion. He had to take out the chief to save the soldiers. As he ran into the street for a shot with his bow, two dozen soldiers converged on the Merkils, seemingly out of nowhere. Hellion knew the chief would never surrender. He took the moment of surprise to aim his arrow through the crowd and right at the chief's chest.

The arrow flew. The big chief stepped right, closer to his prisoner.

Impact was made left of center. Hytan screamed and fell to a knee. The rest of his men looked like they'd seen a ghost. The soldiers closed in. The warriors looked ready to fight to the last man. Then, a second bolt of lightning struck down another dearth. The man was cut in half, his scream like a whisper after the violently loud rumble from the earth. The dearths laid down their weapons while the soldiers stared before them in disbelief.

Jada came running out to Hellion, who walked toward the surrounded natives. Out of their center walked the unharmed three captured soldiers. The largest of the three, wearing a large plumed hat, walked straight toward Swash.

"That was a hell of a shot, young man," said Commander Burin. As he approached Hellion, he extended his hand to thank and congratulate him until their eyes locked upon one another in the opening rays of the morning sun.

He jerked his hand back as if he'd touched a flame. "You! Ferly, Theo, grab him!" The two men responded to the man's words like the sting of a whip.

"Just a minute!" yelled Jada. "He just helped save your lives!" What do you think you're doing?"

Commander Burin straightened his hat and walked past a restrained Hellion toward Jada. "That arrow was probably meant for me," he said calmly, stopping with his face inches from her own. "This man is a known deserter and worse. Everywhere I've chased this man, I've found nothing remaining but a pile of bodies. This coward is none other than the notorious Hellion Swash! Arrest him!"

"How dare you!" scoffed Jada. She was so quick with her slap the commander didn't have time to block the blow to his wide-eyed face. His men stood in awe of the woman. Not a word was said for a moment.

The captain was not about to lose face. Not in front of his men and not in front of all the villagers now witnessing her open defiance. He backhanded her, and she crumpled to the ground.

"As I was saying," he barked, "arrest this man and put him in jail!

The lass also. She might be an accomplice but in the very least needs to learn a lesson in respect. I'm thinking public whipping."

Jada started laughing hysterically from the ground. "You really think you're in control right now? Did you see what just happened to that cooked native still smoking on the ground? My husband will enjoy burning you where you stand, you piece of donkey excrement. Take a look around you!"

Commander Burin and his men lifted their eyes to see an entire army of natives now surrounding the town.

"It's a trap!" he yelled. "Grab the prisoners! Retreat to the ship!"

The soldiers began pushing the natives, Jada, and Hellion toward the dock. The commander instinctively ran ahead to the shore and began slicing through the ropes of every boat but his own. There were a few hundred warriors now ascending upon the town with war whoops and screams, terrifying the soldiers as they began to break formation and run for the boats. The retreat was on.

There were only the commander's two rowboats left at the dock to haul the soldiers back out to the ship. Each boat could only carry six men. It was clear not everyone would be escaping. Commander Burin threw Jada into his boat despite her protests. Next came the wounded and hand-bound chief. Two soldiers hopped in with Hellion, and the first boat shoved off. The remainder of the men, upon seeing the circumstances, released their prisoners and jumped at once for the remaining boat. Seven fought off the others and paddled away from the dock, narrowly avoiding complete submersion. As luck would have it, the morning winds were calm and the two boats rowed with haste toward the anchored ship.

Chapter 42

WHEN THE GHENZI army tightened its collective noose around the city, both the remaining warriors and soldiers laid down their arms.

"Where are Hellion and Jada?" demanded Pike. None of his warriors could answer. "I SAID, WHERE ARE THEY!" he yelled, slamming his spear into the ground. What remained of the Mammoth Inn collapsed into itself with the deafening roar he created.

A runt-sized soldier stepped forward. "The commander took the man and woman as hostages, sir," the scared soldier stammered.

Pike looked out toward the enormous lake. The large ship was already on her way east. Granger mentally reached and found his melody. He grabbed onto it and felt the energy build. The hair on the back of his neck stood on end, and he could feel the potential in the air as the winds began to blow, the waves began to rock, and the sky rumbled lowly. No one said a word as warriors, soldiers, and townspeople alike watched in wonder at what was happening. He saw the boat rocked violently by a stray wave and heard the collective gasp as the townspeople around him saw the boat partially submerged. Pike instantly let go. The sound died back down to a whisper in his head.

He couldn't control it. Oh, how letting go tortured him! Power without precision would kill everyone on that ship. His friends would either sail east or be drowned by his own hand. The wind and thunder hushed to normal. Everyone let out a collective breath of relief as the boat recovered from the sudden onslaught of waves. He stared out, defeated, realizing his powers were useless.

When he lifted his eyes again, they fixed on the little soldier who had broken the news to him.

"What's your name, little man?"

"I'm Pippendale, sir. I'm the personal messenger for Commander Burin."

"Is that so?" asked Pike with anger replacing despair. "Where is the commander heading?"

Pippendale wanted to bite his tongue. He'd just seen this man wield a power that none in the world could match. How could he not tell this man the truth? "My guess is east to Sisterton for both the native chief and the deserter's trials."

So the commander had managed to capture Hytan as well. "I wouldn't call my friend a deserter, little man." He paused as Pippendale glanced downward. "What's the penalty for such an accusation?"

Again, Pippendale looked downward. "If proven, death by hanging, sir."

Pike dropped to a knee. The sound in his head grew so loud he had to set the spear on the ground. He raised his hands to his head for support. The sound stayed briefly before slowly dying away to the familiar hum. The light background noise seemed to stay with him longer than before. When he laid his head upon his pillow at night, he could still feel the energy within reach, even without the spear. He'd told no one this.

His friends were beyond his reach. He recalled the warning of Horton Conner that he'd already broken. He'd never intended to mix the two worlds, but Hytan had forced his hand. It no longer mattered, because what would come next could not be stopped. What was a man's worth if he deserted those he cared for? The commander had brought this on himself; no, the world had brought this on itself.

"We will march east," he finally said.

Chapter 43

"Fortune has finally seen fit to smile upon me, dear Hellion," bragged Commander Burin as he stared toward the empty horizon. Within days that horizon would give way to civilization and sweet justice for the menace known as Hellion Swash. "Because of you I was banished to this puddle in the middle of nowhere. It was you that kept me away from the glory that awaits me on the battlefields across the ocean. Finally, I'm returning to Sisterton victorious. On this very ship I now have in my control the most deadly, most dangerous, most wanted, vile, villainous traitor known in perhaps the history of men. Add to that a local dangerous native, and I think I've had quite a day. Tell me, what smart quip do you have to answer for that?"

"I'd say you're omitting me in your description of yourself and the savage. No hard feelings on the matter, of course. I'm just a small fish in this ordeal," replied Swash, while cracking a cocky smile.

"I hope you laugh walking to the gallows. I assure you, the trial will be very swift once we reach Sisterton."

"I'm not too worried about that, dear foolish commander," rebutted Hellion. "A man much more dangerous than I will be coming for you soon. You saw just a whisper of his strength before you fled his town like the insect you are. You should have counted yourself lucky to be safe and unknown, protected on your anthill of a fortress. As a matter of fact, if I were you, I'd anchor this boat and drop us all off on the nearest shore. It's likely the only way you'll survive."

Commander Burin's face glowed red with anger. "Your stories don't scare me, deserter. You've always dealt in lies and shadows. Was the treasure you promised to the soldier who stabbed you in the back ever real? I know it's certainly not where he thought it was. Why else do you think he reported it to me? When he tried to steal it all for himself, he must have realized he'd been double-crossed. Perhaps you moved it. When I get promoted off of Fort Tuttle, I'll comb over every inch of that island until I find it. With a discovery like that, I'd be even more famous than you. Deny it all you want. Keep up with your desperate lies about make-believe friends and special powers. We'll just see what happens to you in the bright light of justice."

"If you don't believe it was he who burned those hostiles like roasted corncobs, perhaps you should question the savage. Better yet, question the girl you took with me. I certainly hope for your sake that you're treating her better than me. You do realize you have me handcuffed, legs bound, and shackled to the wall, all while being inside a locked cell. That's the definition of overkill. You, sir, are redundant."

"Tell me," asked Burin with malice in his voice. "Do you care for the girl? Perhaps I'll remove her from her cell and keep her in my personal chambers for the remainder of the voyage. Do you think she's my type?" He was studying Swash's expression for a hint of weakness at her mention. "Listen well, criminal. Your friend and anyone else that has aided you will swing in the gallows soon enough. Oh yes, we will return to Mossport with more men after your trial has been dealt with."

"I have a bold prediction," replied Hellion soberly. "I wager my friend will meet you in Sisterton as soon as we arrive."

The commander laughed at this. "With no boat? If he tries it, he's as good as written his own death warrant. The desert will claim him if he tries his way south. The rock cliffs along the shore would take a lifetime to travel if it could even be done. And my men will be waiting at Fort Tuttle should he ever make it that far."

Hellion shrugged his shoulders. "You've been warned, Commander. You allowed the savages to burn his town, rowed off like a thief to your ship with his wife, and now you threaten me, his closest ally, with death. This man will repay those debts sevenfold. I almost feel bad for you, even if you do have that stupid grin on your face."

The commander backhanded Swash hard. His whole body thudded against the wall.

"My goodness, that felt good, Private Swash. Perhaps I'll have to make a routine of this." He kicked Hellion in the chin and his head banged against the cracked pine wall. Blood crept from the corner of his mouth. "I don't deal kindly with threats, even if you are desperate to save your pathetic pestilence of a life. Sleep well, Hellion."

He exited the cell and locked the door behind him. "Sargent! See to it that this door is guarded at all times, day or night."

"Sir, he looks unconscious."

"I don't care if he's dead inside there. You do not leave this post for anything!"

"Yes, Commander Burin."

The commander strolled back onto the deck above. It felt good to be in control again.

"Private Ferly!" he roared.

"Commander?"

"Is the savage secure?"

"Yes, sir. He's hog-tied under the deck. We have the girl down there as well."

"I'd like her brought to my cabin."

"Sir, she's already bitten one of the men."

"Then restrain her for me. And put a gag in her mouth. If she breaks my skin, I'll have her pretty teeth out. See to it that she understands."

The young man charged off to follow his orders. All these men who surrounded him were weak. Few had seen a real battle, as most had been stationed on this lake their whole careers. The only other killer besides himself on this boat was Hellion, and he had him more than accounted for this time. Oh, how he wished he could deliver his sentence right now on the boat and be done with it. But it just wouldn't do. He needed to follow the book to get back in good graces and get the advancement he so desired. Vengeance was only part of the equation. Perhaps the biggest part was destiny. Or perhaps the two were equal. The public humiliation of hanging and gasping for breath and struggling for life in vain while the certainty of death lay at the end of a simple rope was poetic justice. It was pure elegance in a barbarian ritual. He almost convulsed with excitement at the anticipation of what lay ahead.

Chapter 44

KHAWNA STEWED ANGRILY in her private heated bath as her attendant washed the dust off her beautiful tanned skin. Her husband should have been in the bath with her, enjoying the privileges of the new status he had attained. It was not so, for her groom had decided to run back to his own people just moments before their ceremony was complete. True, he had good reason to go, but that didn't make it any easier to accept. It was humiliating that Jada, his other wife, had been allowed to accompany him. Khawna knew she would never care for the pale woman as a friend, but still, there couldn't be a worse start for the arrangement that they would have to live with. Since Pike had left her in charge during his absence, she didn't feel the least bit guilty sending a scout to follow her soon-to-be husband's whereabouts and report back to her.

For the time being, she had to lead her own people. These same people who had once held her own fate and chose to send her to be eaten now relied upon her. She supposed it wasn't all bad, being in charge, that is. Khawna did enjoy some aspects of being the acting chief. She was not at all reserved about directing her people to what needed to be done. Indeed, the sheep that they were and had long been could scarcely survive without someone like her in charge. Deep down she knew it was the main reason she had to be left behind, but she didn't have to like it.

Dressing and acting the part of the chief's wife was as necessary as it was practical. That was perhaps the only thing she had learned from her predecessor. She had sent for the weavers with the softest, finest material. As Khawna rose from the bath and droplets of water beaded on her body, her attendant covered her with a towel and proceeded to pat her legs dry as the girl kneeled on a wicker mat. Before she was to be dressed, the measurer came with a tape and took measurements from her waist to her chest and to her arms and legs. The girl's arms trembled at the honor of doing the measuring. Khawna wanted to smile at the girl with pity, but believed it was better to remain without emotion. The girl was not her friend, just a servant hired for an important task. Kindness was too likely to be mistaken for weakness.

If there was one aspect about her new life that the chief's wife would defend ruthlessly, it was her husband's post and image. Her job was to fight like a lion for his honor, and yet do as he requested at the same time. He had earned that honor, first by saving her life and second by holding the sacred spear. However, he needed her help more than he knew.

The measurements were completed, and her attendant massaged her skin with oil from head to toe. Her entire naked body now gleamed in the mirror, and she felt very powerful indeed. She was then dressed in white robes, which gave her pause at the impracticality of keeping clean, and yet she also knew that she would be carried on the platform if she needed to leave her fortress of a home.

With her fresh gown flowing behind her, Khawna walked to her balcony to watch over the village. How long until her messenger would return? It had, after all, been three days since she'd sent the man.

She heard a grunt behind her and spun around in surprise to see the Tarmigan.

"May I speak with the chief's wife?" the reptilian man asked in his raspy voice.

"I suspect I have little choice now, but yes, Tarmigan. Why don't you start by telling me where you've been?"

The reptile snorted. "I merely go where you cannot. I may be bound to this land, but I am not bound to the present world. I see things. Some have come to pass, and some things are still to come. I seek you now because I fear Pike is off course."

"He is lost in his own land?" she asked, surprised.

"Not in a directional sense. He has a clear destiny. He alone was able to obtain the spear for a reason. His job is to save our world, to restore balance, and to unite all songs into one."

"Yes, Tarmigan, I know he was able to hold the spear for a purpose, and I know of the cycle of song. This is why he is chief. What's happened?"

"You do not know the meaning of the cycle of song." He hesitated after saying it, then the giant reptilian man edged closer and stooped lower to the ground to conceal his words. "His judgement is clouded. He is not ready to do what he's started. He needs more time and your help. This is a man powerful enough to remake the world, yet he also holds the power to destroy it. It nearly happened before."

"You knew this risk before you took him away from me?" Her eyes narrowed on the monster that would frighten even the bravest man. "Tell me what happened before."

The Tarmigan took a step back. "I've said too much." The beast rose to its full height. "His heart is pulled in different directions. It could become torn apart. Heed my words…you cannot let this happen. He is traveling now to a place you've never imagined."

"Will he come back?"

"I cannot say. The way is clouded. If you don't go, it is not likely. But it's not just his return that should worry us, as I've said."

Khawna nodded. "I will go to him."

"He is far ahead of you. You must go swiftly. You must also make sure your people are taken care of while you're gone."

She eyed the beast-man quizzically. "Can you lead them in my absence?"

"No more than a shadow can harvest a plentiful bounty."

She bit her lip as she thought about what to do. She was afraid for her people and yet even more afraid for Pike. She lifted her eyes to the distance beyond the village and saw clouds part to illuminate her tribe's returning warriors. She sucked in air with surprise.

"He sent the majority of his force back to protect you, although you no longer need fear the Merkils."

"So he won the battle."

"He did. But the other two pieces of his song are in peril, and he goes to them now."

"Tell me, how can I protect him more than the spear?"

"The spear protects its owner no better than a pebble lying on the ground. The pebble can be slung and bring down the mightiest warrior, but it must be used correctly."

"I will guide his hand and his head as need be." She thought carefully before choosing her next words. "It's sad to me that a creature like you can live forever but can't intervene in our struggle. I wonder whether this weakness frustrates or comforts you."

Without waiting for a response, she set off on foot to meet her returning warriors, white robes and all. Whomever Pike had selected to lead them would surely be able to fulfill her duties to her people.

Chapter 45

COMMANDER BURIN HEARD a struggle that preceded the wild-tempered woman being thrust through his door with hands tied behind her back. She staggered a few steps forward before collapsing on the floor. Though her eyes were veiled by strands of her now untamed hair, she raised her gaze to the object of her present detestation.

The commander raised his eyes from her to his guard and nodded. "I'll send for you if any…assistance is needed tonight. I think she'll be much more comfortable with me this evening. For the time being, give us a little privacy." He smiled darkly.

"Shall I stand guard outside your door, sir?"

"Won't be necessary. See to it that the rest of the men are taking care of their duties." The door closed, leaving the commander alone with the cold-eyed woman. She rose to her feet slowly and stood proud and defiant with her head up and chest out.

"You have better posture than half my men, Miss…I'm sorry, what was your name?"

"Jada," she said, staring straight through him.

"Such a pretty name. Very fitting. We don't see many pretty girls out here very often, you know."

She gave no response to acknowledge his comment.

Burin sighed. "I suppose you can't have it all. While you are pretty, you definitely have no manners. A simple thank-you would suffice. Still nothing? I've been told you bit some of my men…is this true?"

She couldn't hold back the smile before returning to her stoic glazed expression. The commander started smiling as well, in a creepy manner. He began circling her slowly as he spoke. "You and I are going to have some fun tonight, Jada. Do you really intend to keep glaring like that all night?" He placed a rough hand on her shoulder and squeezed to give her a feel of his power. "This doesn't have to be unenjoyable for you, you know. It really makes no difference to me whether you're willing or not. I've been stationed on a rock with hundreds of men and not one woman for the last year. Your friend downstairs is the reason why I'm here…but we'll get more into that later."

He violently ripped the back of her blouse to expose her back. "I should warn you, now is your only chance to talk. Soon enough I'll shove your own clothes in your mouth and tie them in place." He could feel her start to quiver from the touch of his hand. "Now's a good time to make a deal…or at least give me some information that I might find useful. Of course, you could continue to keep your jaw locked and endure what's coming. But I should warn you, if you do that, I can guarantee you'll end up at the end of a rope with Private Swash."

Jada couldn't hold it in anymore. "You have no idea who I am. Do you think I'm going to wilt and cry? I've been with men far worse than you in my past, and do you know what happened to them?"

She could tell he was intrigued. "Now is the time to ask before it's too late, Commander."

He pulled a chair from his desk and sat down, swinging one leg over the other and placing his hands on his knee. "Of course," he replied. "Please continue your story."

"They're all dead. Soon you will be too."

He chuckled and crossed his arms. "You know I find your hatred almost intoxicating, Jada. Tell me, were you a whore in your past life?"

She smiled. "Just let me know if you have any symptoms in a day or two. And don't say I didn't warn you."

"I've fornicated with every woman that ever peddled her tricks in these parts, my dear. I think you'll be the one finding some discomfort after our little dance tonight…that is, if you live long enough."

"The only thing I know for sure is that you won't." She spit in the commander's face.

He rose quickly to backhand her, and she fell to a knee. He grabbed her under the chin and shoved a wool rag in her mouth. "Your time for groveling is over." He smacked her again in the face. The rage in her eyes would have given him pause if her hands weren't tied securely behind her back.

He spun her around and continued the rip down her back until her clothes just hung on her. She lowered her chin to keep her top from tumbling to the floor. "I hope this brings back good memories," he shouted and shoved her onto the floor.

Just then, there was a pounding at the door.

"What could it possibly be?!" he shouted.

"The native, sir. It appears he jumped overboard."

"What?!" he shouted, buckling his pants back up. He ran to the door shirtless to find his guard wide-eyed in surprise.

"Wipe the astonishment off your face. The girl is a whore, after all. Is the native dead? Who let him out?"

"No one, sir. He chewed through his restraints. I dispatched a rowboat to search, but he's probably already drowned."

"That man was a war criminal against our outpost! Do you realize what you've cost me? I want every rowboat we have dispatched with a lantern! Bring me that savage dead or alive! I need proof for our losses we've sustained. Get me my coat and get that two-bit whore out of my cabin! I ought to have her flogged for distracting me!"

Chapter 46

DESPITE THE PAIN, it felt invigorating to be free. Hytan was embarrassed the soldiers had captured him so easily in the first place. Once again, the man with the spear had ruined everything. Had he not showed up, the chief's warriors would have cut down every soldier in the city. They were not warriors. More like animals in uniforms, animals that needed to be slaughtered. It was unfortunate that revenge wasn't in his cards tonight. Survival, however, was.

Hytan floated on his back, staring at the stars above. The current was taking him south. He knew better than to fight it. He needed to save his strength for daylight. The fools from the ship had boats all about in the night with lanterns ablaze to warn him of their approach. None even came close, and it amused him to watch them fruitlessly search from a safe distance. The fools should have known better than to tie him up with rope. He spit out some remaining fragments of twine and smiled, knowing he was the most dangerous man in the world, save the man with the spear. That would change someday. He would have the spear for himself.

A new thought came to his mind as he floated. If the rest of the people from beyond the wall were as weak and careless as his captors, who could challenge him and his dearths from enslaving them all? He'd always held great ambitions, and even though he was wounded and alone, he couldn't help but dream of a bright future in this new land.

Morning came, and to Hytan's delight, he saw land. His fingers were pruned and he was both exhausted and freezing, but in a few hours' time, the current would deliver him to solid ground. With any luck he'd be able to make a warm fire and have time to plot his next move.

When the chief did reach shore, he realized his struggle wasn't over. High cliffs surrounded the lake as far as he could see. It took nearly every ounce of strength he had left to pull himself out of the water. He found a ledge above the water and had to settle for a stone warmed by the sun instead of a warm fire. He had pushed himself too far to risk climbing any higher at the moment. His stomach yearned for food, but he knew he would have to rest without any nourishment for now. He'd certainly already drunk plenty of water during his overnight float. The only choice now was to rest his muscles and try the climb later that day. Although, with the fatigue he was feeling, it was more likely to be an endeavor for the next day.

GROM SURVEYED THE remainder of his town. The Mammoth Inn was half burned to the ground and its owner had been kidnapped. His own store had been raided at some point in the night. He still wasn't sure who the guilty party was, but they had taken whatever they pleased before disappearing in the night amongst the confusion. The boats had all been cut by the commander before his retreat, and many had sunk while a few had eventually washed back to shore in poor condition. Everywhere around him were death and destruction. Yet with no one else volunteering to take charge, it was up to him and his council to oversee the rebuilding.

The Merkil warriors had been rounded up by Pike's own natives and marched back north. The one advantage Grom did have as the temporary authority of the town was the jurisdiction to put Commander Burin's soldiers to work on repairs.

"A fair day's work will keep you fed and comfortable until they send a ship for you boys," he'd told them. They still stared about in wonder at how their superior had left them to the mercy of the Ghenzis without hesitation. All in all, they listened to Grom as well as could be expected while without a commanding officer.

There was no shortage of work to be done. They needed a large amount of lumber to rebuild the town, which meant many trips to the western woods. The whole town, in time, banded together like never before to help their neighbors get back on their feet. Food was shared, and every spare room in the town and outskirts was used to house those in need. It was a compassionate gesture of grand scale, and Grom couldn't be prouder of his little town. Everyone who had lived more than a season in Mossport knew their lives depended on unparalleled cooperation to rebuild before winter.

After a few days of the new normal for town life, a beautiful native girl arrived in town with a guard of warriors. She was delivered to Grom immediately upon her arrival. Grom noted her elegant clothing and keen eye. She was definitely here on business.

He spoke loudly and slowly to her. "I...hear...you're...some type...of native princess."

She put a hand on his shoulder kindly. "Please don't speak like that. I know of your language."

Grom was taken aback by how well she spoke. "My apologies, princess. We've had many...savage...err...visitors about lately, and not all seem to know the language."

"You are kind. My husband-to-be is our chief. Perhaps you know him? His men brought word of what happened back to our village."

He looked her up and down in amazement. "If you're talking about Pike, you might say I do. I was the one who sent him to find the beast, after all."

She smiled. "Then I should thank you far more than you can know. Are you the chief of this village?"

Grom scratched his head. "We don't have chiefs here, but I suppose that would be a comparable term fer the time being."

"Good. I need you to tell me where he has gone."

Now old Grom turned redder than an oak leaf in the fall. He was still trying to get over the fact that Jada and Pike were said to be together. Did this woman know about the other one he was chasing after? "Pike was hardly here long enough to give tale about your beauty, princess. I can see now that words would never have done you justice." Flattery was his only defense when put in a rough situation. It was a skill learned quickly in the arena of politics in the big cities, and Grom was well versed in knowing when to play the card.

"I will soon be his native wife. He will take a wife among your people as well."

Grom breathed a sigh of relief before realizing what he had just heard. Did the man have a death wish? Two wives Pike had come back with! Could there be a worse idea in the history of man?

"I'm sure you heard as much as I know. He took half of his men and headed after Jada and Lion. I also recall him saying something about the Merkil chief being captured with those two. Boats were all cut loose, so he went south around the lake, which typically is a death sentence, although I'll not put any money against him after what I've witnessed the man do."

"He is in danger. He needs my help."

Grom rubbed his beard. "Are you here alone, or did you bring another army with you?"

"Just my guards with me now, but I'll travel alone from here quicker. It's my counsel he needs."

"Oh, I see," said Grom. *Bet he could use a little more than just counsel where he's at.* "You really shouldn't go into the southlands at all. To go alone is a death sentence. They literally charge people in Sisterton with crimes and send them walking this way as punishment. It's a way of execution. Not a one of 'em ever showed up here before."

"I appreciate your concern. What can you tell me about where he is headed?"

"He believed the ship was headed back to the coastal city of Sisterton. Even if you did make it, alone in the desert, the city's a dangerous enough place fer a woman on her own."

"How many warriors are there?"

"There are soldiers aplenty there. Of course, at any given time it depends how many are dispatched across the ocean. The buildings are much taller than anything we have out here, and it's so overcrowded, it's easy to get lost. There's bad people about too, princess. They'd try to take advantage of you first thing."

Khawna patted her hip and produced a sharp knife and a grin. "These things you speak of do not scare me."

"Well, that's good, I guess. I really don't think Pike would approve of me letting you head out alone like you seem to be intending."

Khawna scowled. "I need no approval. I am in charge because he left. If he is angry at my decision, he should be angry at himself for putting me in charge." She sheathed her blade.

"I see," said Grom, with his eye on her blade hand. "I'm not sure he'd see it that way, but I'm not fixing to get between you and that knife."

Khawna smiled. "I like you, Grom. You are a wise man."

Grom laughed. "Har! That's a new one. Wish my wife heard you say that. Is there anything I can get you fer your journey? Pike is a dear friend of mine, which puts you in the same category."

"Thank you, friend Grom. Some extra food and drink for my journey would not be forgotten."

"You shall have it. And if you insist on going on your own, I've got something else for you."

"What is it?"

"Have you ever ridden a horse?"

Chapter 47

THE FOURTH DAY of the desert march had brought the frustration level to a new high for Pike and his warriors. There was no fresh water to be found anywhere. Three men had been bitten by vipers, and if the first two were any indication, the third man would be dead within hours. Pike had always heard that the south lands were cursed, and now he knew why. Nothing grew here. Nothing seemed to survive here unless it slithered or flew. The little food they had brought with them would run out soon, which left a hollow realization in the eyes of all of Pike's men. Perhaps Grom had been right. No one could ever survive this land.

The mountain cut off any chance of traveling north toward the Mammoth. It wasn't as high as the Greater Mortapenums, but it was surely as steep. To go further south would lead further into the heart of the wasteland they were currently enduring. Finally, to head back to Mossport was to give up on Jada and Hellion. They had no choice but to go east now.

Granger had twice made the skies open up with rain, but it turned into a dense fog by the time it reached the ground. The heat was too much, and the soil would not hold the water that did reach the ground. Morale was low, and he knew he had to do something. His men trusted him and believed in the power of the spear above everything else. But how could he use his power to overcome this land? He wouldn't do anyone justice if he killed his army on their march.

Pike could feel the weariness mounting in his warriors as they dutifully followed him. Finally, it became too much for him to stomach anymore. He called his newly appointed second in command, Foxskin. He was a man the others seemed to look up to. His confidence in Pike helped invigorate the others. The new chief needed such a man, especially now that he was beginning to doubt himself. "Have the men rest. I need to perform a sign."

The man with a red hide over his shoulders needed no further explanation. He ran excitedly to spread the news to the others. The men gathered on a dune of sand, staring down at Pike and a valley of nothing that waited to greet them. They seated themselves on any clothes and rugs they could find or make from their battered supplies and reclined during what they believed to be another speech or another attempt at rainfall. Despite their low morale, the group still believed wholeheartedly in their leader. They also had come to believe in the wickedness of the land they were in.

"Friends," Pike began while studying his men's expressions carefully, "I have led us to a part of the world no man has ever traveled. You followed me bravely, and for that I commend you. I believed I could help us overcome the stories of how vile this land was. We have endured just four days, and it feels already like an eternity in damnation. I believed that because our cause was just, the land would let us pass. But now I realize I was wrong."

There was murmuring amongst the warriors. "We can pass it!" yelled Foxskin angrily. "Our legs still work! We are not afraid if death waits in the valley below! We will follow you, Nytel!"

The outburst was received with a thunderous rumble of agreement from the men. Their confidence was shaken, but they still believed. Hardship was to be expected in any endeavor of greatness. Their chief had a destiny, and it was their duty to make sure he succeeded.

Pike allowed the men to settle back down, and again they looked to him for guidance. "Part of being a chief is acknowledging when you are wrong. The other part is fixing your mistakes. This land may very well kill us all in its present state. That is why I have no choice but to change it. You've seen what this land does to rain, but now I must dig deeper. I must strike harder. Now is the time to awaken from this world of nightmares!" He raised the great spear above his head for effect. "I will break this land before it breaks my people!"

The warriors quickly rose to their feet, cheering and yelling and throwing sand into the wind that was beginning to build.

"We cannot kill what is already dead, but with the spear, I will bring this land back to life!" Pike Granger yelled at the top of his lungs. The intertwining melodies danced in his head, and he searched for the one he could control. His cries matched the ebb and flow of the frequency and seemingly magnified each other, both in his head and in his vocals as he watched his men cover their ears in pain. At the peak of the flow of the energy, he mentally grabbed onto the power source as he had before. It was so strong he struggled to direct it for a moment. It took all his strength with both arms to take the spear that was above his head and pull it back down to slam it into the earth at his feet. As he did, the ground beneath them buckled, and the men's faces turned from cheer to fear at the deafening sound of snapping rock. The valley below them grew a crack that stretched north and south. The earth groaned and the winds suddenly stopped, almost in astonishment, as the mountain due north split in two before the men's eyes! The sound that followed was different. It was foreign to this land of death as it grew while it sped south.

The froth and awesome power of a river of water raced past them, filling the valley with fresh water and extending further south into the desolation.

"This land will live again!" yelled Pike, releasing the sound in his mind. He had seen much in the moments he had held onto it. "It has been dead for too long! Likewise, the civilized world must be reborn upon our arrival as well. Nothing can remain the same! Now go and drink from the Mammoth River! Tonight we will eat fresh fish and renew our strength! The world awaits us!"

All recovered their feet and cheered as they ran eagerly toward the new river below. When they raised their eyes from the precious water toward the lesser Mortapenums, they could now see all the way through to Mammoth Lake.

Chapter 48

HELLION'S HEAD THROBBED. The dark, stale air in the bowels of the ship gave no hint of how long he'd been unconscious. The latest beating he'd received from Commander Burin was unprovoked. He had held his tongue this time at the man's taunting, and for what? The sooner he knifed the sadistic bastard, the better. He pictured it vividly whenever he looked into the man's eyes. Swash thought the last beating had been more out of frustration than due to his previous digs at the man. It was almost as if something had not gone his way. The thought of him upset was one of the few things presently that could bring a smile to the outlaw's face.

His chance to kill the man would come. Death had a habit of following Hellion. It danced with him often but always found another partner to take home before the song ended. He knew he'd made a mistake not killing Burin the night he'd escaped from the army. He'd been hasty and left one too many strings dangling. He'd reached the point now where he didn't even care if he swung in the gallows…as long as he got Burin first.

Hellion's nutritional intake consisted of room-temperature broth. There was one occasion on which the chef must have mistakenly left a sliver of potato skin in his bowl. The bite brought bliss for a brief second and then agony at the prospect of not getting any more.

To date, he'd heard no updates involving the other prisoners on board. He could only hope Jada was still okay, but he wouldn't put anything past Burin. The poor girl, though quick to lash out savagely with her tongue, was the only innocent person on this ship. He himself, Hytan, and Burin were all killers deserving of the blade or rope that would end them someday. If only the girl knew when to keep her mouth shut. It was no wonder she'd never settled down. The more she crept into his thoughts, the more he worried about her. Even Swash had to admit the girl was easy on the eyes. In some ways, Pike was a lucky man. But on the other hand, she was always pushing, always aggravating, always arguing with those narrowed eyes and pursed lips. All that baggage would be wearisome for Pike. As far as dealing with Commander Burin, her antics would not go over well at all. Swash was just as guilty as she was at times with running his mouth, but at least he could back up his boasts. If he could get untied right now, oh how he'd back up every boast. Until that time came, he had to wait for someone to slip up or for Granger to arrive.

When the ship reached the port of Sisterton, he'd be regarded as a dangerous villain. Swash knew they wouldn't wait long to hang him. Perhaps he deserved it. After all, who had killed more men, Burin or he? At least he'd always had the decency to kill a man himself. The commander had others do his bidding. Of course, that little fact was probably the reason Swash was still alive today. Or perhaps it was the only reason Burin was.

It wasn't easy to live with at first, taking someone's life. Watching the fright in his enemy's eyes and then the realization that death was taking their hand was dark business. But that was how he'd come to think of it. Just business. Some men turned coward after their first kill, and Hellion understood why. Like anything else in life, the more the bodies piled up for him, the less he thought about it. The surprised look on his enemies' faces barely registered a response in him anymore. If anything, it had made him laugh on occasion. It was pretty sickening when he thought about it. The other soldiers had thought him a madman for laughing during battle. Perhaps they were right.

He hadn't always been a two-legged killing machine, but he had always been a survivor. If that endpoint meant a few other heads had to roll, he'd dispatch them on their journey. Up to this point, he'd always come out on top in the end. There was something dangerously different about this time that bothered him deep down. This time he actually had a friend. For whatever reason, Pike considered him as such, against his own wishes. Having vulnerability like that could prove deadly in battle, for either him or Pike. He didn't want to care, but the truth was, he did. While combat was supposed to be about fighting as a unit, worrying about other men could get you killed. Therefore, Hellion was always selfish during battle.

Indeed, many soldiers who fought alongside Hellion had fallen either before he could deliver the death blow to their enemy or before he could retreat to more favorable ground. Now he also had Jada to worry about while likely counting on Pike to save him. The irony pissed him off. If he and Granger switched places, it was likely he'd be a goner.

Yet Pike was a different kind of man, and he did possess power beyond most people's imagination. Hellion wasn't sure if he admired or pitied the man for his honesty. Who else would have befriended a miserable, mangy cutthroat like himself? He owed it to Pike to help Jada as well. Of course, if she didn't make it, he'd probably be doing Granger a favor. He still thought two wives, especially with Jada as one, was the most ill-conceived idea in the history of man. He rolled his eyes, smiling. Pike wouldn't find it at all funny, even if it was a joke. Friend or not, the truth was the two-wife course would likely be Pike's undoing, that is, if befriending Hellion didn't kill him first.

PIKE HAD NO way to know for sure, but he guessed the newly formed Mammoth River had been the halfway point to Sisterton. He hoped that put them just a few days behind Hellion and Jada. Things had changed in a short amount of time, and it wasn't just the confidence of his men. There hadn't been any more snakebites or even serpent sightings. More birds were seen above them, as a result of either the newly formed river or the approaching end to the desert. Perhaps he'd imagined it, but the air itself didn't feel quite as blistering as it had days before. It was also comforting to know they'd stocked up on plenty of freshwater. The men moved faster too, sensing something big was going to happen in contrast to a slow death, being ravaged by heat and dehydration.

Pike looked proudly behind him as his warriors marched fearlessly. When he turned back around, he saw Foxskin on the horizon. He sent the man ahead periodically to scout the land, although there wasn't much change most of the time. Generally there were just sandy dunes broken up with the occasional rock. Foxskin was waving his hands and jumping up and down excitedly. They couldn't have come to the edge of the desert yet, thought Granger.

By the time Pike and his men reached him, they beheld with their own eyes what the excitement was about. A man's head protruded from the sand. A gigantic, worn, stone head.

The warriors murmured amongst themselves at its conspicuous location. Nothing but flat sand surrounded them.

"This looks ancient," observed Pike to no one in particular. "Everyone stand back. There's no time to dig this out by hand. This could be lost under the sand for another hundred years if we wait for our return." *If we ever do return.*

The tone rang in his head clearly from the moment he laid eyes on the head. With little effort he harnessed the power while raising the spear into the air. The wind picked up, causing his warriors to cover their faces, save a slight crevice to witness the power that their Nytel now wielded. The wind came from the south and the north and grew in intensity, swirling Pike's long hair. All eyes rose to the skies where the clouds slowly started to circle.

"Evil cloud!" yelled one warrior in fear.

"No!" yelled Granger through gritted teeth. "Power and evil are not the same! I have it controlled! Behold!" The winds grew in ferocity while the clouds swirled more quickly and began to lower toward the ground. The monstrosity sounded like an angry beast, descending from the clouds to devour them all. But Pike was closest in proximity and it was clear he wasn't scared. He could feel the power growing both in him and above him, but it was far from the power he'd controlled previously. Around and around the cyclone twisted in fury. He could barely make out his men yelling to one another over the sound both in his head and in the sky. They sounded frightened, but clarity of words under the present conditions was impossible. The cyclone sucked sand, air, and words all upward. Now its tail reached down directly upon the statue, eliminating all visibility for everyone. Everyone lay against the ground with their eyes closed in fear that the mass of wind would steal them from this world. The sound's intensity had increased so much that the warriors covered their ears as well as their eyes as the sand pelted them painfully. They felt the sensation of falling but had yet to be pulled from the ground. What was happening? Where was their chief? Their senses were useless. They couldn't see, couldn't hear, and they'd likely soon be buried under mountains of sand if it didn't all let up soon…

And then the winds weakened. The sound lessened. Not all at once but slowly, as if under total control. That control was from their Nytel, the most powerful man to ever walk the world.

Pike allowed the excess sand to rain down upon the desert harmlessly, far south of his men. They now sat in a great valley of sand. The ground had been removed from under their feet. Before them stood the full statue of a man. It was far taller than any man ever seen. Much taller than Pike himself. But the most terrifying aspect was what the man held in his hand. It was an exact replica of the great spear that Pike now held in his hand. The statue-man glared eastward, almost angrily.

Pike had Foxskin translate the writing etched into the bottom of the enormous statue.

You are entering the prosperous lands of Victor the Just. Friends are welcome but enemies be warned the great city of Joventin will be the last you ever see. All visitors must obey the three laws of Victor:

DO NOT bring false testimony into Victor's lands

DO NOT take anything with you that you don't have claim to

A trespass against Victor's people is a trespass against Victor himself

"So much for prosperous lands," observed Foxskin.

"I knew I could feel life in this desert," said Pike. "Something very bad happened here. It is a cursed land. This same spear in my hand ruled these lands many lifetimes ago. Perhaps this land serves as a warning for the power of the spear. I feel a need for our return to find this city the statue speaks of. It lies somewhere in the middle of this barren land."

"What can be gained from this useless land?" asked Foxskin. "This land is dead. Perhaps we should leave before it kills us too."

Pike could feel the uncertainty growing in his men. "Do not be afraid, brave warriors! To learn what happened here means we can prevent it in our own future. This land has been awakened by our presence. We will return when the time is right. Now we must go east! I can feel the end of this desert coming to meet us!"

His men cheered both at his words and the prospect of escaping their surroundings. Their march now turned into a jog. The final stretch of the race had begun.

Chapter 49

KHAWNA HAD BEEN on Pike's trail for three days. She rode in his footsteps and knelt to softly touch the ground where he'd laid his head. She found a grave for one of her future husband's warriors. She knew Pike's strength but feared for his safety in the vile land. If they all should perish, she knew in her heart he would be the last to die.

The heat was almost unbearable, but Khawna knew her man's life depended on her alone, whether he accepted it or not. She pushed her borrowed horse, Harley, onward over sand and stones until she thought she heard a gull cry. *How could it be?* She squeezed her mount's ribs like Grom had shown her, and within moments she saw green ahead. *Was this real? Was she losing her mind in the heat?* There was no way she'd traversed the whole desert in three days. With renewed hope and curiosity, both rider and horse galloped toward the marvel ahead.

She came to a stop and dismounted in front of what should not be. Before her feet were the banks of a great river cutting through the lifeless sand. Along the edges sprouted young grass beginning to cover the cool sandy banks. She stepped into the river to assure herself it was real. A cold, powerful sensation of refreshment greeted her.

She stooped to her knees and drank the precious water that now flowed abundantly in the land of desolation. Harley followed suit. *How could it be?* The river looked out of place in the landscape. She peered upstream and saw daylight through the mountain. Judging by the sharp edges that could fit together like a puzzle, it looked as if the mountain had been ripped in two. The realization that perhaps it *had* been ripped apart crossed her mind. She had seen for herself the passage Pike had created on his way to Mossport. She beamed with pride at her husband's work. He had likely saved her life, although he didn't know it. Now it would be up to her to return the favor.

Khawna and Harley swam across the great river and ended up much further downstream. Although the river wasn't terribly deep, the current was strong, and she and her horse were already in a weakened state. When she'd once again found her betrothed's trail, it was nearing dark. It could be treacherous to continue on during the dark night. She gathered the few dried up cacti and burnables she could scavenge and made a small fire. She feasted on Grom's provisions of dried meat, hard bread, and her now full waterskin. The warm fire felt good, as she had learned the desert could get rather cold at night. Her belly full, she thought of nothing besides catching up to Pike. She would not fail him.

Familiar reservations snuck into her head as she lay on the ground alone. The fact that it was not just Hellion he was chasing but the pale-faced Jada made her green with envy. Jada did not deserve Pike's attention. She was disrespectful, impulsive, and unfit to be a chief's wife. The Nytel needed a wife who listened and was tactful in advising him. She must be both wise and obedient, most of the time. Above all, she must be loyal.

Khawna stretched her lean frame out on a blanket beside her meager fire. She'd tied Harley up nearby to a cactus since there was nothing else to tie a rope around. Although she'd mostly ridden, she was surprised at how sore her muscles were from the strain of the journey. It would all be worth it to reach her hunter. It felt dangerously good to lie down with the sound of the river lulling her to sleep. The remnants of her soon-to-be husband's power made her feel safe in the cruel, foreign land. The world was right again now that her people were finished with being weak and defenseless.

As Pike's sole hope to reach his destiny, she wished she had more of a plan to help him. The Tarmigan had been vague about his trouble, and she still didn't know how to advise him once she did reach him. Had she made this trip just to tell him to be careful? How foolish would that look? She could not bear the thought of appearing as foolish as Jada. What else could she do? She could listen to his plans and watch his back. She could give him advice if he asked for it. She understood his people far better than he. What she didn't understand were the people south of her home. Particularly the bad people and why they wanted Hellion and Jada.

Her sense of purpose restored, she was easily able to drift into sleep.

She must have been out for a while when a flash of light burned in her closed eyes and within her head itself. *How long have I slept? Why does my head ache?* She was having a difficult time seeing as she struggled to get to her feet.

Another jolt of light exploded in her head. Now she knew why her head hurt as she dropped woozily back to her hands and knees. She cried out in pain as her blurry vision kept her confused as to what was happening.

A bare foot pushed down on her throat as she lay supine, struggling for breath. To her horror, a bracelet with little bones was attached to the foot that had her subdued.

"The gods have returned you to me for a purpose," a voice said in the darkness. It was a deep voice, in Merkil language. She tried to yell, scream, beg for air, but the more she struggled, the more pressure she felt on her throat. It was collapsing, robbing her of oxygen, and so painful, tears ran from her eyes. Her muscles struggled, trying to stop her neck from snapping. Khawna's face twisted in pain and horror at what she knew was coming.

"I'm awful hungry, Khawna. What part should I eat first? I need all the strength I can get before I slay your friend."

Khawna shuddered. She stopped fighting and felt the foot loosen enough for her to inhale a small amount of precious air. Her lungs burned as they started to expand again. She could only manage five words. "My...husband...will...end...you," she managed in Merkil.

This caused Hytan to pause. After a moment he sheathed his knife that had looked like it was about to come down on her one final time. As if he'd had a change of heart, he promptly rolled her on her stomach and tied her hands behind her back. Then he bound her legs so tightly she lost feeling.

"Don't look so upset. You were destined to be eaten. You should be honored it's me that does it. But before I cook you, I have one last job for you," he said, smiling.

The last thing Khawna remembered was the pointy filed teeth of Hytan's half-burned face before he delivered a final smack to the back of her head that made the world go dark once again.

Chapter 50

THERE WAS A change in the ship's movement. *Had they anchored? Were they at port?* Hellion knew he wouldn't have to wait long to learn his fate. All that awaited him in Sisterton were the formalities. He might have a day or two before they hanged him. Would it be enough time for Pike?

Commander Burin presented himself with a dark smile. A guard stood on either side of him.

"I hope you enjoyed your final voyage, traitor. I've already sent for the magistrate to read you your crimes. You'll be charged momentarily; then we'll come to the small business of scheduling your execution. Do you prefer morning or evening?"

"I've never been a morning person," replied Swash. "Push it back to the evening at least."

"That settles it, boys," laughed the commander to his guards. "First thing tomorrow morning it is!"

Hellion scowled.

"Oh, don't look so glum. You've stretched out over a year since your last execution. You should be grateful. And don't expect any chance of escape this time."

"I'll be grateful when I piss on your ugly corpse," growled Hellion.

The words rolled off the commander like a dinnertime joke. He laughed heartily, the way people do when they see a dog wearing glasses or a squirrel atop a saddled horse. In a word, he found it comical.

"Unfortunately for you, we don't live in fairytale land. I suppose all a killer like you can dream about is killing though. It's almost sad. Isn't there something you can be grateful for that's happened in your miserable, retched life?"

Hellion kept silent while staring at the man with hate.

"Come on, Private; tell me, one military man to another. You're better than an animal surely, though not by much. Can you think of nothing save violence and lashing out at me, a humble man that provides justice in a cruel world?"

"Your bastardized version of justice will come to an end soon, Commander. I promise you that. But in truth, I have found something else in these days since my last death sentence worth celebrating."

"Oh, do tell, Private."

"I'll let you know when the time is right."

Commander Burin looked annoyed. "I do detest waiting, Hellion. It bores me. And so do you, presently. Guards! Do not divert your eyes from this criminal for a second. He'll cut your throats quicker than a surprise sneeze. Sweet justice is on its way. If you'll excuse me, I have a girl in my room to attend to." Once again he smiled malevolently and left.

Hellion had tried to talk with the guards previously and found them quite dull. They wouldn't even humor him with conversation. He sat in his chains and closed his eyes, trying to think of a way out. If he escaped on the docks, they'd have him in a flash. It would take a little while to transport him from the ship to the jail. They'd definitely keep him there overnight. If he was in jail, it was likely he'd be in with other criminals. With others around it was possible someone would have a blade. If he could get his hands on a blade, he could provide true justice before they cut him down.

JADA ALSO WAS trying to come up with a plan. She was no stranger to the port of Sisterton. She'd worked the port on a few occasions in the past. However, the inner city was where she'd spent the bulk of her time while destitute. The justice system would definitely hold her for questioning, but there was little that could be done to her now that they'd reached civilization. She'd escaped the cruel commander's desires just long enough. Now, after at most a few days of questioning, they'd have to let her go. There were no witnesses to prove she had aided Hellion in Mossport. Once they let her go, she would try to find Pike. He was undoubtedly coming for them. But what if he didn't make it in time? Could she save Hellion?

Sure, Swash was mangy and quite irritating to keep around as company, but he was close with Pike. At least the man had a sense of humor, unlike Commander Burin. And he was in this predicament because of her. True, the crimes he'd done on his own, but he had tried to protect her. Had she not seen her inn aflame, she wouldn't have run ahead of Pike and caused Hellion to follow. *Why had Hellion followed and not Pike? Pike probably ordered him to follow me. I can't believe I'm even considering this, but I have to help him if I can. Pike might not make it before it's too late.* She sat on her bed, thinking. She'd been locked in a small, private cabin for the remainder of the journey. She believed the separate arrangements were made because the commander was afraid she'd cut his throat while he slept. He was right about that.

She had two real options. Either figure a way to help Hellion escape or find a way to delay the execution so Pike could arrive to stop it.

A knock at the door made her jump.

"Excuse me, Miss Jada?"

It was one of the guards. The courteous address had changed considerably from previous addresses of "Hey you" and "Stupid girl."

"Yes?" she replied in a guarded tone.

The door opened enough for the guard to pop his head into her cabin. "It appears someone has paid your bond. You'll be free to leave the ship and stay where you wish in the city. You will be required to show up at the sentencing for Private Swash. Failure to show up could cost your benefactor a good deal of money."

"Who paid my bond?" she asked astonished.

"That's above my pay grade. I just do what I'm told." He hesitated. "I hope you don't think all of us are like the commander. All we do is follow orders."

The statement caught Jada by surprise momentarily. *Perhaps the man has some remorse.*

"How much is Hellion's bond?" she asked quizzically.

The soldier shook his head. "There is no bond for the fugitive. We all got a cut of the bounty for bringing him in though." The man grinned, patting his pocket. "Again, I'm sorry if the commander treated you badly on the trip. I can tell you're a true lady." There was a pause. "I'd love to take you to dinner sometime while we're in port. Just want to make it up to you for how you were treated. Do you like the shows?"

Jada fought the vomit threatening in the back of her throat. *This must not have been the one I bit.* She straightened her back and tried to act the part of a lady. Confidence, gentleness, and all that nonsense. "Where are you staying?" she asked.

The man's eyes lit up. "We'll be staying at the Jolly Roger Inn near the courthouse."

Jada's mind raced with ideas. "I'm not sure where I'll be staying yet, but I'll keep your offer in mind, Private…what was your name?"

"Ferly, Miss."

"Ferly," she said out loud, flashing the fakest smile she could muster. The idiot turned red.

"Could you spare a lady a coin to get a decent room in this city?"

The man couldn't reach into his pocket quickly enough.

"You're a good man, Ferly," she whispered in his ear as she left. "I hope we can meet up for that dinner before you leave."

Chapter 51

THE GOVERNOR OF Sisterton was pleased to receive good news. It seemed it was rare in the city these days. Word had been sent that the notorious army criminal had finally been captured. The man had done well to stay hidden this long, especially with his picture plastered over nearly every port around the globe. Galvin Huxworth was beginning to give up hope of ever finding the infamous private. His escape had been a bad omen for the fabled mercenary army. It made people wonder if the world-renowned force was as mighty as it claimed to be. But now these fairytales could be put to rest for good.

If there was one reason that the governor was able to remain in power for all of the last two decades, it was his image of strength. That extended both to and from his military force that he employed all over the world to the highest bidder. Despite what many people had to say, money could be made from war. That was especially true when it was your country's primary export. One of the byproducts of the gruesome occupation of a mercenary was that it could, from time to time, create a man who could become a danger to his own nation. If such a man could ever gain a following, it could spell the end of Sisterton. The hard truth was sometimes you had to put down a violent dog before it turned on its master. Hellion Swash was the perfect example of a dutiful soldier turned threat. Based on the reports of Swash's commanding officer, he had killed his own man in battle, presumably because he would not follow in Swash's plans for a mutiny against Commander Burin. From there, the man's plans could easily have led to a coup or some other type of instability. This was a matter neither the army nor its capital city could take lightly. Now that they had the defector back in their possession, his execution would make a grand spectacle for his city. There was no finer entertainment in the city than a hanging, especially one whose name was known by nearly all inhabitants around the world. It would also give the governor an excellent platform to address his constituents and remind them how lucky they were to have elected him.

Huxworth called General Code to his office.

"I want all your men present for this execution, General. This needs to be a grand show of strength for our city. The message must be received that anyone who revolts against us will be put down quickly."

The general nodded approvingly. "I can have five thousand men on hand if you give me two days."

"You shall have it, General," replied the governor. "I'll postpone it until the evening so the whole city will be awake and watching."

"Brilliant idea, sir. Though, I do fear Commander Burin may become quite cross with the need to postpone."

"Well, he can throw a tantrum on his own time. He is, after all, the one that let the man escape the first time. He should be grateful I let him anywhere near the city! If anything, he is partially to blame for the creation of this malicious soldier."

"You speak the truth, Governor. However, the man has paid for his mistakes with a demotion and yet somehow successfully brought back the traitor alive. Such resolve should not go unnoted."

"Oh, it's noted, General. Now you can note this. The only reason that man's still in my army is because of his family's wealth and ties. I sincerely hope the army isn't giving the man a medal for simply fixing his own blunder."

"Governor, it's nearly impossible not to. He captured the man that had more kills than anyone to ever don our uniform. And he's half my age. Hellion Swash never lost a battle, no matter the odds. This capture is a huge success for the commander. And the commander managed to do it while defending Mossport from an attack by hostiles."

"I've heard these tales as well. I suppose we better send for Burin at once to testify to these reports of natives and magical beasts that have been surfacing from the western frontier as of late. I know what's out there, General. I've been to Mossport a few times in my life. It's a whole town of nothing. Just scared townspeople afraid of their shadows, I'd have to wager. No more beasts there than anywhere else. And hostiles? More likely a band of outlaws. That I could believe. How else can we account for the successful hiding and survival of Private Swash?"

"If it's a band of outlaws, they just lost their ringleader. Public enemy number one will be swinging in the gallows soon enough for everyone to see."

The governor smiled. "Bring me the reports from Mossport as soon as the commander's men are debriefed. I'll arrange the judge and verdict ahead of time."

"What shall we do about the girl out on bond? Burin claims she aided Private Swash."

Huxworth considered for a moment. "Cut her loose when she shows up. If we try her, we'll probably have to hang her. Hanging a woman would take away from the entertainment. I'll not have half the crowd booing me before my address. She won't be able to interfere with our plans."

"As you wish, Governor." With that, the general left him to write his speech.

As Jada walked the length of the docks, she scanned the shacks that lined the walkway. Everyone acted in a hurry as they pushed past her toward their various destinations. How nice it must be to know where one was supposed to go. She had been so surprised to be released from the soldiers, she wasn't sure what her next move would be. She did have distant family in the city that she hadn't seen since she was a little girl. She could only imagine their surprise to find her on their doorstep, begging for a room. The idea had never materialized in the past when she was broke, and now was not the time to open that chapter. The sun beat down upon her, giving her a headache that made planning nearly impossible. Her instinct led her to an alehouse in one of the shacks that sat above the water. At least it would be dark inside, and it was a setting she'd grown accustomed to for passing time.

Entering through the door brought back the familiar smell of tobacco smoke and stale beer. The air was cool and the lighting, dim. It was as she had hoped. The only other patron at this hour of the day was an elderly man at the end of the bar who seemed to be a few pints in already.

"What can I get you?" asked the gruff barmaid. She was middle aged with what looked to be a permanent furrow in her brow from years of wariness or perhaps just fatigue. Was Jada gazing at a mirror of herself in a few years?

"Do you have arbor wine?"

The woman looked agitated. "Let me take a look in the back." Her brow furrowed even more.

No sooner had the barmaid stepped out of sight when the old man put on his hat and half ran, half stumbled to the door. He might have made his escape had another man not opened the door at the perfect time to step in front of the drunken, bill-dodging customer. The old man collapsed in a heap, making a loud thud when he hit the ground.

The barmaid came running back to the sound of commotion and was on the old man before he could get back to his feet. He raised his head high enough for the woman to cuff him twice on the cheek and bounce his head off the half-rotted floor. She reached in his pants and pulled out the now unconscious man's wallet. She stuffed some bills in her apron and threw the wallet onto the man's chest. Only then did the barmaid look up non-apologetically at the new customer and Jada.

"The lousy wretch had the money. If there's one thing I can't stand, it's thiev'n." She bent back down and put the man's wallet back in his pocket and dragged him by the boots out the front door. Upon returning she dusted her hands and stepped back behind the bar. "We don't have any arbor wine, ma'm."

"I'll just have your house ale then. I'm sorry about that customer."

She nodded, then turned her attention to the man who had stopped her customer from escaping. "Your first drink is on the house, Gordy."

The man had a hard face. "Give it to the beautiful young lady, Gertrude. And put my usual on my tab."

"She looks a little young for you, but whatever you say, Captain."

The barmaid went to pour the drinks and the captain sat down next to Jada. She stared at the man with her best business face and started, "I'm not interested in whatever you're about to…"

The man put a finger to her lips. "Keep your voice down, Miss. We have business."

"Excuse me?" asked Jada. "You don't even know who I am."

The man exhaled. "I paid your bail."

Now he had her attention. "And why would you do that?" whispered Jada.

"Not for you. It was because of your friend. There was no way they'd let him go. He was worth too much."

"How did you even know we were on the boat? We hadn't been docked an hour. I find your story hard to believe." She could feel herself flushing with anger.

"Calm down, little lady," the man said. "The business I have is with your friend, and if he doesn't survive, I don't make money. I know everything that comes and goes on this dock, both legal and not. I pay good money to know, but I always know."

"What do you want from me?"

"More information, and possibly your help, if you'll lend it."

She narrowed her eyes at the man. "How do I know you're really trying to help Hellion? He's said before he doesn't have any friends."

"You don't," said the man. "But I can guarantee he'll live longer if I succeed. And if I don't, I'll be swinging next to the bastard."

"Let me guess. My fate would be the same if I help you and you fail?"

"There is no certainty in life save death, but your guess is probably dead on. I've already told you enough to get my neck stretched, so if you won't help, be gone and forget we talked."

The man got up to move further down the bar when Jada put her hand on his shoulder. "Sit back down," she said firmly. "The man saved me once; I suppose it's the least I can do to help you."

The bartender returned and set down their glasses.

"The best way to complete an agreement is over drinks. Know any toasts?" asked the captain.

"Quite a few from my profession. I heard one a little while back I liked though."

"Let's hear it."

Jada almost got chills as she repeated the words.

Let us drink to past, present, and 'morrow,
To sweet love, may we give more than borrow,
To life, that it be fulfilled not hollow,
To all who can't drink away their sorrow,
Last to the dead, who we'll all soon follow!

"Sounds fitting for what I'm about to propose," said the captain after lowering his mug and wiping his mustache with his arm. "Where'd you hear that one?"

"Hellion Swash," Jada replied coolly.

Chapter 52

THE DEAD MAN rose from the corner of his cell. He touched two fingers to his neck where the black raven was now fully healed. Things weren't looking good. He was kept in solitary confinement, meaning no chance to conspire with any other jail mates. The gallows were calling and he would not be able to get a blade. No news had been reported about any parties arriving from Mossport. It sure didn't look like Pike would make it in time. The man had unlimited power if he could get here, and yet how could he possibly arrive before the following evening?

Hellion began tapping the raven, trying to drum up some way out of this nightmare. He had, after all, been counted out before in his life. As he looked around, all he could concentrate on were the iron bars and solid stone floor. It would take two lifetimes to chisel out the wall. The only way out of the cell was through the locked door.

When a man knows death is near, he can't help but reflect on his life. The monster he was accused of being was the same reason he had escaped so many other previous scrapes in this life. He was indeed a ruthless butcher. He had become exactly what the mercenary army wanted and needed. How thankless was this life that the one time he'd tried to do something good, something almost righteous for friends, he'd sealed his own fate? The fact that he had cared had made him weak, vulnerable. Yet, he still felt this bond with Pike and Jada. He bore them no resentment. He was proud to be their ally or if the word should be used…friend. Perhaps someone in this world would actually miss him after he checked out.

Truth be told, Swash had been too vile a man to deserve much less than the gallows up to this point in his life. If there was truly any justice in this world, he would not escape what awaited him the next day. He was never meant to be a hero, only a villain, and he'd embraced that role a long time ago. At least until he'd met Pike. The man, just like Hellion, had no friends, and yet could there be a more direct opposite to himself? He had befriended Hellion after he'd warned him not to. Far from the villain that Swash was, Pike was a sheltered hero, never introduced into the world to become what he should have been…until now.

The power he held would change the world, but the world was lucky for it. Hellion shivered at the thought of what he would do if he held such power. He had no illusions of how bad it would be for everyone else. Thank the stars Pike was the chosen one.

While he lamented his life and choices, Swash's ears pricked up when he heard a familiar voice outside the jail.

"May I trouble you to have a word with the accused?"

"He ain't just accused, Miss," responded a gray-haired military man clothed in scarlet with a green sash. "That there is the infamous Hellion Swash. He admitted as much. He's more of a butcher than a man. A pretty little lady like you ought have no reason to talk with a dead man."

Jada contracted her fingers into a balled fist and squeezed to keep her anger under control. "I knew him a lifetime ago. Surely it wouldn't hurt anything to have a last talk with the boy I used to know." She smiled as sincerely as she could muster while grinding her teeth underneath and cocking her head sideways as if she thought the guard would go along with her request. She started forward before he raised his hand to stop her from entering.

"I can't allow it, Miss. The boy you knew is gone. He'd probably murder you on the spot if he could get a hand on you. It's likely he'd use your bones to pick the lock before he killed us all. The orders are no one sees him and no one gets to talk to him."

Hellion came closer to his cell door to listen. Jada was impulsive, but definitely not stupid. What was her plan?

"Well, I'm not scared, mister soldier." She swayed her body as if that made a difference. "You could stand right next to me if ya want. I swear I won't take but a minute. Please, sir?"

The guard sighed. "You're really not too bright, are ya?"

"My pappy always said I was smart enough for this mean old world. I can cook too, ya know. Mayhaps you'd like me to bring you back something to eat later tonight for your trouble?"

"Not interested. Listen, I already told you I can't. Why won't you just move along?" His voice was rising, and he was getting frustrated.

Jada rose her hands to her face. Her hair fell over them, and to Hellion's surprise, she started sobbing loudly. "There… must be something… I can do to see him one last… time," she wailed into her hands.

The guard was not having it. "You can get out of my doorway and come to the gallows tomorrow like everybody else."

"Come on, Charles!" spat another guard who had overheard the conversation. "Let the poor girl have a word. She can't hurt nothing. It's not like we won't be here the whole time watching her. I can't stand to see a pretty girl like her cry."

Jada quickly turned toward the man, sensing weakness. "Oh, please, sir! It would mean the world to me!"

"Fine," replied Charles, visibly uncomfortable with the whole situation. "Just get on with it quickly."

Jada hurried past the men toward Hellion's cell. She wiped away what appeared to be real tears from her eyes.

"Hellion, Hellion, it's me, Annie, from grade school!"

Swash did his best to play along. "You still remember me, Annie?"

"Of course! You haven't changed a bit, Hellion. I always knew you'd be famous. I just wish it wasn't for all this."

"I never was good at being perfect, sweet Annie. There's always been a darkness inside me, I'm afraid."

"I always saw light where others saw none. Where there is light, there is hope."

Hellion lowered his voice to a whisper. "Is there any hope?"

"Do you remember a Captain Gordon?"

"Yes."

"Well, he seems to think you will pay him handsomely for helping to rescue you."

"I may have mentioned it before to him. What's his plan?"

"To create a distraction when they take you to the gallows. I have to persuade a guard to help us."

Hellion stared at her. "How, pray tell, are you going to do that? I don't suppose you have any money?"

"Don't concern yourself with it. I'll do whatever it takes. I owe you, and that's the end of the story."

"Since when did you ever care what happened to me?"

"Who says I do?" she asked, smiling. "Be ready, you'll know when the time comes. You'll have to be quick."

"Stealth and speed are my calling cards. Tell the good captain he'll have his reward. And one other thing..." he beckoned her closer.

"Young lady, not another step closer!" yelled the guard from the door. He started in the doorway.

Hellion whispered softly, for only Jada to hear. "There is a cave on an uninhabited island off the coast of Cape Zigon across the sea. Crescent Moon Island. It's a burial tomb filled with skeletons from the armies. Buried under them lies what the captain wants. Tell no one. If I don't make it, it is for you."

The guard laid a hand on her shoulder and began to push her back to the entrance. "Goodbye, brave Hellion," she called out to him. "I will think of you always."

"Perhaps had we reunited sooner, I might have stopped my wicked ways. The world is cruel, my Annie. Thank you for your kind words!"

The guard practically threw her into the dusty street.

Mouthing a few choice words in the opposite direction, she popped back up and dusted herself off. Then she turned around and smiled back at the guard who had allowed her in. "Can I bring you some sweets later?"

Now they both stood with arms crossed. "Miss, you'd better not come back here. He just saved your life, and you don't even realize it."

Jada shrugged her shoulders and walked off. She had more work to do.

Chapter 53

COMMANDER BURIN'S VICTORIOUS day had arrived. The verdict was in, and his only surviving adversary would be swinging in the gallows after a quick passage from the jail and a speech from the governor. He'd wished the deed had been done earlier, but the foolish politician wanted to use the event for his own promotion. It infuriated Burin, but he decided he could use the governor's boost in popularity to his own advantage in time. There was no way they could send him back to Fort Tuttle now.

The streets were lined with uniformed soldiers. A military band had started playing at noon that day, and the drinking had begun long before that. The weather was good, and the crowds were large and still growing. The commander strolled victoriously past the guards to the cell that held his greatest enemy.

"Come to gloat, have you?" asked Hellion as Burin approached the cell in military dress with all his accolades displayed on his chest. "Or have you had a change in heart. Perhaps trial by sword, man to man would be better? No? Too chicken shit as usual?"

Burin grimaced at his words. "You know, when a man hangs, often there are bets placed on if he shits his pants as he dies. I think I'll put my money on your brown trousers."

"If you'd have told me that yesterday, I'd have skipped my last three meals. No matter, just as easily as I've beaten you in life, I'll beat you in death."

The commander sneered. "You've won nothing in life. You merely delayed the inevitable. If anything, arresting you, the greatest traitor in the history of the army, will make me even more famous. I'll likely ascend the ranks even faster than ever before."

"Even faster than by lining others' pockets with money? You're a sham. Everyone knows it."

The remark hit the victorious man in the gut. All he could do was lie to deny it.

"If you weren't already sentenced to death, I'd put you on trial for that outrageous accusation!"

"The truth hurts, dear commander. The men know, of course. They may not say it directly, but word has spread about how your detractors often meet an eerily similar fate to what nearly happened to me. I wish you had the guts to kill me yourself, but you're weak. At least you realize it. Speaking of which, you never thanked me."

"For what?"

Hellion smiled as if the commander were a child. "For saving your life in Mossport. You know in some cultures, that would make you my slave."

"That's nonsense."

"Oh, but it isn't. That Merkil chief that suddenly disappeared? He would have eaten you were it not for my arrow, and you know it. Make sure you never forget that."

"And here I believed you might have some regret for all the crimes you committed."

"And here I thought you knew me better. Alas, we both disappoint one another. Go. You better get out there to brownnose the governor or whoever else of importance requests a good cleaning. Don't waste any more time here. You've got a whole grand celebration to enjoy."

The commander glared at him, wanting to have the guards hold him down as he punched the insubordinate's face to a bloody pulp. He couldn't get away with that kind of action here, so he swallowed and forced a smile. "All I can say is you're taking this way better than most would before defecating themselves in public at the end of a rope. Perhaps you still think you're going to somehow escape?"

"A man can always dream," replied Hellion.

"Whatever pleases you," scoffed Commander Burin. He turned on his heel and headed to the execution site to wait for his prisoner's final escort through town.

FERLY ARRIVED WITH eleven other guards in total to escort the doomed man to the gallows. There was only one other man with them from Commander Burin's men. The rest of the guards were inhabitants of the city, most likely more loyal to the governor than anyone else. Ferly counted himself lucky to be included in the procession. He was under no illusions that had he not been so close to the prisoner, his date with Jada the prior night would not have gone so well. She was feisty and beautiful, everything a woman should be. She needed him for her grand scheme, as luck would have it. Still, the night could have gone better before it ended. But if everything worked out as he hoped, he would have plenty more opportunities with the beautiful creature, Miss Jada.

All twelve men entered the small cell. Hellion Swash's face was stoic to their commands. He rose from his heap in the corner and complied without a struggle as they chained both his hands and feet together. They led him out with three pairs of soldiers in the vanguard and three pairs in the rearguard. The sun was beginning to fall as they ushered him into the streets with lanterns illuminating the vast crowds gathered to watch his walk to the gallows.

The crowds were rowdy and drunk. Many had waited all afternoon to secure a good spot to see the notorious Hellion Swash walk by. Ferly was positioned directly behind Hellion with his partner. As they followed the sentenced man, they could hear the crowd's jeers.

"Thought you couldn't be captured, did ya?" said one man with big eyes.

"That can't be him! I could whip that sap in a fight!" yelled another man.

"Justice belongs to Governor Huxworth!" cried out a middle-aged woman.

The procession made about a hundred paces before the crowd began hurling objects at Hellion. Mostly they pelted him with rotten fruit and vegetables. Ferly got hit with a tomato and swore at the man with poor aim. One man threw a particularly hazardous piece of driftwood, which Hellion unexpectedly caught in his chained hands with a menacing look in his eye. The coward that threw it ran into the crowd before any of the stationed guards on the street could catch him. To Ferly's relief, Hellion dropped the piece of wood to the ground. It was said that the man could kill as well with a spoon as a weapon. Ferly had no interest in dying tonight. He had a simple, yet vital part to play.

After the ceremonial walk through the city, they arrived at the steps of the platform for the gallows. Here the number of people gathered was greatest. The gallows were built near the channel that connected Mammoth Lake to the sea. Further east up the channel were the docks and boardwalk area of the city. Across the channel to the north, within viewing distance, were the slums of the city of Sisterton. Those banks were also filled with people watching for the big moment.

Two of the twelve guards led Hellion up the steps where Governor Huxworth waited along with General Code, the judge who had given the verdict, and a masked man who would pull the lever to drop the floor beneath Hellion's feet.

Hellion was escorted to his rope's end. The governor raised his hands to quiet the crowds. After a few moments the crowds hushed, and he began his address facing the largest mass of people, directly east up the street Ferly had ushered Hellion through.

"My friends, welcome!" he yelled, raising his hands in excited animation. "Today we see what happens to the enemies of our people. Justice has been overdue for the likes of Hellion Swash!"

The crowds erupted in cheers at his words. He waited for them to settle down before continuing.

"Let this man's fate serve as warning to all who would do harm to our army, to our people. We will never stop searching for you. We will find you, and you will pay the price of justice!"

The roar of the city's entire population once again erupted. The governor gave them a few moments to gloat, when suddenly the night erupted in a flash of light and a *boom* that sent the already nearly hysterical crowds into a frenzy. The lanterns whisked off in the streets while panic overtook the crowds as well as the soldiers standing beside Ferly. It was time for the soldier to play his part.

Chapter 54

JADA STOOD IMPATIENTLY on the docks. *Would they make it through the crowds?* With arms crossed, she scanned the docks in the starlight. The city had gone dark, and people were scared. There was no telling what was happening at the gallows. *Could Ferly pull this off?*

Resting beside her, *The Rose Tattoo* was ready to sail. The only problem, other than missing the most infamous man in Sisterton, was Captain Gordon had dispatched half his crew to extinguish the street-lights that would illuminate Hellion's escape with Ferly to the docks. A major drawback of the plan was that one rarely could guess how large groups of frantic people would react. Could Hellion make it through the chaos? Would the rest of the crew make it back to the ship?

She saw a dim light approach and quickly realized it was Captain Gordon's pipe. He had been watching the events play out from the edge of the crowd.

"What is happening out there?" she whispered.

He hurried closer, glancing nervously around before he spoke. "They had Swash on the platform, standing at the rope. The governor was giving his speech when the powder was lit at the three locations. In the panic, no one noticed my men take out the lanterns as far as

I could tell. It's going to be treacherous to get through. There's likely some people trampled in the panic."

"Serves them right," said Jada with a curled lip. "There's too much celebration for a man about to be killed unjustly."

The captain was taken aback by her response. Then he shrugged. "It can't be helped, I suppose. I just hope my boys are okay."

The two heard footsteps running toward the docks. They shrank into the shadows without a word. As they watched, two men emerged. It was Hellion and Ferly.

Jada ran out to hug Hellion, who had an enormous grin on his face. When she looked at Ferly, she knew something was wrong.

"Ferly, you've done well. What's the matter?"

He solemnly looked down the pier where four men now approached. Even in the shadows their drawn crossbows could not be missed. In the night, a chilling, familiar voice called out.

"Planning on leaving at such a late hour, are we?" Commander Burin appeared behind the bowman.

Jada scowled at Ferly. "You ratted us out?"

The man turned his gaze downward and said nothing.

"Oh, yes, he most definitely did, Miss Jada. Do you want to know the most romantic part of it? He insisted that you be released to him. Isn't that just heartwarming?" Commander Burin laughed. "Apparently your seduction worked like a charm."

Hellion glanced at Jada in surprise. She ignored his gaze and spoke pointedly. "I'm no one's property. I'll swing in the gallows beside Hellion proudly. He's more of a man than any of you."

Commander Burin threw his head back and laughed again. "You think you're going to get a trial after all of this? How stupid do you think I am? All of you, get on your knees now and put your hands on your heads!" he barked.

Visibly upset, Ferly started to walk toward the soldiers when the archers shifted their aim to him.

"Wait just a minute!" he yelled in disbelief. "I helped you catch them! How about some gratitude!"

The archers didn't waver.

"Ahh yes, gratitude," said Burin. "For making demands of your commanding officer regarding a whore. Here is your gratitude. I'm about to spare you the indignity of a public hearing and humiliation before you're executed. On your knees now! I will not say it again!"

The man looked at Jada before taking another step forward. The single arrow caught him through the heart before he could make his final plea. The large man fell on the wooden dock, clutching his chest as he died.

The commander approached the remaining three already on their knees.

"At least you three know how to follow directions. Just in case you're thinking I'm not going to get away with this, you couldn't be further from the truth. Your bodies may wash up on shore eventually, but what is about to happen will remain a mystery. And guess what, Private Swash? In the end, I still win. Guards, it's time to end these three. They've caused our city much grief already. On my signal, each gets an arrow."

The commander backed up to the edge of the dock to let the archers have a clear shot.

Captain Gordon groaned as if already in pain. Tears streamed down Jada's eyes as they locked on Hellion.

"I'm sorry," Swash said. "You deserve so much better than this."

Commander Burin started. "Okay, men! Ready…set…"

Darkness turned into daylight for the second time that night.

Chapter 55

PIKE COULD FEEL waves of fear from the city's inhabitants roll over him like an endless ocean of ice. He shivered from the sensation as he stood on the gallows in the midst of the smell of burnt ozone. His warriors surrounded him below on the ground, but it was clear there was no one running to storm his perch. After hearing of the public event upon his approach into the city, he was relieved to find no one at the end of the rope. But where was Hellion?

Again and again he showered the skies with forks of lightning, trying to glimpse where his friends were being hidden. The people who hadn't fled the streets yet were surely trying now.

"Where is Hellion Swash?!" Pike's voice boomed loud enough for the entire city to hear. His voice was stronger and louder than anyone had ever heard shouted from one man.

An inaudible voice called out from behind him. Pike turned around to see a large man approach with a lantern in one hand and something over his shoulder. Disgusted it clearly wasn't Hellion, Pike pointed the spear at the man who continued to approach. His warriors also raised their spears.

The man raised the lantern such that it illuminated his now scarred face. Pike gasped, but before he could mentally reach for the familiar melody, the man pulled the hood from his shouldered load to reveal Khawna in the lantern's light. Those wretched teeth formed a smile, much like that of a wolf, as Hytan unsheathed his knife.

"Nobody move," Pike instructed his men. He calmly walked, spear in hand, toward the Merkil chief, wondering if he could control his power enough to not hurt Khawna, assuming she was still alive.

When he reached twenty paces away, Hytan put a hand up signaling him to stop. Pike hesitantly complied.

The man grunted communication, but Pike couldn't understand. "What are you saying?" he boomed into the darkness.

The chief pointed to Pike's spear, then he motioned to the ground in front of him. He pointed at Khawna and then back to Pike.

He wants the spear for Khawna.

Pike glanced at his surroundings. Without the spear he carried only his large hunting blade. If Hytan could actually use the spear, it made the oversized knife about as useless as a pebble to throw at him. Pike glanced at his warriors now surrounding him. Any would throw him their own spear should he outstretch an open hand. With much trepidation, Pike set the spear on the ground and kicked it between them.

When Captain Burin got back to his feet, he realized what was happening.

"The man from Mossport is here! Kill them now!"

The bowmen were frightened and confused, staring at the man in disbelief.

"A man did that?" asked the middle bowman. "You knew of this man and didn't tell the governor he was following you?"

Commander Burin spoke very slowly. "Turn around slowly, men. The next time you turn your back on that man on his knees, he's likely to have already run you through. Stay calm, and kill them now."

The rattled men glanced back behind them, at the three on their knees, and back to Burin before taking aim again.

"That's much better, men. Best to do it simultaneously. Ready… set…"

"Commander Burin," Swash interrupted the tense silence. "I think the time is right for me to tell you about that secret I found. Remember you wanted to know what I've found worth celebrating since my last death sentence?"

"I must confess I no longer care," replied Burin. "As I was saying, men…"

"Friendship, Commander. I found friendship." Hellion grabbed both Jada and Captain Gordon's hands and held them tightly. "Do you have any friends?"

"Ha! My friend is my sword. And it's about to signal your end. That was a touching soliloquy of bullshit." He raised his sword into the air to commence the execution. "Ready, aim…"

The water erupted in an explosion, blurring everyone's vision. They heard the commander scream. The guards whirled around to fire their bows at the enormous creature that had Burin in its jaws.

"The Tarmigan!" shouted Jada.

Blood spurted onto the dock before the Tarmigan pulled the commander's flailing body below the water's surface.

It was more than enough time for Hellion to spring into action. He snatched Ferly's dagger and ran at the first bowman to turn around. As he buried the dagger with one hand in the man's chest, his other arm was pulling an arrow from the man's quiver. He grabbed it by the fletching and threw it so quickly the second man caught its point in his neck. The last man shot his bow, catching the dead man Swash now held in the back. The bowman raised his sword and charged before Hellion could dig his knife out of his first victim. Swash rolled away from the swing of the large blade and bent down to loosen and pull up a plank from the dock. He smiled as he held the arm's length piece of wood with two hands. "Surrender now or join your friends."

The guard nervously laughed, but his approach was much more

measured with his long blade. "Only a fool would fight steel against wood."

Hellion shrugged. "I guess that makes you the fool." He attacked with his awkward piece of wood and deflected the swordsman's blows one by one. He didn't look to be working half as hard as the sweaty bowman turned swordsman while he almost casually misdirected all the man's power of each swing with a simple flick of his wrist. As the fight continued, his wood got thinner and thinner until it was almost pointed at the end. It was obvious; another misdirection would be the end of his plank. For the final blow, the guard charged, and rather than parry the oncoming blow; Hellion feigned left, then rolled right and slid under the swipe of the guard's sword. He popped to his feet and threw the sharp chunk of wood, and it buried itself in the guard's back. The man fell to his knees and dropped his sword.

"I gave you warning," said Hellion. The man tried to talk but fell to the deck.

Jada ran to Hellion's side. "Get on the ship! We have to get you out of the city!"

More footsteps came running to the ship.

"It's the rest of my lads!" shouted Captain Gordon. "Don't hurt them, Swash!"

The sailors' eyes went white at the bodies and blood on the dock.

"What's happening out there?" asked Gordon.

The men were breathless but tried to explain the series of events.

"Lightning! Fire! Savages!" The rest began to blend together as all started to shout at once.

"Slow down!" said Gordon. "Just one of you. What's happening in the city?"

The boy called Orr excitedly started reciting the events. "A man showed up and lit the sky on fire. He wanted to know where Hellion is. I don't know if he wants to help him or hurt him. Then another man came with a woman on his shoulder and wanted the first man's spear. The man looking for Hellion set down his spear. Last I saw, the man wearing bones picked up the spear, and now he's fighting the man that set the sky on fire!"

Hellion walked away from the group and picked up the fallen guard's sword.

"I think you better listen to the lady and board my boat," said Gordon. "Sounds like some bad things are happening."

"They're about to," said Hellion. "Captain Gordon, get on that ship and take Jada."

"Like hell. We had a deal. I risked everything for your reward."

Hellion sighed. "If I don't make it back, Jada will take you to the treasure."

Captain Gordon looked at Jada, astonished. "You knew all along? You trusted this barmaid with the secret?"

Hellion swung around, sword in hand. "She's a friend. If you try to cheat her, that would make you my enemy." There was no smile with the words.

The captain threw his hands in the air. "I meant no offense. I'm just surprised, is all."

Jada ran to Hellion and put her arms around him. "Just come with us. We can leave this place."

He shook his head. "Your husband needs me."

"I need you!" she shouted angrily. She shook him by the shoulders. "I'm the one that's needed you all along! He can't be my husband! He chose the native girl first! I won't be second choice a moment longer!"

Hellion took a step back, eyes wide with realization. "I thought you were helping me for Pike."

"It was you who rescued me, not him! And just when I thought I evened the score to rescue you, once again you save my life! Pike has his native wife. He doesn't need me!"

"It's not true," said Hellion. "He is a good man. He does need you. We're all connected, Jada. You'll see when it's all over."

"This is how we're connected!" Jada threw her arms around him and kissed Hellion on the lips. He stared back in astonishment. For once in his life he had no quip, no smart reply.

"And now you see," replied Jada. She stared at the speechless man for a moment. "If the army doesn't kill you, Hytan certainly will if he has the spear. Pike would want you to live!"

His eyes almost looked soft for the first time Jada could remember. "It wouldn't have even been a choice before," he whispered. "But things have changed. Pike would do the same for me." He took her hand gently. "Please understand, this isn't because I don't love you, dear." He turned over his shoulder and yelled, "Gordon, get her out of here now!"

Swash turned his back on his escape and walked toward the burning city alone with sword drawn and the sobs of Jada fading into the darkness behind him.

Chapter 56

KHAWNA DREW IN deeply, filling her lungs with fresh air. The hood had been suffocating. She had heard the thunderous voice of her husband, and even though her eyes still hadn't adjusted, the hush of the city told her something big was happening. In the moonlight, the first object she saw upon her hood's removal was the familiar posture of her husband-to-be.

She saw him lob the underhand toss and heard the rattle of the spear as it landed on the ground in front of him. She looked up to see the toothy grin on Hytan's face as he set her feet on the ground but held her captive tightly by her hair. *He's going to get the spear and kill us all.*

Khawna tried not to panic, though her chest grew tighter and her breath grew more intense. She had come for a reason. The Tarmigan had said Pike needed her, so how could she help like this? Pike's men now stood behind him as he approached closer with a hand outstretched for her. The Merkil chief held a dagger to Khawna's neck and slowly moved toward the spear with eyes darting back and forth.

"Kill him, husband," Khawna said calmly to Pike as the steel pressed against the soft skin of her neck. "He will kill you all if he gets the spear!"

Hytan slapped her head with the back side of his knife, causing

Khawna to see a burst of light before she crumpled to the ground. The force of the chief's hand around her hair held her up, and she quickly regained her feet from the jolt of pain.

Pike fumed and started to look toward the spear, but the chief's dagger went quickly back to his betrothed's throat. Pike ground his teeth and waited. In that instant, he heard something in his head. It was another internal sound but different than normal. He placed a hand to his forehead and fixated his mental energy on the new sound to see if he could concentrate it. The frequency jumped and stopped, started and hopped, making its next move difficult to anticipate. He reached out but caught nothing in his head. *Is it possible without the spear?*

Hytan now stood ten paces away. The spear was between them. With one hand still on his temple, Pike reached out the other hand for Khawna. She pulled forward to meet him, but Hytan pulled her back twice as hard. He wanted his hands on the spear first. He'd dreamed of this moment for too long to be hasty. He stepped forward slowly and quietly, like a wild animal. Pike stood still. All that Khawna could hear for a moment was her own breath as everyone present watched, unmoving.

Hytan took another step, glanced around, and then took another. With one final step, he reached the spear. He squatted to the ground, pushing Khawna's head all the way to the ground with his eyes on Pike. With his free hand he grasped the spear and his eyes went white with wonder. He released Khawna—who quickly rolled away and ran to Pike—and used both his hands to hold the spear.

The spear glowed in his hands, and his laughter echoed like Pike's voice had, just minutes before. Pike's warriors glanced at him, and he held a hand up to stop them from attacking.

A young warrior cried out and charged at Hytan. The chief lowered the tip of the spear and green light erupted from its shaft, colliding with the unfortunate warrior. His skin changed color, and green flame erupted out of his mouth and eyes. To everyone present, it was almost as if the man was cooked from the inside out. Then the chief pointed the spear at Pike and smiled.

"Get behind me," he whispered to Khawna. She complied. He could feel her shaking in fear behind him. But with her proximity, he also was able to hear a familiar tone mixed with the new ones in his mind. The familiarity gave him hope. *Can I do this? It's now or never.* In one giant mental leap, he wrapped everything around the pulse of sound he could now so clearly hear in his head. In that instant, what was happening outside his body could only be heard like distant voices from another room. He crossed the divide, and the frequency was so powerful, so strong, that it took all his concentration to channel it. He focused it forward at the same time that Hytan unleashed his green flame, and to everyone present, it looked like he caught the Merkil chief's beam in his hands. What they couldn't see yet was his own light, struggling mightily against the energy trying to incinerate him and his love. But he now had mastered the power, spear or no spear, and the two men were equal in power.

The Merkil chief grunted and groaned with strain as Pike pushed himself toward the man clad with bones. Each step became easier, as if the spear recognized his right to hold it. Khawna could feel the energy growing in Pike from her touch. She dared not release her husband now, so she followed him with a hand on his shoulder. The hate in Hytan's eyes resembled the color of the glowing melted rock from Serpent's Spittle. The energy being released in the battle of light soon began to manifest itself as heat, and each step, although easier, grew hotter. Both men pushed with everything they had toward each other as the drops of sweat formed at their temples.

Pike felt as if his strength was surpassing Hytan's. He reached out to put a hand on the spear. In that instant, the force between them stopped and erupted angrily from the tip of the weapon. The energy hit the wooden gallows, and they exploded in flames. Khawna screamed, realizing the danger she was now in, and ran for cover. The energy from the tip of the spear did not stop. The two large men had both hands on the spear and were fighting to control it. Pike managed to divert the spear's destruction into the air, and although nothing was hit, the air lit up as if on fire and glowed in a trail for a few moments as the aim shifted up and down. All the citizens of Sisterton unable to find cover now watched, lying flat on the ground, believing they were witnessing the end of the world.

Hytan soon realized he was unable to overpower Pike and loosened his grip for a moment. Taking the chief's bait, Pike tried to pull the spear away and got hit with a kick to the stomach. The power spewing from the tip of the spear was now pulled back to the ground. Hytan turned with the weapon while pulling Pike along. The hunter struggled for breath while the force demolished buildings instantaneously. Screams erupted as a tall building collapsed onto itself, likely crushing many within it.

Pike realized with horror what was happening. *He's going to kill them all, whether I hang on or not.* "Khawna, you have to get out of here now!" he shouted.

Hytan's eyes went straight for the girl, and he pulled the spear's destruction to where the native girl had stood seconds before. The ground opened up with a mighty roar.

Pike still couldn't catch his breath. With little strength remaining, he was merely along for the ride as Hytan pulled his weight to finish off the native girl once and for all. She ran quickly, but her speed was no match for the wave of power that would easily cut her in two. The spear slowly turned, despite everything Pike had left, until something else stopped it. Two more hands now gripped the spear and pulled the destruction back to the sky.

"Swash!" yelled Pike.

"Thanks for coming, friend," grunted Hellion. The power of the two frustrated Hytan as he tried to jerk the spear in another direction but couldn't. His eyes went to his dagger. Before Pike could warn Hellion, the chief let go of the spear with one hand, and in one graceful motion produced the blade to drive through Hellion. Pike released the spear with both hands and grabbed the chief's arm. The change of hands on the spear caused a shift in the balance, and the tip was driven into the ground, causing the entire city to shake. Pike used all his strength and rolled to the ground, pulling Hytan's armed hand with him and flipping the cannibal onto the ground.

Hellion now stood alone, holding the spear with a look of terror in his eyes.

Hytan, being the experienced fighter that he was, landed on top of Pike and tried to wrestle his arm free to drive the dagger home.

"Use the spear, Swash!" yelled Pike. "Fire at him now!"

Hellion just stood there with the spear in his hands. The power had stopped. "I can't control it, Pike! It's in my head!"

"You have to!"

Confusion overtook Hellion's mind as it felt as if a blend of sounds conspired to split his head open. Swash shook the spear angrily. "Get out, get out, GET OUT!"

Hytan laughed as he pinned one of Pike's arms to the ground with his leg. Pike's one hand would now be unable to stop what was to come. He yelled and pushed the man's wrist as hard as he could. The man in bones laughed hysterically, pushing the dagger downward with the weight of his body, until he erupted in a horrifying scream.

The knife dropped from his hand to the ground. His screams turned to green flames that shot out of his mouth and eyes. Pike twisted sideways to avoid the consuming fireball. Behind Hytan stood Hellion. In his hands was the butt end of the spear he'd just driven through the Merkil chief.

"You did it, Hellion!" yelled Pike. He scrambled to his feet from under the pile of melted flesh that had been Hytan, but now paused. Something wasn't right. Swash's eyes glowed red.

Chapter 57

Hellion pulled the spear from the dead man, a deadly look on his face. An ominous tone pulsed loudly in his brain. He raised the spear and pointed it back at the city.

"Snap out of it, Swash! You have to let go!"

He turned to Pike. He shook his head in a firm *no.*

Pike slid away from the smoldering corpse and put his hands up. "Just relax, friend. You are in control."

"Liar!" he roared. "It's in my head. I can barely think with this racket in my brain! All these people want me dead! I can't stop until they're gone. It won't let me stop! It knows I want to do this. All these people coming to watch me hang! They deserve it!" Red light began to sputter in sparks from the end of the spear until it reached a solid line of destruction. He pointed it at what remained of the gallows, and in an instant, there was nothing left.

He's stronger than Hytan, and he has no control. "Just set the spear on the ground, Hellion!"

"Nooooo!" The roar that came back shook Pike with its force. "You have to take it away!" he screamed. "It passes through me in waves. I can't hold back what I'm about to do!" His pitch grew higher and shrill. "Take it away! I was never supposed to have this!"

Pike slowly rose to his feet with his hands in the air. "You're not what they say you are. I don't think you're who *you* think you are. I know you don't want to do this." His pleading eyes burned into the retinas of Hellion Swash.

Hellion lowered his eyes to the ground. "I told you who I was once," he said in a now calm voice. There was no light emitting from the spear currently, but the winds were picking up again, swirling the burning embers of Hytan around the two men. "You chose not to listen. Look at all these people! They will *never* stop hunting me! How else can it all end? Tell me!"

"It can end with no more bloodshed. You can let go of the retribution and your fear and just embrace your friends! We've come for you! Let's go away from this place and start anew with the Ghenzis. Please listen to reason, Hellion!"

"If you're truly my friend, strike me down when I turn my back. Be quick, or you will not find me a friend at all. That is the best I can promise, Pike. I can't stop what's already begun. As long as there is air in my lungs, this city will fall!" Swash raised the spear and turned his back on his friend.

Pike realized what was happening immediately. *He's gathering too much power! This could kill everyone!* Pike thought of Khawna, of Jada, of his warriors ready to lay down their lives. He alone knew the unspeakable power of the spear. "Throw it down, friend! I beg you!"

There was no answer, but there was now a glow coming from Swash. He was too far committed and probably couldn't hear Pike now. Pike looked at Foxskin, who held up his weapon and pointed it toward Swash.

"No!" called Pike. He held up a hand to stop his loyal scout. He shook as he summoned the tone in his brain. He connected with a different frequency that he had not used before. Power surged through him, but would it be enough?

"Turn around, Hellion!" he called. "Please take this last chance!"

The man was shaking violently. Was he sobbing? Was he trying to fight for control? "If I do, you die! If you hesitate, everyone dies. I'm sorry, friend. You truly were a friend to me, Pike. I am the monster they say I am. I've fought it as long as I could."

Pike raised his palms toward the back of his friend. The air felt unnatural. Whatever the man was planning far exceeded Pike's imagination. Could he do this?

He closed his eyes for a second before he could hear the upcoming summoning his friend had performed. There was a crash of water as the first wave from the Mammoth crashed over the banks and into the city. The water swept into the streets and pulled frightened citizens with it. *He's going to drown us all.* Pike thought he heard something from the east. An ocean wave?

"I'm sorry, friend," was all the hunter could say as his shaky hands released their light. Swash immediately erupted in radical colors of light and heat. The night turned into day for a brief moment, and then, in the same instant, his friend was gone.

"Nooo!" he heard the terrified scream of a woman. It was Jada.

He ran to where Hellion had just stood and found the spear, fully intact, next to a scorch mark on the ground. He was really gone. And yet there was no time to replay what had just happened. Pike needed more power to fight the waves that would be coming. With tears still running down his face, he grabbed onto his familiar frequency and gathered as much power as he could in the short amount of time he had. It was so much easier with the spear. When he unleashed the power, it split east and west and met the incoming tidal wave out at sea that would have surely crushed them all. The two energies met in a deafening collision. Pike could feel the weight of the water lift into the air.

"Take cover, everyone! The sky is about to fall upon us!" He focused again and intensified his energy on a wind from the west. He needed everything it had. Raising his hands, the power surge of wind ripped through the city. A few damaged buildings began to fall, but he couldn't stop now. The wind increased, and debris flew from west to east. Everyone else in the street was on their knees or stomachs, trying not to blow away. The winds caught the mountains of water and pushed them back over the ocean. The sea swelled, and Pike knew there would still be flooding, but perhaps for the time being, he had saved the city.

Then the winds died down and the sounds of the night turned to nothingness. No one dared speak or cry out for a moment. How could words describe what had just happened? Breaking that silence, a single voice rang out.

"I hate you!" Jada screamed at the top of her lungs through sobs. "You were his friend! His only friend!"

Pike had no words to respond with, although there was plenty he wanted to say. Swallowing his feelings, he could not shake the pity for himself, for his friend, for his betrothed.

"I would kill you myself if I could! You're a monster, Pike Granger!"

"I've only done what he begged for." *What else can I say?*

Khawna came running to Pike with tears running down her cheeks. She jumped into his arms, hugging him like a frightened child. "Let's go back, let's go back. We must get away from here!" was all she said, squeezing him as hard as she could. He could feel his power growing again, but this time, he would not reach out for it.

"I'm sorry," was all he could manage to say.

"Goodbye forever!" shrieked Jada. "You've completely destroyed my life! Everyone's lives! I have nothing to return to!" She sobbed heavily, her chest rising and falling. "I'm leaving for good! And don't you ever try to find me, you monster! Captain Gordon! Ready your ship, I have a promise to keep to a true friend!"

"Yes indeed, Miss Jada." He looked toward Pike to make sure it was indeed okay. Pike nodded, and the man scampered back toward the docks, following Jada.

Pike looked to his men who now huddled around their leader, no doubt relieved that the night was over.

"I'm sorry, but it seems our trip was in vain. I've failed my friends, but I won't fail my new people. We cannot stay here. It is not safe. Follow me and I will take you to a new home."

Chapter 58

When the sun's rays fell upon his once great city, Governor Huxworth swore. His home looked like a sacked city in a war zone. Alleys were flooded. Buildings were reduced to piles of bricks. The dead lay scattered everywhere. His magnificent army had failed to keep the peace during the ensuing night, which had led to looting and open lawlessness in the streets. The only good thing to happen was that the man with the spear and the natives appeared to have left. They had destroyed everything and yet took nothing. A single question ran through the governor's head over and over. *What kind of power had they unleased?*

One thing now was clearer than ever. The city was not safe. Huxworth could not remain until it was rebuilt. He had General Code secure him a ride on the next military ship across the ocean. The general would be left in charge of rebuilding. He would be given all the men and materials he needed. Huxworth's friends overseas would see to it. He would fulfill his duties as governor from Altanica, the twin city of Sisterton. When word of what happened reached their ally, they would take great interest in dealing with the new threat to the civilized world. Until then, it would be a full month's voyage by ship to cross the sea.

Commander Burin had obviously led the man with the spear to

the city. He'd love to hang the fool if only he could find him. It was likely he'd run when the threat emerged, or perhaps he was one of the countless fatalities from the night's events. The man with the spear would eventually need to be brought to justice for his crimes. The governor did not know how yet, but he knew the world would never feel safe again until it happened. Sisterton's armies were spread all over the world fighting and collecting wealth for their capital, and now it lay in ruins. The rest of the world was sure to take notice of the temporary weakness and rise up. He would need to be tactful in reassembling his fighting forces. Many resources he'd acquired were at stake. And yet, what were his men fighting for if their home had been destroyed? Even though they were a mercenary army, their loyalty was to Sisterton. He needed help and advice that could not come from the continent on which he now stood.

The people left behind would have to endure more hardship. Thank fate that the warmer days were coming; otherwise, they'd all be dead. There were simply not enough boats to take the refugees to the sister city.

When he boarded the military vessel, he spat on the ground before leaving it behind. All of this because of Hellion Swash. He shook his head in disbelief. At least the bastard finally got what was coming to him. It was the only consolation the governor had.

AT THE WESTERN end of Mammoth Lake, Grom had accomplished much in little time. Just three weeks ago he'd seen Pike off on his death march to the south. He'd heard nothing from the east since. Not even a ship had arrived to bring any news, or supplies for that matter. Grom didn't know if no news was good news, but all he could do was hope that Pike and Khawna had made it in time. During the presently uncertain times, the small town of Mossport had really pulled together. The Mammoth Inn now boasted a roof and stairs once again. The interior was still a work in progress, but at least the elements wouldn't destroy Jada's livelihood.

Grom figured if any of his townspeople made it back from Sisterton, it would be Jada. She was, after all, innocent on all accounts and didn't have to make the trek through the desert. She was also one woman whose wrath Grom didn't relish receiving. He'd already planned to run her hotel for her and deposit her profits into a separate account. He could only hope someone else would do the same for him if he and his wife ever disappeared unexpectedly.

The rest of the town had now been patched up handily. In fact, Grom was getting worried he'd soon run out of work for the soldiers. He knew when that day came, he'd have to find a way to ship them off himself if need be. Bored soldiers with no work would not be good for Mossport.

The sun had started to go down, so he'd called a halt on the work for the evening. The displaced soldiers were all served meals in the new Great Room of the Mammoth, and after overseeing that, Grom decided to close up his shop and retire for the night. He was reading a book on commerce when there was a knock at his door.

"Someone's at the door!" yelled his wife.

"I heard it, woman! Would you give me a minute to get out of this chair? I've worked all day, you know."

He gingerly limped to the back door where he found Pippendale at the top of the stairs with excitement in his eyes.

"What is it, Pip?"

"A native has arrived! All he would say is your name, Grom. You have to come to the inn now!"

"Feed him and keep him there. I'll be dressed and over promptly!"

"Yes sir, Mr. Grom."

When Grom arrived, he recognized the man with the red hide of a fox covering his shoulders. The native had left with Pike, but where were the others?

"Any friend of Pike is welcome here always," said Grom, sitting down next to the man as he ate the barley soup.

The man's expression gave no hint of his emotion. Grom wasn't even sure he understood language.

Foxskin reached into his pouch and pulled out a sheet of parchment. Grom recognized it, as he had included it in a pack with Pike's supplies before he left.

"Chief has a message for Grom."

It was all the man said. He turned his attention back to his soup.

Grom reached for his glasses and held the letter up to read.

My Dear Friend Grom,

I regret to inform you that our journey to the city did not go as planned. Sisterton has been destroyed. I swear I tried to stop it. In my attempts to rescue both Hellion and Jada I have failed miserably. I tried to do them right in the end, but I fear Jada will never forgive me for the choice I was presented with. Someday I hope she'll understand my reasons. I'm sorry for the destruction I've unleashed on your village. I've come to realize I'm not cut out for your world any longer…perhaps I never was. I will remain in the desert, my new home with my new people. Foxskin is on his way to retrieve the rest still north of the Mortapenums. We are starting anew, and yet we are not. This land we are presently in isn't all that it seems. There's much more history than we could have ever guessed.

Should Mossport need any supplies, my people are here to help. We will soon be transporting all our seeds and grain stores to our new home. The Mammoth River has awakened this desert. I know it will be tough without Sisterton, and again, I apologize. I wish it could have ended differently. I can change going forward, but the past I regretfully cannot. Thank you for remaining my friend. You will always be welcome in Joventin, where I now dwell. Be well, Grom.

Your friend,
Pike Granger

Chapter 59

Aﬀﬀﬀ ﬀﬀ ﬀﬀﬀﬀ AFTER SPENDING NEARLY two months at sea, the boy glimpsed a speck of land on the horizon. He crawled out of the crow's nest and scampered down the rope ladder until he reached the deck.

"Captain Gordon! Our destination is within sight!" he yelled excitedly.

"Good work, Orr!" shouted the captain jovially. He eyed Jada, who stood against the main cabin with her arms crossed, fingers rubbing the hilt of her knife.

"I'd have thought you'd be happier we're finally here," said the captain.

"I am," she replied.

"Why must you look so serious all the time? No one here will cross you. You've got Captain Gordon's word on that. My word is always good."

Her expression remained the same. "I wasn't good at trusting before, but now, I'm through with it."

The captain shrugged his shoulders. "Keep the current setting, boys! Linden, make sure our rowboat is ready for launch!" He paced up and down the deck restlessly with his hands intertwined behind his back.

Finally, he came back to Jada and addressed her privately, so no one else could hear.

"So when do you plan on giving me the rest of the details?"

"Not a moment before our feet are on sand."

"I figured you'd say that. Don't know why I asked. What if there's nothing there?"

Jada stared at the water blankly. "It will definitely be there."

The afternoon sun was torturous, and time seemed to slow as they all watched the speck of land grow into the size of a thumb, then a hand, and then a large desolate island with rocks, sand, and palm trees.

"I must say it doesn't look inhabited," said Linden.

"That's the point," replied Jada.

"Enough talk, Linden," said Gordon. "Drop anchor here. I don't want to get hung up on the reef. I dare say we'd be stranded here for eternity."

After the ship was anchored, Captain Gordon, Jada, Linden, and another mate were lowered into the water and began rowing for the shore. The waves were large for the little boat, making for glimpses of shoreline interrupted by walls of water. After much rowing, the boat rode a final wave onto the surf and beached. Everyone hopped overboard and began pulling the rowboat further into the dry sand.

"Care to tell us the rest now, lass?" asked the captain.

"There is a cave on the east side of the island. We will find soldiers buried in a tomb there. Under the soldiers lies the treasure that Swash stashed away."

"This had better be worth it," replied the captain.

As the four marched down the beach, the only sound was the waves in the surf. The island was not overly large, but they had to walk its entire length. Jada was fixated on the hill of rocks ahead when something caught her eye near the tree line. What in the world…

"My friends have arrived!" screamed a frantic man's voice. He had an unkempt beard, a rag over his head, and his clothes hung upon him in tatters as he ran toward the startled crew with arms wide open. Jada could feel tightness in her chest when she realized there was something familiar about the voice.

She put up a hand to shade her eyes. It couldn't be…

"Hellion!?"

Hellion Swash came running to meet them, complete with cat eyes and a wicked grin.

"How can it be?" asked Jada as the man she'd mourned for two months embraced her in a hug.

"I told Pike the day I met him he wasn't a killer," said Swash. "Guess I was right."

"How'd you end up here?" asked Captain Gordon.

"I can't say because I don't know. It was the last place I was thinking of before…the end."

Now Captain Gordon embraced the man. "Please tell me you're not going to say that there is no treasure."

He shook Gordon's shoulder with giddiness. "I hope you're ready to row, good captain. It's going to take a lotta trips in that little rowboat to haul it all in."

The captain's eyes lit up with glee. "What comes next, Hellion?" asked Gordon.

"First, I get a new name. Pike knew he was doing me a favor by killing Hellion Swash. Won't be nobody hunting me anymore. Next, I need a business to invest in." He eyed the captain. "I'm thinking shipping. I can make you an even wealthier man if you help me."

"We'll have to discuss terms, of course, but it seems you're good to your word," said the captain. "On everything except for a certain map, that is." He couldn't suppress his grin.

"I know who has it," replied Swash, grinning even larger.

"And what about me, Hellion?" asked Jada.

"You, my dear," he said, taking her hand and pressing it to his lips, "after what you did for me in Sisterton, you shall have whatever you like."

She pointed a finger into the man's chest. "I want the Swash that's not a scoundrel."

"I was talking about gold, my beautiful, angry lady. But what about your husband?"

"That's over," replied Jada. "I told you I require all that a man has to give for myself."

"Sounds like you want all my gold. As far as myself, I would love to give everything to you, my dear, but I'm afraid I'm unable to separate the scoundrel."

She took his hand. "Perhaps not, but a good woman can."

He smiled. "Well, it would certainly take a strong woman. And we all know that's exactly what you are."

Chapter 60

ALONE, A YOUNG man wanders the vast desert. Everything that surrounds him feels, looks, and even smells new; yet, deep down he knows he has done this before. He is in no hurry, just taking each step forward urged by both destiny and curiosity. When he reaches the river, he smiles. The way is south.

Within days, he reaches a green, lush site ahead. It has the feel of home, and yet it can never be. He will not stay long, but before he goes, he just has to know. The man dwarfs the warriors who are astonished when he asks to speak with the Nytel in their native tongue. They eagerly usher him through the ruins that are presently being restored. *So many memories, both joyful and painful.* They bring the young man to a large open room with only one chair, a throne carved for a man so large that it's almost amusing to behold. The Nytel enters with his native wife.

"Welcome to Joventin, the lost city of the Ghenzi," he hears Pike say. "You are our first visitor. I will see to it that you are well taken care of."

The young man's eyes went to the Nytel's empty hands, and Pike immediately noticed his confused look.

"Perhaps you were hoping to find something, friend?"

Khawna stood beside her husband with her arms crossed. "He's come to see the spear. He does not know."

The man bowed gracefully. "I do know of the spear, and also of the man born to wield it. Do you find your new home to your liking?"

Pike and Khawna exchanged glances. "It suits my people well," he finally replied.

The man laughed. "It should. It was built to withstand time itself for them. No enemy ever successfully attacked the city fortress."

"Where have you heard this?" asked Pike with interest.

"I will tell you all that you ask, but I have one question for you first."

"No one disrespects the Ny—" Pike raised a hand to stop Khawna's outburst. She smiled sheepishly and bowed to her husband, but she could not hide her eyes, which pierced through the intruder. Pike gestured for the man to continue.

The large man looked around at all the guards and then back at Pike. "What has become of the spear?" he asked.

"I put it in a safe place, far away," replied Pike.

The man smiled. "You will be a wise leader. Much wiser than I ever was."

Pike could feel the man giving off his own frequency now. "What is your name, friend?"

The man turned sideways as if surprised. "You don't recognize me, do you?"

"I've never seen you in my life. Surely, I would remember it."

The man was smiling from ear to ear. He started laughing so hard the guards looked worried. "My name is Victor, but you used to call me Tarmigan."

Gasps filled the open room.

"How can it be?" asked Pike.

"Every reign can turn bad, my friend. Put your trust in your friends and keep faith in your people, and you will fare better than I. If you dwell on power and in particular, the spear, you may end up cursed like me. You see me in my true form now because our people have been restored to their homeland. I also chose to interfere on your friends' behalf, which means eternity is now over for me."

Pike lowered his eyes. "I am sorry to have cost you so much, friend. What can we do to help? Will you stay with us?"

"I will die much happier knowing my curse has been lifted off my people. For me to stay is not meant to be. Besides, there is a whole world to see before my sand falls through the hourglass. It has changed much since I nearly destroyed it."

Pike and Khawna exchanged glances.

"The power you possess is far more powerful than you yet understand, Nytel. You have only scratched the surface of your capabilities. And therein lies the danger. Do you think that our homeland was originally in a wasteland? Do you wonder why the animals beyond the wall are different? Do you wonder why oceans separate civilizations? It was because of me. I broke this world, almost beyond repair. Thankfully, the world adapted. I tell you this as a warning. Do not share my fate. To lose everything only takes one mistake."

"Is the spear evil?" asked Pike.

"No," replied Victor quickly. "But it is not good either. We make it what it is. Few are capable of the control you have shown. Your people's journey is just beginning. Even if you are a better leader than I was, be warned that others will learn of your power. They will plot against you out of jealousy and fear alike. Your response may well define your rule."

"Do you still have the spear's power? I can sense your frequency from across the room."

Victor nodded his head, smiling. "You have already discovered this. The power does not originate from the spear. It's a different song inside everyone, waiting to be realized."

Pike thought about that comment for a moment.

"Tell me, wise leader," asked Victor. "What has become of the Merkil tribe that tormented our people?"

Khawna interrupted before Pike could speak. "He was more lenient than any other ruler could ever be." She paused. "But that is why he is our Nytel."

"I sealed them back where they belong," replied Pike. "They can either evolve into a prosperous people or eat each other until none are left. The choice is theirs."

"A very wise leader indeed," remarked Victor. "I can see I have left *your people* in good hands."

Pike cocked his head at Victor, noticing significance in his words. "It has bugged me for quite some time how a foreigner like me was meant to bring these people full circle to Joventin."

"Why it had to be you, I cannot say. But know this: you are not a foreigner."

Pike gasped. "Do you know of my family?"

"Unfortunately, I do not. However, your bloodline stems from your people now. My guess is that you will find the answers you seek in time. Remember, your powers have many more dimensions than you yet know."

"I wish to know so much more, Victor. There are questions I should have that I don't even know to ask yet. I know you said that you cannot stay, but will you at least join us for dinner?"

"That, I would enjoy greatly. While our parts have only overlapped briefly in the collective song of life, I could not be happier your turn has come to be heard." The man's eyes showed optimism and happiness for the first time in centuries.

www.ingramcontent.com/pod-product-compliance
Lightning Source LLC
Chambersburg PA
CBHW071247300726
48975CB00002B/584